Premedicated Murder
A Medium with a Heart

Book 1

Erica J Whelton

Publisher: Sunseri Design Publishing
ISBN-13: 978-1-956069-02-0
Second Edition

Printed in the United States of America

To my Grandmother Levin and Aunt Detna Kacher,
who would both have loved this story.
I miss you both every day.

Books in this series:

Premedicated Murder (book 1)
Replicated Murder (book 2)
Organized Murder (book 3)
Inherited Murder (book 4)
Crafted Murder (book 5)
Destined Murder (book 6)

Other books by this Author:

Mandy's Story: A Glenn Lake Novel (book 1)
Becca's Story: A Glenn Lake Novel (book 2)
Caroline's Story: A Glenn Lake Novel (book 3)

The Haunting of Anna-Rose (Paranormal Suspense)
Decoding Us (Women's Fiction/Friendship)

Chapter One

If Tessa didn't return soon with the sign-in sheet, I was going to wear a hole in the floor from my anxious pacing. We scrambled to do our research before my turn on stage. When I felt I could wait no longer, she barged in with the sheet, trailed closely by my other assistant, Micah.

"I have the list!" she announced, thrusting it toward me.

I snatched it from her, quickly skimming the names. I started typing them into the computer before passing the list back to her and Micah, so they could do the same.

I had an auditorium full of people who had paid to see me speak to the dead. They didn't know I was a fake, and I worked hard to ensure the secret never came out.

"I've got some excellent stuff, Boss. Excellent," Micah declared. He read off a few things.

"Those are a good start. Write it down."

More tapping and clicking of the keyboard and mouse as we all worked.

"Oh, I got it! This is gold." I read them a story from a blog.

"Oh yeah, that's perfect for the finale," Micah said over his laptop.

"If that doesn't get them crying, I don't know what will," Tessa agreed.

"How much longer until I go on?"

"The magician has another 20 minutes, and then it's you," Micah confirmed.

We consolidated our notes, worked out what I would say, and then I took a few minutes to practice. I'd been doing this so long I could perform with little prep time.

"Two minutes," Micah cued.

I took a few deep breaths as I checked my reflection in the dressing room mirror before making the long walk down the cement gray, cinder-block hallway toward the stage.

"Okay, Boss, ready?" Micah smiled from the top of the stairs as the illusionist on stage wrapped up.

The crowd erupted in applause. I peeked around the heavy purple curtain to see Julio taking a bow to a standing crowd.

He was the perfect opening act, long enough that we could get our research complete, but not so long that the audience became bored.

He was entertaining and got the crowd into it. I was glad to have him as part of the team.

He didn't know what we did while he was on stage. He just did his job and did it well.

The curtain dropped, and the stage cleared behind it. Micah winked at me before walking out in front of the curtain to make my introduction. I stood in the wings, watching him. His long legs made it to center stage in a blink. He looked sharp in his dark blue sports coat paired with a crisp white dress shirt and khaki pants. Relaxed and confident, he turned with a smile to the crowd.

"Wasn't he wonderful! Give it up one more time for Julio the Great!" The audience went crazy with applause. When they quieted, he continued. "Now up next, the woman you all came to see. She has a special connection to the other side, giving us all hope that our loved ones are still looking out for us. Because of her, I know I have a few guardian angels." He paused and put his hand on his heart, closed his eyes while bowing his head.

Micah was good, too. Damn good.

He opened his eyes and pretended to wipe away a tear. The theater filled with a soft murmur as the onlookers reacted to him.

"Let's give a warm welcome to Joanna, your Medium with a Heart."

The audience came to their feet with cheers mixed with sobbing. They were ready to believe. This was going to be a great show. I took a deep breath before walking in front of the curtain with my best pageant queen smile.

"Oh, thank you, thank you. Please, please..." I held my hands up for quiet. As they took their seats, the cheering quieted, but the gentle weeping continued.

It occurred at almost every show. People felt hope that they would hear from a loved one or two. Only a handful would, well, sort of.

I put my hands over my heart. "I'm humbled by your welcome. I hope everyone is doing well this evening. I've been backstage, clearing my mind and preparing to connect with the other side. I can already feel them waiting. Let's see..."

I paced slowly to one side of the stage, paused, and then moved back to the middle of the stage. "Hm, so I'm hearing from a woman. She's telling me a story about an olive-green dress with *far too* many bows." My statement was met with low laughter from the audience. "A prom dress?

No, wait... a bridesmaid's dress. It caused disagreement and compromise."

There was a gasp from the right side of the audience. A woman in her mid-fifties stood. She had a tissue already pressed to one eye.

"My sister. I hated that dress," the woman stated.

A muffled laugh rolled through the crowd. I gestured for her to join me on stage.

The rest of the show went smoothly. I had picked the perfect stories, and the audience was eating them up. I felt good about the performance. The finale was the real tearjerker, a story about a mother and daughter and a rose garden they had planted together.

While my assistants did their things out front, I went to my dressing room to unwind and change into my everyday plain self. It felt good to dress up and put on my alias for the hour-long show, but it was even better to relax after.

Now in my soft, oversized t-shirt and yoga pants with beat-up sneakers, I washed my make-up off and shook out the fancy updo, pulling my hair into a ponytail. I gave a sigh of relief once I was back to plain ole Jo.

"Much better," I said to my reflection.

After I changed, I tidied the dressing area while waiting for my assistants. I wasn't one to sit idle. When I was satisfied, I scrolled through social media and my emails.

It was about an hour later when they finally joined me in the dressing room. They had a stack of receipts, cash overflowing the cash box, and empty boxes.

"Great night, Boss," Micah said as he set down the boxes with what was left. "Everyone was commenting on the rose story. They loved that one."

I peeked inside. Not much. A few shirts, some other miscellaneous items, and a few books. We had brought several dozen of each product.

"We thought they might," I confirmed. "Everything's cleaned up, so we should be good to go."

We gathered our items and turned to leave. As we turned, I noticed a man in the doorway watching us. Was he a fan looking for an autograph? He was dressed too nicely to be the janitor.

"Oh, I'm sorry. You can't be back here."

I looked over my shoulder at Micah and Tessa for confirmation. They stared at me, confused.

"Who are you talking to, Boss?" Micah asked.

"Him." I gestured toward the man standing by the door.

They looked at each other and then at me. Blank stares all around.

"You can see me?" the strange man asked.

"Um, *yeah*. What kind of question is that?"

"You *can* see me." He became animated and walked toward me. "Wow, I came here for your help. When I realized you were faking it, I was disappointed. But you can *really* see me. So, you can help me."

An icy prickle crawled up my spine. I took a step back.

"Okay, this is freaking me out. Who are you?"

"Boss?" Micah sounded concerned.

I looked at him and then at the stranger. Who was this guy? Why could I see him, and Micah and Tessa couldn't?

"They can't see me. I'm dead." His tone became more serious. "You're a medium, or whatever it's called, right? That's what the marquee out front says anyway."

My mouth dropped open. Every childhood memory I'd buried, every spirit I'd blocked out, came rushing back. This wasn't supposed to happen. Not anymore. I'd been faking the medium thing, trying to get my childhood powers back. I'd just never figured out how, and I couldn't believe this was really happening now. Or perhaps this was a trick?

"Okay, so you're telling me you're dead... I can see you, but you're... dead." I looked around the room for an exit.

"Yes. I am, and you can." He had a pleased look on his face, like he had just won the lottery. "I need your help. That's why I came to your show. I heard you can speak to the dead, and I need you to speak for me."

I had to ignore for a minute that he just named the most dangerous, powerful man in our town and try to focus on what he wanted me to do. I couldn't do this. Could I? What was in it for me? I couldn't think of anything. Not. One. Thing.

Plus, why would I help a womanizing con artist? *Says the fake medium,* I thought.

"What if I don't agree to help you?"

"Well, I have nowhere to go and nothing to do but follow you around. I can be pretty annoying."

That sounded like a threat, and based on our limited interaction, caused me to visibly shudder. I imagined he could be quite annoying. I could try to block him like I had with spirits from my childhood, but not knowing how I was seeing him now, I wasn't sure I could block him.

"What's he saying?" Tessa asked, her voice quivering slightly.

"He says he wants me to help investigate his death. Says he was murdered."

"Oh, this is crazy awesome!" Micah was grinning from ear to ear and swaying like an eager little boy. He seemed to enjoy this.

Micah was over six feet tall and thin as a rail, with a full hipster beard. To see him act childlike was amusing. If I wasn't so annoyed and spooked by this stranger's request, I would have laughed.

"Look... um, wait, what's your name?" I realized in the rush of information, he hadn't introduced himself, though he looked familiar. I just couldn't place him.

"Jeremy Landon."

"Oh, I remember hearing about you. From Creekview, like us. But the news said accidental poisoning. Not too many of the people that were interviewed seemed upset you were dead... you weren't a nice person."

"Yeah, well... I didn't deserve to die for being an asshole." He paused, running his hands through his hair. "A lot of people are assholes, and seriously, it was murder. Like you said, many people didn't like me and had good reason to kill me. I just need to prove it. Again, since you can see me, I need you to tell my side of the story."

I'd never investigated a murder. Never thought I would ever be asked to. What skills did I have? Maybe my research skills could help us, but that was really the only skill I could think of that might translate to sleuth.

"Can you at least give me tonight to think about it? Don't do the whole stalking ghost thing until I have time to think."

"Fine. I'll come see you in the morning." He turned to leave, but then stopped, pointing at me. "And for the record, my wife and girlfriend were both upset that I died. They still cry for me."

He continued his departure from the room; I followed him to watch him head down the cinder-block hallway until he was gone. Slowly, I turned back to my assistants.

"So?" they asked together. Their hands clasped, begging me for answers.

"He said he would give me until the morning to think about it. Can I really do this?"

"Yes!" they said simultaneously.

I stared blankly at them, trying to determine my next move.

Tessa seemed over her fear and now matched Micah's excitement over the situation. A freaking ghost had just asked me to help solve his murder. How had this turned into my life?

Chapter Two

~Joanna~

The next day, bright and way too early, I was startled awake by the feeling I wasn't alone. In the chair next to the bed sat Jeremy. I shrieked, jumping nearly out of bed.

"Holy crap, Jeremy! I wasn't expecting you this early."

"I told you that you had until morning. It's morning." He gestured toward the window, where faint light was starting to peek through the curtains.

"Ugh, too early, guy. Too early. I'm not a morning person." I fell back on my pillows, closing my eyes.

"Well, I need an answer."

I peeked at him through half-closed eyes and heaved a sigh. I desperately wanted to say 'no,' but I pictured Laney sitting at home wondering why her husband had cheated. What could she have done differently? What did she do wrong? I didn't know her, but I had lived through those feelings not that long ago. I knew the emotional rollercoaster: anger, grief, sadness, rage.

So many questions and no one to provide the answers. I could give that to her and maybe help Jeremy with his own peace of mind in the process.

And the cherry on top, I didn't want him to haunt me. From this early-morning wake-up to his lack of remorse about being an adulterer, I had a low opinion of Jeremy Landon and didn't want to spend any more time with him than was necessary. He'd actually smiled when mentioning his pregnant wife *and* girlfriend. Like it was something to be proud of. The man had no shame.

"I don't have the experience for this, and honestly, there isn't anything in this for me." I glared at Jeremy, trying to decide what to say. "But I can tell this won't end well if I don't agree. You clearly have no boundaries."

"No, no, I don't," he stated flatly. "And I won't leave you alone until I get my way. I didn't make my money by slacking and letting things go. I had to push my weight around." He flashed me a million-dollar smile.

"I just want to make it clear. I'm not just doing this because of your threat. Okay, well, maybe a little, but as a medium, I give people peace and closure. That's what I'll do for you. And also, being that we are

both from the same hometown, I'll help a fellow Creekview citizen." I
shrugged.

"Great. So, when do we get started?" He rubbed his hands
together.

I shuddered. Had I made a deal with the devil? Yikes. But if it
helped Laney find answers, maybe it was worth selling my soul for a few
weeks.

"I need a shower and coffee, in that order. Then we can talk."

"Excellent." He settled in like he planned to stay while I showered.

Studying him, I was fascinated to realize he wasn't exactly sitting
in the chair as I first thought when I woke. He was kind of hovering.
Weird. But I dismissed the thought immediately. He couldn't stay while I
showered and dressed. I'd figure that out later.

"Um, no. No. Nope. You have gotta go. You can wait downstairs in
the lobby, but I need privacy. That's rule number one if this is going to
work. *Privacy*."

"You're a prude. Lobby. One hour."

I turned my head to watch as he faded into the wall and was
gone.

"How did I get here?" I said to the empty room.

I wanted to lie there for at least another hour, but instead, I sent a
text to my assistants letting them know Jeremy had ordered us an early
wake-up call and to meet me in the hotel lobby in an hour. I received
delayed responses that were not polite, but they were, at least, awake.

An hour later, I was showered and dressed, then headed
downstairs as promised. Stepping out of the elevator, I fought a yawn as I
scanned the lobby for the hotel's coffee shop. I needed coffee, stat.

"Right on time." Jeremy snuck up behind me.

I practically jumped out of my skin. He was going to give me a
heart attack if he kept sneaking up on me like that.

"I can't be seen talking to you because it will look like I'm talking
to myself," I whispered.

"Fine."

I fumbled to put my cell phone to my ear to make it look like I was
on a call. "I'm going to get coffee, and then I'll be right back. My assistants
will be down any minute."

"Yeah, hipster guy is here already. I haven't seen goth girl yet."

"Um, thanks." I walked away but then turned back, still holding
my cell phone. "She isn't goth, just... artistic."

He flashed me a slow, smart-ass grin. Arrogant prick. I desperately hoped this would be an easy mystery to solve because I didn't know how long I could stand being around him.

I saw Micah when I walked into the coffee shop. He nodded his greeting. Micah wasn't a morning person, either. He collected our order and turned to hand me a cup of coffee.

"Lifesaver," I mumbled as I took the cup and sipped the bitter nectar, sighing when it hit my soul.

"Did you see our friend yet?"

"Yeah, he's outside. He's nicknamed you hipster guy."

Micah perked up.

"Oh, yeah? Cool. I like it." He grinned and stroked his beard.

"He called Tessa 'goth girl.'"

"Ouch. She *won't* like that."

"I know."

We walked back out to the lobby. I looked around, then nodded in Jeremy's direction. Micah followed me. At least now I could speak without looking like I was talking to myself.

"So, where is 'artistic girl'?" He did the air quotes thing.

"I'll text her."

"He asked about Tessa?" Micah asked.

"Yeah." I typed a message into my phone.

She replied she was on her way.

Micah inspected where I'd indicated Jeremy was standing. Jeremy stared back at him.

"What *is* he doing?" he snapped, crossing his arms over his chest.

"I think he is trying to see you."

"I am," Micah confirmed. "I wish I could see and talk to him without you."

Jeremy rolled his eyes and glanced out the window. I didn't relay this message. It would only disappoint Micah. He wanted so badly to be a medium.

Finally, Tessa made her appearance. On closer inspection, she did look a bit goth. I, for one, had always liked her style. She was unique.

Today's outfit was a black crop top with a gray wool cardigan over it paired with a black and white plaid skirt, fishnet stockings, and combat boots. Her hair was black with dark purple highlights and pulled into a messy bun. A typical Tessa outfit.

Not many people around dressed like this. It made her stand out.

"See? You see it now, don't you?" Jeremy said smugly.

I didn't answer but turned to my assistants to discuss our next move. We needed to check out of the hotel, then travel to the next city for the last show of our tour before heading home. It had been a long month on the road, and we were all getting worn out.

I was ready to be home. Tired of fast-food and wanted something home cooked, to sleep in my own bed, and I wanted a break from standing in front of the crowds and being 'on' every night.

"I guess we need to work out who you think might have killed you, then make a plan to talk to each person and research their motives."

"Sounds good to me," Jeremy confirmed.

We checked out of the hotel. Micah drove, and we grabbed one more coffee before the three-hour drive. Jeremy and Tessa in the back, me in the front.

Once we got on the highway, I pulled out a notepad to take notes on the whos, whats, and hows. I turned so I could see him and started taking notes.

"Okay, let's start at the beginning," I said, pen in hand.

Jeremy launched into stories about his wife, his girlfriend, his business partner, and his brother. They all sounded like they had reasons to kill him. He had cheated on his wife, and both women were six months pregnant. His business partner felt betrayed by a deal he'd made without him. His brother thought he'd used their grandmother as a guinea pig for his drug trials.

"Wow, you really were an ass," I said.

"Yeah, I know. I told you that already. But I also did good things. I gave to charity, helped my employees, built a successful company that helps people." He sounded defensive.

"Okay, okay. I'm just saying, you gave a lot of people motive."

We spent the rest of the drive narrowing down the list and making a plan for how to approach each person. By the time we arrived at the next hotel, I had a solid list and felt slightly more confident about this whole investigation thing.

Maybe I could do this after all.

We arrived at the hotel around noon and checked in. After getting our room keys, we parted ways with a plan to meet up in a few hours. Tessa would come to my room to help me get ready for the evening's performance, and then we'd pick up dinner before heading to the show.

Jeremy followed me to my room, talking the entire time. With his non-stop chatter, I couldn't hear my own thoughts. I just wanted to lie down for a few minutes and relax before showtime.

Once in the room, I set my bags down and scanned the space. Nothing special about it. A standard hotel room with a queen bed covered in white bedding. A generic forest scene hung on the wall behind the bed. The window was adorned with the usual paisley-patterned curtains seen in every hotel room. There was a television across from the bed on a credenza with a single-cup coffee maker. The usual ice bucket and water glasses shared the tray with the coffee machine and its accessories.

I excused myself to the bathroom to wash my face and clear my head away from Mr. Chatty. It didn't work because I could still hear him talking, though I couldn't quite make out what he was saying.

Give me strength, I thought to myself as I stared at my reflection in the mirror.

"Are you nearly done in there? I have more to tell you."

"Yes, almost. I just need a minute alone." I answered.

"Fine. Fine. I'll be back in what? An hour?"

I opened the door with a little too much enthusiasm. "Yes, that would be perfect. Thank you."

"I think I will go spy on your assistants. The boy seems interesting."

He turned, disappearing into the wall. Maybe I should warn Micah? Nah, I wanted some peace.

I used the time to do a bit of research on my new BFF, Jeremy. I needed to find out the things he wasn't telling me. There were always three sides to every story: "yours," "mine," and the truth.

I found some information about his business deals. He seemed slimy, the stereotypical used-car-salesman slimy. He sang a good song, but the product was subpar.

It appeared he got lucky with Remarpax, but that didn't mean he hadn't taken shortcuts and stepped on toes to get there. Not to mention the experiment on his grandmother.

Next, I looked up his wife and girlfriend on various social media sites. They shared updates on their lives, preparing for their babies, and pictures of their growing bellies. I hoped I looked that cute if I was ever pregnant, but you probably have to date for that.

With my work schedule, job, and bitterness toward my first marriage, I didn't date often. The few dates I'd been on, the guys thought my job was weird, or my schedule was a hurdle they couldn't get past. I understood, mostly.

Plus, I was now a bit cynical when it came to guys. Ted left me with a lot of trust issues. I was thankful that we never had children. We had talked about it, but we had put it on hold with his supposed work travel. Little did I know back then that he wasn't traveling for work, or at least not as much as he said he was. My heart squeezed at the memories.

Now the idea of children hurt my heart. I didn't think I would ever want one. I would just enjoy my nephews.

All this Jeremy business was bringing memories back fast and hard. I had done a good job of not thinking about Ted, at least not as much as I did right after his death. Out of sight, out of mind, maybe? I had nothing in my house to remind me of him. I'd gotten rid of his things years ago. Not a picture, not a gift, nothing remained. Plus, he'd never lived here with me, so no random memories of happier times.

I felt I had a much clearer picture of Jeremy following my research. I didn't know if I would tell him everything I found. For now, I would keep it in my back pocket and use it only if needed.

"So that Micah is a strange fellow. You know he's gay?"

"Um, yeah. So?"

"I don't think I have ever been around a gay man before. At least, not that closely. I listened to him talking to his boyfriend."

"I don't want to hear this." I didn't need the details of my assistant's personal life, or anyone's, for that matter.

"No, no, not like that. It was like normal stuff. I don't know what I expected, but something... different." He sounded sincere in his fascination, and why not? Micah was a neat guy. That's why I liked working with him. "I have learned so much about people since being dead."

"I guess the whole 'life's short' thing is true?"

"Yeah, that, but I didn't spend much time with people that were different from me. I know me, but you and your friends are fascinating."

"Wait, what's fascinating about me? I'm plain... me."

"Oh, you know, not the rich country club, shopping-obsessed type of woman that I'm used to."

I didn't reply, not knowing if I should be insulted or flattered. I knew some rich country club ladies, and they were the sweetest, but his tone led me to believe he meant it negatively. He was blunt, matter of fact, and a bit of an ass, but he seemed sincere in learning about new people.

I decided to let it pass. I actually liked being plain Joanna. I had my stage persona, and that's what most people presumed I was like, but I was really an unassuming, quiet homebody. I preferred life out of the limelight, which I know with my job sounds contradictory.

On stage, I was this glamorous medium who spoke to the dead. I wore my hair in fancy styles and glittery, flashy makeup. Catsuits and kimonos with stiletto heels completed the illusion of Joanna: The Medium with a Heart. It was a flashy look, but people loved that Joanna.

Offstage, I typically wore jeans or yoga pants with baggy shirts, my hair in a ponytail, messy bun, or loose hanging to just below my shoulders. I seldom wore makeup. Maybe a little lip gloss occasionally, but rarely much more than that. This look saved me from being recognized, at least most of the time.

Only a few diehard Joanna the Medium fans saw through my plain Jo facade. They would laugh and comment on how it was smart of me to hide my identity. I played along, but the medium was the real disguise. I was plain Jo.

"So, what's the plan now?" Jeremy asked.

"I need to start getting ready for tonight's show. Tessa should be here any minute to help with my hair and makeup, and then we'll go pick up dinner before heading to the theater."

"Have you ever thought of actually talking to other dead people like me? There are more here. It isn't just me." He gestured around the room.

I cringed and looked around. I wondered how many more were here. Was I ever truly alone?

"I don't know how. You're a fluke. I have no idea if I can do this with anyone else."

I didn't mention that I used to be able to see dead people all the time. I had worked hard to block that ability and now didn't know how to get it back. After meeting this ghost, I wasn't entirely sure I wanted to meet more.

"I can teach you," he offered.

"How?"

"I don't know yet, but we'll figure it out."

"Why would you help me?" I asked. "There's nothing in it for you."

"To get you focused. This is your job; don't you want to do it properly?"

I stared at him. I wasn't sure if he was insulting me or genuinely trying to help.

"Well, yeah, I guess."

"Great. And the sooner we get through your BS, the sooner we can get to figuring out who killed me."

Ah, there was his motivation. It wasn't to help me, but to get to his case.

There was a knock at the door. I opened it to Tessa, loaded down with all the bags that would turn me from everyday Jo to Joanna the Medium with a Heart.

Tessa started unpacking my bags. She laid out my outfit for tonight. It was a kimono with gold fringe and embroidered gold floral accents that would go over a black catsuit. I had black open-toed stiletto heels to complete the look. I felt these outfits gave me a mysterious allure.

When I was dressed, Tessa painted on my face. Since she wasn't talkative, we were mostly quiet while she worked.

She applied the glittery gold eyeshadow, black eyeliner, and thick black mascara. We used a powder with a shimmer to it. The spotlights shining on me would make the makeup pop, but I always thought it looked goofy in the hotel room's plain lighting.

"Wow, I have seen your show a few times, but this is my favorite outfit so far," Jeremy said.

"Thanks. So, you like?" I posed for him.

"Oh shit, is he here? I didn't even think to ask you." Tessa looked around the room. I pointed toward where he stood.

"She's a character, yeah?"

"Yeah, a bit," I replied. "We need to get packed up. Where's Micah? He should be here by now."

I fired off a text, then Tessa and I started gathering the laptop bags. We had our merchandise shipped ahead to the theater. They would have it ready for us when we arrived. One less thing we had to worry about.

A few minutes later, my phone was still silent.

"No answer from Micah. This isn't like him."

Tessa tried to call him. "Straight to voicemail."

"We'll just go to his room."

We grabbed our gear and headed down. I knocked. Nothing. I knocked a little harder and heard mumbling, a curse, and then a thud like something fell. Maybe Micah. The door swung open.

With crazy hair and a wild, sleepy look on his face, Micah appeared at the door. "I'm so sorry, Boss. I am so, so sorry. Give me two minutes."

"No rush. We still have plenty of time before the show. Tessa and I will load the car and grab some coffees. Meet us downstairs?"

He nodded and turned back into the room, letting the door slam behind him. I giggled as we headed to the car. I guess I wasn't the only one who hadn't enjoyed Jeremy's early-morning wake-up call.

Chapter Three

Micah apologized for the entire drive to the venue. "I can't believe I fell asleep. We *just* checked into the hotel a few hours ago, and I was only supposed to rest for a minute."

I tried to reassure him it was fine. We were all exhausted. The tour always took so much out of us, and after Jeremy's early-morning wake-up call, it was no wonder he'd passed out the moment his head hit the pillow.

"Seriously, don't worry about it. We all needed the rest. Besides, we made it with time to spare."

When we arrived in the dressing room, we got everything unpacked. It was the same as most we visited, yellowed walls that might have once been white, bright lights lining the mirrors, and long counters that we commandeered for our tech setup.

Micah and Tessa went to set up in the lobby to start selling shirts, books, and all the Joanna the Medium must-haves. I stayed behind to get the tech side of things set up.

Our opening act was once again Julio the Great. He stuck his head in when he arrived to say hello.

"Hey, Jo."

"Hey, Julio. Ready for the last show?" I smiled.

"Oh yeah, and ready to get back home. Baby's due any day."

"Congratulations! Break a leg tonight."

He left me and went to take the stage.

He was an incredible illusionist. He didn't do your typical magic show, but more of a visual display of mind puzzles. The audience was always on the edge of their seats, almost literally, through the entire show.

I dreaded the day he would realize he'd outgrown being my opener because he was going places. Whenever I told him he'd be headlining his own shows someday, he would laugh it off, but I think he knew it too.

"Are you going to cheat or trust me that you can do this?" Jeremy asked.

"I don't call it cheating. I call it... giving the people what they want." Okay, maybe it was cheating, but I wasn't admitting anything to him.

"Semantics. Okay, look, there's a guy here. His wife is going to be in the crowd tonight. He's standing right here next to me." He motioned to his right.

I stared and tried to focus.

"Jeremy, I don't know..." But as I spoke, I started to see an older man, a bit short and overweight, with the worst comb-over. I guessed even in the afterlife, bad hair was a thing. He had nervous energy, rocking slightly on his heels, hands fidgeting. "Wait. I think I see him. Is he wearing an orange Hawaiian shirt?"

"Yes, that's him," Jeremy said, becoming animated. "Joanna, meet Larry."

"Nice to meet you. I'm so glad you can see me. I need you to give my wife a message." Larry spoke with a slow Southern accent.

"Of course, but don't you want to wait for the show?"

"Um, yeah, I guess. Wait, no, I should tell you now." He looked at Jeremy and then at me. "I know she wants to hear from me, but she'll also hate hearing from me. She hates me."

"Why? What happened?" I was a sucker for other people's drama. I didn't like it in my own life.

"I died... Oh my." He looked down at the floor but then looked up at me again. "I died while having sex with another woman... her sister."

"What? I mean, oh." I needed to act cool and professional.

But what was wrong with guys? What were the odds that both dead people I could currently see were adulterers? It had me looking around for Ted, or maybe a hidden camera from some prank show.

"I know. It's horrible. I need to apologize. But that isn't even the worst part." He ran a hand over his face. "I spent all our money. We were in debt up to our eyeballs. Her sister wanted new boobs..."

He shrugged, and Jeremy laughed.

"Hey, man, I get it. I bought a pair for my girl, too."

"What the heck? I am starting to hate this job." I mumbled to myself and turned to face the mirror. He was exactly like my husband. "Are there any normal dead people?"

"Not really," Jeremy said. "Most regular folks go wherever they go. Heaven, Hell, whatever you believe in. Those of us wandering Earth? We're stuck. Unfinished business." He gestured toward Larry. "Apologies to make, or in my case, not satisfied with how they say I died. Like Purgatory, I guess."

"So, you're saying that if I meet others, they will probably have more stories like yours? More cheating husbands or other people who did bad things?" *Of course. Just my freaking luck.* I had a cheating husband, and now I was stuck with a bunch of them.

"Um, yeah, probably." He shrugged and said it so nonchalantly, like it was normal. "There are others, though. Just unhappy people. Like me, they don't like how they died and want to know more. Then others want to tell their loved ones they love them one last time but have no way to do it."

"Okay, so are there any more people here?" I glanced around the room, trying to figure out how to unblock my powers. I still didn't know how I was seeing anyone.

"Not in the room, but they're here. I can go get another one or two, or as many as you like, if you want to try to see them."

I could only manage a nod.

When Jeremy and Larry walked out, I collapsed into the closest chair, trying to process this latest experience.

His story wasn't the kind I thought I would be telling in this job, but I guess that's why I wanted to try. When Ted died six years ago, I wanted to learn how to channel spirits again so I could get closure on his death and lies. Though for all the crap Ted put me through, he hadn't cheated with my sister.

My brother-in-law had bought me gifts in the past, but things like books I had wanted or a glass figurine of sisters holding hands. That was the limit of our intimacy. I couldn't imagine him buying me boobs. The thought made me feel sick.

I didn't know if I really wanted to do this. These weren't the type of spirits I remembered as a child, but then would middle-aged men, like these, tell a ten-year-old girl about their affairs? Probably not. They had all been nice and told me funny stories.

I rubbed my temples. It sounded like I was going to meet a lot of people I probably wasn't going to like. A headache was starting to form at the thought.

"What have I gotten myself into?" I said to the air.

"Excuse me, Ms. Joanna?"

"Yes?" I turned to see a stunningly beautiful young girl. She couldn't have been more than eighteen years old.

"Hi, I'm Kelsey. Mr. Jeremy sent me." She gestured over her shoulder toward the hallway.

My next tragic story. What could this sweet girl have done?

"You have unfinished business with a loved one or something you want said?"

"Yes. My mother and sister are in the audience tonight. I have been following them since I died. I need them to know I'm sorry and tell them they did nothing wrong."

I hated to ask, but I knew I had to. "What happened?"

"Heart attack. I was a cheerleader, healthy, athletic. I died during practice. My mom... she blames herself. She thinks she should have known, should have seen the signs. But there weren't any. I just... died."

Her voice broke on the last word, and I felt tears prick my own eyes.

"I'll help you," I promised.

Jeremy returned with two more spirits, and we spent the next hour going through their stories. It was unnerving. Had they been there all along? It was fine when I didn't know, but now knowing, I felt almost violated.

Jeremy had found some good stories for me, which was helpful. Like Kelsey's, most were heartbreaking tales of life gone too soon, and people who needed to say something.

After hearing them, I felt the need to make a bunch of phone calls. I sent a few texts instead, just to be sure a message got out. This afterlife thing was a lot more fun when it was fake.

My sister's reply put a smile on my face.

Okay, weirdo, I love you

She was a good sport about my job, not thinking I was strange or insane, and had always been supportive when we grew up. She must have thought I was becoming as nutty as our mother, just with a different ailment. I replied I loved her too and left it at that.

During our prep time, I gave Micah and Tessa a rundown of the stories and the new spirits I was seeing.

"That's exciting, Boss," Micah said.

"Yeah, so I don't think we'll need to do our research this time."

"What?" Tessa asked. "Are you sure?"

"Yes. I know what I'm seeing, and I can do this without it."

"You don't even want to have some information for backup? What if your powers fail as you go on?" Micah held the list out toward me.

"No, no. I don't think I need it." I knew what I was seeing, and it would be good to actually do this for real.

With that settled, I touched up my makeup and then made my way toward the stage. I nodded and smiled at the various dead people as I walked through the hallways.

Seeing them was a strange yet exhilarating feeling.

I got to the stage just in time to catch the end of Julio's show. I wished I knew how he did his tricks; he was so talented.

The audience came to their feet as Julio took his final bow. I could feel my nerves firing up as Micah made my introduction. I took a deep breath as I prepared to perform for the first time without notes.

Micah wrapped up my intro, and I walked to center stage as the audience applauded. I felt my second persona take over, the one who loved to be in the spotlight.

"Thank you all, thank you for that warm welcome. Please sit down. Wasn't Julio brilliant? How does he do all those tricks?" I paused as the crowd gave another round of applause for Julio. When the applause slowed, I continued with my opening. "I think we will have some wonderful messages for you all tonight. I have had the pleasure of meeting some of your lost loved ones ahead of time. Typically, I wait until I'm on stage."

The reaction from the audience was mixed. Some gasped, a few whispered, while others wept. These group readings always had that emotional effect on people.

"They wanted to make sure I got their messages exactly right." I paused for a brief round of applause. When it died down, I began. "Our first message isn't quite as heartwarming as most are. We're talking about betrayal and heartbreak, but I'm hoping the ending will be one of forgiveness and a soul that can rest at peace."

I almost gagged on the words. I wasn't picturing Larry, but Ted's face. I didn't want him to rest in peace. I honestly hoped he was miserable and rotting.

Refocusing on Larry, I launched into his story while he stood anxiously next to me. I spoke for Larry.

"So, I'll speak exactly as our guest, Larry. 'My Lulu bell, I'm so very sorry for hurting you. I want you to remember the us from the early years. The us that ate pizza in our hotel room after our wedding because we were too busy enjoying the moment to eat. Or the us that brought our beautiful twin girls home from the hospital, and we stayed up all night watching them sleep. We couldn't believe how beautiful they were and how in love we were. Remember painting the living room that awful color? We tried everything to cover it.'"

I heard a half-sob, half-laugh from the left side of the audience and assumed it was his widow.

"'And I know I strayed, but that was because I had failed you and let you down. I didn't think I deserved you anymore, and I sabotaged our relationship.'" *Really? That's what you want to say?* "Whoops, sorry. Yes, that's what he wants to say." That was unprofessional of me to break character, but this way of doing readings was going to take some getting used to. I'd have to be more careful to not let my feelings get the better of me.

I heard Luanne's soft weeping change to heavier sobs. Then her chair scraped back, and she pushed through the row, stumbling slightly as she made her way to the stage. Larry nodded to me and rocked back and forth, anxiously waiting for her to join us.

"My husband... he's here?" Her thin face was red and streaked with tears.

Luanne was a tall, slim woman with frizzy blonde hair. She and Larry made an interesting pairing.

"Yes." I gestured to my left.

She looked at the empty space next to me, fresh tears falling from her eyes.

"Larry, I don't know if I can forgive you. You left us in heavy debt, and you *slept with my sister*." A gasp from the audience. "I lost the house. I'm on antidepressants now. You're gone, and I can't even see you to tell you how angry I am." She balled up her fists and waved them wildly. She seemed caught up in the moment and oblivious to the room full of strangers. "I wish I could see your face when I tell you how much you hurt me. I'm a broken woman. Broken!"

Tessa appeared with tissues. Luanne took several, wiping her eyes. "You got out of this the easy way. Gawd, I was stupid... but fine, fine. You said what you wanted to say. I heard it. Now what?"

Larry looked at me, desperate. "Tell her I'll wait. However long it takes, I'll wait for her forgiveness."

I relayed his message. Luanne's face crumpled, and she turned away without another word, walking off the stage as the audience sat in stunned silence.

Larry looked over at me. He hung his head even lower, turned on his heel, and sulked off. I knew he hadn't gotten the closure and peace he had hoped for. His story was a hard sell, but I thought she would get there. Someday.

The next was a mom who had lost her battle with cancer. In her last days, she went into cardiac arrest, and after a few days in a coma, the family had to make the tough decision to stop her life support.

She wanted her family to know she was okay, that they made the right decision, and she was no longer in pain. There were tears, a few laughs, and what everyone loved to see: peaceful closure.

A few more heartwarming stories like this, families happy to hear from their loved ones, moments of forgiveness. This was what I had built my brand on. Granted, that brand had initially been faked, but this turned out to be my best show, minus Larry's story. Strike that, even with Larry's story, because it was real.

Kelsey was last. I signaled to her that I was ready, and she stepped forward to stand next to me.

"Our last spirit tonight is a sweet girl who wants to apologize to her mother. They had a silly fight, her words, before she passed suddenly from a heart attack."

I heard a gasp, and a female voice say, "Kelsey."

Kelsey whimpered. I knew she was going to have a hard time with this. Dead or not, she still had feelings.

I continued, "She was a cheerleader and track star, healthy, but like most teens, a bit on the rebellious side. Trying to balance becoming an adult and learning who she was with still being a child."

"It's my Kelsey, isn't it?" A woman stood from the fourth row and made her way forward.

"Yes, ma'am, it is."

Kelsey started crying quietly at my side as her mother and someone I assumed was her sister followed behind. As Kelsey had mentioned, she was also in the audience.

"She was too young. This shouldn't have happened. I should've known." Tears streaming down her face as she joined me. She hugged me once she got near enough. "I found her, and at first I thought she had killed herself, but... when they said heart attack, it just blew my mind. Where is she?" She looked around the stage, trying to see Kelsey. I gestured to my right. "Kelsey, baby, our fight was so silly. I'm sorry. I love you very much, and you will always be my baby."

"I love you too, Mom," I said for her.

"Aw, I wish I could see her just one more time. Does she look good? She was such a beautiful baby."

"She is very beautiful," I said as I looked over at the stunning beauty to my right. She could have been the homecoming queen.

After a few more tears and words of love, they said their goodbyes. I wrapped up my show, then took my leave from the stage. My assistants went to the lobby to sell our merchandise, and I went backstage to undo my stage persona.

"That was a great show!" Jeremy snuck up from behind me as I was entering the dressing room. "Much better than last night."

"Oh, Jeremy, thanks."

"You like the people I found?"

"Except maybe Larry. I know he says he's sorry, but he hurt his wife." I stopped short of saying I knew exactly how much pain she was in.

"I guess you don't like me too much either, huh?"

"That's a loaded question." I didn't answer directly. Instead, I went into the bathroom to wash my face. Jeremy didn't follow me. He respected rule one, privacy.

I was thankful for it, needing a few minutes to unwind after that show. It had been more draining than in the past. They were all emotional, but the difference was that this was real.

I hadn't faked it for a good show or a sympathetic reaction. This was raw and real, physically and emotionally draining for me as I relearned how to actually channel the spirits and face my own demons.

I shook away the unhappy memories and got back to changing into my plain ole Jo self.

"Much better," I mumbled to my reflection. I heard Micah and Tessa come back and joined them in the main dressing room.

"That was quick!" I quipped as I came out of the bathroom. I checked the time; maybe thirty minutes had passed since the end of the show. Fastest in our history.

"Yep, and you'll be proud, Boss. All sold out." Micah turned one of the boxes upside down to show me.

"Wow! That's amazing. Any comments on the show?"

"Yes, they loved it. Best reviews in a long time." Micah grinned ear to ear, but then he reached for my hand, and his eyebrows raised in question. "How are you doing? I mean, with the Larry story, I thought it might bring up some feelings about..."

He didn't have to finish that statement. I knew what he meant.

"Oh, yeah, no. Yes, it did, but I'm okay. Well, I'll be okay. I haven't thought about him in so long."

Tessa reached over and took my other hand. They were the most supportive friends.

"What am I missing here?" Jeremy asked as he looked on.

"I don't know that I want to share that part of me with you." I snapped sharper than I intended. "I'm sorry, Jeremy. That was harsher than I meant. It's just that your and Larry's stories are so much... like my own."

Micah and Tessa looked at me and then at the space where I was looking. They never let go of my hands. I met them only months after Ted died, when I was still struggling with the fallout. They saw some of my darkest moments and walked me through it all.

"In what way?"

I sighed. There was no point hiding it now.

"My husband died about six years ago. And when that happened, I found out he had been cheating on me for our entire marriage. He ran up a bunch of credit cards I knew nothing about. Then his girlfriend's family sued our insurance and his estate for damages. I didn't even know that was a thing. They didn't win, but I had to spend a small fortune in attorney and court fees. It was a financial mess that I'm finally out of. So, yes, Larry's story hit very close to home." I could feel tears forming, but I wasn't going to cry. I would fight it until I was alone.

"Oh," he replied with no remorse, no sympathy. Just stoic.

I shook it off and added his lack of a sympathetic reaction to the long list of things I didn't like about this man.

"Well, we'd better get the room cleaned and packed up."

One more night, and then I could head home and start work on investigating Jeremy's death, then hopefully get him out of my life. I was so done with him.

Chapter Four

I dropped my bags and collapsed on the couch with a heavy sigh. Home. Finally. I loved my job, my assistants, and being on the road, but after a month of shows, I was drained. Every night on stage, entertaining crowds, connecting with people emotionally, it took everything out of me.

He was eager to get this mystery solved, but based on what I had read, there was nothing to figure out. It was an accident, plain and simple. Nevertheless, I was willing to do what I could to give him the peace of mind he needed, or mostly his widow. I needed to brainstorm how to connect with her when we were ready for it.

Looking around my living room, I daydreamed about staying right here without moving for a week.

Lying back with my eyes closed, I tried to relax and forget about my ghostly shadow.

"How long do you plan to lie around?" he finally asked, breaking the silence.

"I don't know. Hours. Days. A week?"

I kept my eyes closed, knowing he was probably standing right above me, staring down. Not a sight I wanted to see in my moment of relaxation.

"Fine. You take your little break. I'm going to check on my wife and girlfriend. I'll be back bright and early tomorrow, so be ready to work."

With that, he was gone, and I was finally alone. I opened my eyes to see if he had really left, and sure enough, no Jeremy. I didn't see any other spirits hanging around, so I hoped that meant I was really, truly alone. Jeremy had confirmed that I wasn't seeing all of them yet, just a fraction of those hanging around. I still had no clue how this worked.

I basked in the silence for too long, but my to-do list loomed. I did a mental rundown of the things I needed to get done today. Unpack, get my laundry started, then run to the grocery store. After a month on the road, my fridge and pantry were bare.

But first, I had to let my mother know I was home, or she would start the worried, guilt-filled phone calls. She might even send my dad or sister over to check on me. She had done that before and got herself all worked up, which would result in her in bed with a headache or stomachache. I couldn't be responsible for that again.

I tried to keep the call short, but she had other plans, briefing me on all the family news and gossip, the goings-on with her friends, the drama with her neighbors.

An hour later, I was caught up and even more exhausted. She had sucked away all my motivation to complete the rest of my errands, and I only had one thing checked off the list so far.

However, I couldn't put off the rest of my chores for long, so I went to knock out the remaining tasks. Everything had to be completed today, especially getting to the grocery store. I could not eat another meal from a sack.

As I drove to the store, I smiled and felt myself relaxing while enjoying the sights of home. My town. It was comforting and familiar. I have lived here all my life, except for the few years I was away at college.

I thought of all the towns and cities I visited while touring. I have been to small towns and large cities. Creekview was somewhere between the two.

Big enough that not everyone knew you and you could go to the store looking ugly without worrying you would run into someone you knew. Yet small enough that there were people you could count on when you needed them.

I lived in one of the older neighborhoods, full of mature trees and with a mix of quaint craftsmen and newer ranch-style homes. My neighbors were a blend of young families just starting out to the empty nesters who had raised their kids in these houses and never planned to leave. I was not the norm.

Single people like me rented townhouses or bought condos in the part of town called The Ridge. Restaurants, bars, and trendy shops filled the Ridge area. But that wasn't me. I liked my simple life, at least when I wasn't Joanna: The Medium with a Heart.

I didn't exactly feel like a single person. To me, they seemed carefree, just looking to have fun and casually date until 'the one' came along. I didn't want to date, and I didn't feel carefree. For sure, I wasn't looking for 'the one.' I didn't believe in that stuff anymore. From my twenty-one-year-old newlywed self to now, at nearly twenty-nine, a lot has changed.

I bought this house after I dug myself out of the debt Ted had left me in. This signified my independence from him and my ability to stand on my own two feet. I was proud of it.

I pulled into the grocery store parking lot and found a spot. Then grabbed a cart and headed to the produce section. I was looking forward to fresh vegetables, fruits, and anything homemade. I didn't want anything processed or from a cardboard box or wrapper.

Everything looked so good and fresh, so I loaded up my cart. I wanted to buy the entire produce section. I didn't. I left some for the other patrons.

I then headed to the fish counter to look at the salmon and noticed Jeremy standing nearby. When I realized he was watching a gorgeous pregnant blonde, I wanted to run the other way. I didn't want to think about his request to find his murderer and wanted even less to get involved with his wife right now.

I had never seen Laney Landon in person before. She was even more beautiful than her online pictures. If I hadn't already known she was pregnant, it would be difficult to tell, at least until she turned sideways. She had a slim, athletic build with a cute, round belly.

He noticed me, and his eyes got big.

"What are you doing here?"

I had to grab my phone to act like I was on a call. "Shopping. What are you doing?"

"I told you. I'm checking on my wife." He said through gritted teeth; if a ghost can grit their teeth, that is.

"Ah, I see. Well, I'm off the clock, so I'll get back to my shopping. Talk to you later. Bye." I tucked my phone back in my purse, making it clear that was the end of any conversation between us, and marched away. Maybe chicken instead of salmon?

I tried to rush through the rest of my shopping, looking over my shoulder and watching Jeremy's widow whenever she was near. I'm not sure why I was hiding from her, since she was the reason I was doing this for him. I guess I just wanted to finish my shopping without dealing with the situation.

While I might have been a semi-celebrity, I rarely assumed people knew me, especially when I wasn't dressed to perform. I wasn't the arrogant type, and it still surprised me when people recognized me.

But if she did, she might ask me to talk to Jeremy or ask a bunch of questions that I knew I wasn't prepared for. Mostly because Jeremy wanted to have a say in what I said to her, and we hadn't formulated that plan, so it was probably best to keep a low profile and my distance from her.

After I finished most of my shopping, I doubled back for the salmon. I really didn't feel like chicken tonight. I made my selection, then headed to the checkout line. I was ready to breathe a sigh of relief that I would get out of the store undetected. But just my luck. Guess who got in line behind me?

"Hey, aren't you Joanna the Medium?" And, of course, Laney knew who I was.

My semi-celebrity status strikes again.

"Umm, yes," I whispered and looked around to make sure nobody else had heard. Anonymity was nearly impossible offstage, though I tried. This was a part of the job I despised.

"Oh, I'm sorry. You probably don't want people to know." She lowered her voice and stepped closer. "My name is Laney Landon. I recently lost someone and... well, I'd been hoping to get an appointment with you, but when I called, they said you were out on tour."

"Yes, I was. I just got back today. Needed a few things after several weeks on the road." I nodded toward my groceries, trying not to make eye contact with Jeremy, who was standing behind her.

"Yeah, oh, makes sense." She smiled, looking at my shopping cart. "Do you know what your schedule might be? I really need some answers and was hoping..." she trailed off. Her sadness was apparent.

I understood that pain.

"Oh yeah, I can probably see you soon. I just need to check my schedule. I have assistants that normally keep that for me." I saw Jeremy shaking his head. I wasn't sure if he just didn't want me meeting with her or judging me for my assistants. "I can take your number, and one of us will call you once we check."

"Great!"

We traded numbers, and I got checked out, waving as I exited the store. Jeremy followed me.

"What the heck? Are you really going to meet with her?" he said.

"Yeah, shouldn't I? I thought that was the point of all this." Forgetting to pick up my phone.

"I don't think we are ready to meet with her, are we?"

"I didn't even set up an appointment yet. We have time to make a plan." A mother and young child were walking through the parking lot. The mother looked at me up and down, pulled her child close to her, and hurried past me. "Great, now I'm the crazy lady talking to herself."

I gestured to Jeremy with the zipped lip sign, then loaded my food without saying a word and climbed into the car, shaking my head as I left him standing there.

I muttered to myself all the way home. What had he wanted me to do? I'd been caught off guard. We had never discussed what I would or should do if I just ran into her, and if she happens to recognize me. It was a commonplace, the grocery store. What did he expect?

Once home, I unloaded my groceries and then pulled up my schedule to see when I had an opening. It was important for me to meet with her to discuss Jeremy and see if she had any information, but I hadn't planned to make appointments for another two weeks.

I had scheduled this as a vacation after the tour. I was booked solid for months afterward, so I decided to fit Laney in just before my regular appointments. It was a special case.

I would have Tessa call and set it up later. I didn't want to talk to Laney before I was ready, and more importantly, until Jeremy was prepared, since he had gotten so upset with me for speaking to her.

Though I didn't expect to find anything new, I decided to do more research on him. What if I had missed something before? My life revolved around researching people, and he seemed adamant that he had been killed, so I thought there had to be more clues out there.

After about an hour, I'd found some interesting details. Jeremy's business deals weren't just slimy, they were borderline illegal. One article mentioned a questionable patent acquisition where the original inventor claimed Jeremy had stolen his research. The case had been settled out of court for an undisclosed sum.

I also saw some social media updates from both his wife and girlfriend. They had doctor appointments recently, so each gave statuses on their respective pregnancies. They each shared more belly shots. I hoped I would look that cute if I was ever pregnant, but you probably have to date for that.

With my work schedule and bitterness toward my first marriage, I didn't date often. The few dates I'd been on usually ended the same way: guys either thought my job was weird or couldn't handle my schedule. I understood. Mostly. Dating a medium who traveled half the year wasn't exactly easy.

Plus, I was now a bit cynical when it came to guys. Ted left me with a lot of trust issues. I was thankful we never had children. We'd talked about it, but we put it on hold because of his supposed work travel. Little did I know back then that he wasn't traveling for work, or at least not as much as he said he was. My heart squeezed at the memories.

Now the idea of children hurt my heart. I didn't think I would ever want one. I would just enjoy my nephews.

All this Jeremy business was bringing memories back fast and hard. I'd done a good job of not thinking about Ted, at least not as much as I did right after his death. Out of sight, out of mind. Or so I'd hoped. I had nothing in my house to remind me of him. I'd gotten rid of his things years ago. Not a picture, not a gift, nothing remained. Plus, he'd never lived here with me, so no random memories of happier times.

I looked around. A few spirits had started to hang out with me. It had me questioning whether they had always been here. Why didn't I see Ted? Was he here, and I just couldn't see him yet? Or was he keeping his distance from me?

Telling him off like Larry's widow had done might be healing. It was something I was looking forward to someday.

I stretched and shut down the computer. I couldn't research Jeremy any further from my computer. I had to get out and talk to people. The wife was covered, but how was I going to meet Caitlyn? What about the others in his life, like his brother or business partner? Those would be tricky too.

I could just imagine marching up to them and announcing that I was speaking to their dead brother or business partner, and he suspected them of his murder. They wouldn't think he was crazy. Oh no, he was dead. They would wonder what I was after.

I pushed the thought from my head and went to start dinner. It felt good to be home and doing normal, everyday things.

After dinner was eaten and the dishes were done, I poured a glass of wine. I didn't have wine frequently, but an occasional glass or two was nice, especially after a long trip. It helped me unwind and get me back on my regular sleep schedule.

I had a phobia about flying, so we always traveled by car. It made the tours harder, but it was worth it when my fans enjoyed the shows. Of course, I enjoyed giving them what they wanted. Plus, it gave me a comfortable, well more than comfortable living.

We had tried to travel via plane once. It did not go well, even with a sedative. Let's just say I may or may not have been threatened with removal from the plane, but I was definitely seated by the air marshal for the rest of the flight. He claimed to be a banker from Ohio. With that build? Nah. He looked like an ex-Marine and was definitely an air marshal; I was almost sure of it.

We started planning our trips to be strictly by car. It made the trips more difficult in planning and on our bodies, but I wasn't the crying, crazy lady in seat 5A. I avoided being the crazy lady.

I settled in front of the television and grabbed my Kindle, planning for a quiet evening of reading.

When I was in the middle of a good chapter, my phone rang and startled me. It was my sister.

"Hey," I said.

"Hey, Mom said you were back. Can I stop by?" So much for my quiet evening.

Audrey was the exact opposite of me. Bubbly, loud, friendly, and confident. I was awkward, quiet, and insecure; at least that's how I felt, except when I was on stage.

"Sure. Come on over."

"Great. I'm in your driveway."

I smiled and shook my head. *Just like Audrey.*

"Of course you are. I'm heading to the door."

As soon as I opened the door, she grabbed me for a hug. When it ended, she stepped around me and into the house.

"I brought wine! I missed you. Mom has been driving me crazy," she said.

"I bet." I followed her down my hallway to the living room.

"No, this is the worst she's been. I had to take her to the doctor six times. There was nothing wrong with her. Bless Dr. Blevins. If he retires, we are screwed."

She headed to the kitchen for a corkscrew and another wine glass. She came back, pouring herself a glass as she walked. Did I mention she was talented?

"So, Stan has the kids, I assume."

"Yep. Mom's night off. He loves it." It was true. He was one of the best dads I knew.

"I bet they are getting big."

"Oh, they are." She pulled out her phone and scrolled through the latest pictures.

She had two little boys. Harris was five, and Dylan was two. I did the proper amount of aunt gushing over my nephews. They were adorable.

"Okay, so your drunk texts from the other night were freaky. What is going on with you?" She said as she stowed her phone away.

Ah, the impromptu visit made a lot more sense now. She was checking on me, probably to ensure I wasn't going crazy like our mother.

"I wasn't drunk."

"Really? Alright then, what was it? Because I could tell that something was going on."

It was on the tip of my tongue to tell her about the spirits being back. She was a few years older than me and, though she couldn't see them herself, she used to love listening to me talking with the spirits and relaying their stories to her. She asked all types of questions and was sad when our mom 'made' them go away.

"I can see you thinking. Spill it." She moved to the edge of her seat.

"Fine... Do you remember when I used to see dead people, for real?"

"Yes? Oh, my gawd, are they back? Please say they are back." She started looking around the room. I wasn't sure why she looked; she could never see them.

Nobody was here anyway, or at least, I didn't see anyone. I looked around once quickly to make sure.

"None at the moment, but do you remember hearing about that Jeremy Landon, who died a month or so ago? The pharmaceutical guy?" I asked.

"Yeah, I remember him. He'd been in the news a lot being interviewed about that new medicine. I got the impression he was all about the money and fame and then heard about his death."

"Well, when we were in Belmonte the other day, I saw him. He wants me to investigate his death."

"*Really*? Wow! And you said?"

"At first, I was going to say no. What do I know about being a private investigator? I'm a sort of fake medium, right? But he was going to blackmail me into it, so I ended up agreeing."

"How does a ghost blackmail you?"

"Okay, maybe that isn't the right word, but basically, he was going to haunt me until I did what he wanted."

"That's rude, but I have missed the dead people."

I couldn't decide if I missed them or not. All I knew was I wasn't enjoying my latest visitor. I filled Audrey in on my encounter with my newest friend and how my last show went. She was fascinated. I told her my 'drunk text' was a reaction to hearing from them and their stories. They all wished they had had more time to tell their loved ones how they felt. I didn't want to wait until it was too late.

"Yeah, well, the haunting thing didn't bother me as much as the cheating husband thing," I said.

Her mouth fell open. "Seriously? He was cheating on his wife?"

"Yes, and then get this: she and the mistress are pregnant."

"No!" She slapped the couch. She loved drama as much as I did.

"Yep. And to top it off, the second dead guy... same story. What is wrong with men?"

"How're you doing with this? I'm sure it brought up feelings." She squeezed my hand.

"Yeah, I'm okay. Well, I'll be okay." I tried to smile.

"You know I love you, too, right?"

"Yes, as long as you know, I love you."

We hugged and then changed the subject, catching up on all things sisterly. We were always close, growing up. She was the only one that never judged me, never questioned what I saw, and stood up for me against the bullies.

We agreed to have lunch soon, and I mentioned I wanted to see my nephews even sooner. She agreed. We hugged again, and I walked her out. I smiled as I watched her drive away.

For living a quiet life, it hadn't been a bad night.

Chapter Five

~Joanna~

I woke the next day with that same eerie feeling, like I wasn't alone. That meant Jeremy must be around somewhere. I wished he would wait until a more reasonable time. I rolled to look at the clock: 6:00 a.m. Probably a decent time if I had a different type of job, but I worked for myself.

"Ugh. Jeremy, are you here?"

"Yes, and if I could, I would bring you coffee, but I can't hold objects. You understand. Are you ready?" he asked from somewhere in the shadows of my dark room.

"No, you just saw me wake up. Plus, we talked about the not a morning person thing before. And are you forgetting about rule number one? *Privacy*." I sat up, trying to see him in my dimly lit bedroom.

"Boo!" He jumped at me, taking advantage of the darkness to scare me.

"You're an ass."

I threw a pillow at him, but it went right through him. This caused him to burst into a fit of laughter. I gave him a dirty look.

"Will you at least give me a minute to go to the bathroom and wake up a bit? Ten minutes max."

"Fine, but you know if the TV was at least on..." He looked over his shoulder.

I stormed past him into the living room, turned on the television, flipped to the channel he requested, then sprinted to the restroom. I should have done that first, but if the TV bought me a respite, so be it.

After I peed, I washed my face then stared at myself in the mirror for a moment. For probably the millionth time since meeting Jeremy, I questioned how this could possibly be my life. I was a captive to this spirit who was a jerk and enjoyed it.

I ran a brush through my hair, pulling it up into a messy bun. I'd deal with it after a shower, but first, coffee.

Without a word to him, I walked through the living room and straight to the coffee pot. I popped in a new single cup and hit start. Once that was ready, I grabbed my mug and headed back to the living room.

I held up one finger. One minute before he started chatting. I had considered the other finger, but for now, he was at least being quiet. After drinking about half the cup, I felt more awake.

"Okay, sorry. I'm not a morning person," I said.

"Yeah, you mentioned that." He rolled his eyes.

"Well, if you would let me sleep longer..."

"We don't have time for you to sleep. I must solve this because I would like to get on with... well, whatever I'm supposed to really be doing. The 'at peace' part of this afterlife."

"Okay, so what do you want to start with?"

"I don't think it was Laney or Cate. I watched them both yesterday, and there was nothing to indicate they had done it. Laney is the angriest of the two, but she cried over me last night. Cate is just sad, so I'm thinking she didn't do it either. I want to look at either Greg or Aaron more closely. I know Greg was angry with me about our grandma, but enough to kill me?"

"So, you want me to go talk to him? How do you suggest I do that?"

"With Greg, it's best to be blunt and matter of fact. I say we go to his office, and you tell him who you are, that I'm with you, then ask him if he killed me."

"Are you crazy? No way. Nope. Not doing that." I stared at him. "You seriously want me to walk in and accuse your brother of murder?"

"Okay, then what do you suggest?"

I had no idea, but I knew telling him outright that we suspected him of murder wasn't the right way to go. I had to process this crazy plan of his for a bit before I could jump into it.

"Let me think about it. I'm not quite an on-the-fly type of person; I'm more of a planner."

"Maybe that's your problem."

I huffed. "Fine. Fine. Where does he work?"

After a second cup of coffee and a shower, I was standing outside of Landon Construction Company. It was in the industrial park in a nondescript beige building. Nothing about it screamed money, but I knew it was the largest construction company in our region.

I was second-guessing my decision to come. What had I been thinking?

"You can do this." Jeremy stood beside me, looking more anxious than I'd seen him.

I took a deep breath and walked inside. The reception area was as uninspiring as the exterior. Gray carpet, white walls, cheap furniture. A bored-looking receptionist sat behind a desk, filing her nails.

"Can I help you?" She didn't look up.

"Um, yes. I'm here to see Greg Landon. I don't have an appointment, but it's important. It's about his brother."

Her head snapped up. She had clearly heard about Jeremy's death. Everyone in town had.

"Your name?"

"Joanna Webber."

She picked up the phone and had a brief, whispered conversation. I caught the name *Jeremy*. She hung up and gestured down the hallway.

"Second door on the right. He'll see you."

I thanked her and walked down the hall, Jeremy trailing behind me. When I reached the door, I paused.

"Ready?" Jeremy asked.

I nodded, though I wasn't sure I was.

I knocked and heard a gruff "Come in."

Bridget, the receptionist, must have followed me because she leaned forward as I reached for the door handle, her voice dropping to a whisper. "*Jeremy*."

"Jeremy? What about him?" Greg asked, turning his gaze back to me as I entered.

"It would be better in private."

He eyed me up and down.

"Of course," he nodded at me. "Bridget, hold my calls."

He held the door open, so I walked past him into his office. It was as plain and uninspiring as the rest of the place. No personal touches, just chaos. Folders, blueprints, and papers littered every flat surface. Either Greg was drowning in work, or he had a serious organizational problem. I guess he wasn't one of those that went paperless, like so many nowadays.

Once in his office and seated, he started rapid-firing questions at me. "Okay, so what is your name? Why are you here? And what could you *possibly* have to tell me about my brother?"

"I'm Joanna, and I'm a medium." I tried to sound confident, but my voice wavered slightly.

"A what? Like, someone who talks to dead people?"

"Yeah, something like that. I've been speaking with your brother Jeremy, and he had a few questions..."

"Wait. So, wait, are you telling me that you are talking to him? Is he here now?"

"Umm..." I looked at Jeremy, and he nodded to go ahead. "Yes, he is here."

Greg looked me up and down again. Maybe he was trying to decide if he believed me or not. I was used to most people being skeptical of me. At least, in this case, Jeremy was here for backup.

"Let's say I believe all this. What the hell could he have to say to me? What could he possibly have to say?" He crossed his arms and sat back in his chair.

"He says he is sorry for using Grandma for his drug trials, but she is better, and he thinks you should forgive him for that," I said.

Jeremy nodded.

"Oh, yeah? Is that what he thinks this is about?" His expression was unreadable as he pondered his next words. "That's BS. It doesn't even sound like him. What do you want? Money? I don't have any to spare. A job? You want to try blackmailing me? I have no secrets to share."

"No, I..." This was not going well.

"Ask him if he remembers when we were about ten and twelve. He broke mom's favorite crystal vase, and I took the fall for it."

I relayed the message to Greg, and as I spoke, his face went pale. "Son of a..."

I looked at Jeremy, and he just shrugged. Who the heck was this guy?

"Is he here now? Right here?" He pointed to where I kept looking.

"Yes, he is." I looked at Jeremy again.

People had three reactions to these interactions. They either believed instantly, they took a lot of convincing, or they never believed. Greg was the first type.

"You little dick! You have someone come in here to do your dirty work. But then, you couldn't be a man even when you were alive; why should I expect anything less from you now?"

"Now, I'm going to say what Jeremy says to you. I'll do my best to say it word for word." I paused to listen to Jeremy.

"Screw you, Greg. I can't talk to you now, or I would myself. And I was a man when I was alive, always standing up for your sorry ass. I got you out of trouble time and time again. I don't know why I bothered if you weren't even going to remember."

Greg stood and started pacing. I could see the anger and hurt warring on his face.

"You want to know why I'm pissed? It isn't just about Grandma, though that was bad enough. You left me holding the bag on a massive gambling debt!"

"What?" Jeremy's face showed genuine confusion.

I relayed Jeremy's reaction to Greg.

"Don't play dumb. You borrowed money from Hank 'the Hammer' Hammersley for your company. When you died, that debt didn't just disappear. Hank came after me for it. Said family pays family debts."

I had heard whispers about Hank Hammersley. He was a local loan shark and bookie, the kind of guy you only dealt with when you were desperate or stupid. Apparently Jeremy had been one or both.

"I paid off my debt to Hank before I died," Jeremy said, his voice rising. "The company loan was settled. Greg shouldn't owe him anything."

I passed this along to Greg.

"Well, that's not what Hank says. And trust me, you don't argue with Hank the Hammer. I've been paying him for months. So yeah, Jeremy, I'm pissed. You screwed Grandma, you screwed me, and then you went and died before I could even confront you about any of it."

Greg sat back down heavily in his chair. Some of the fight seemed to drain out of him.

"Look, I don't know what game you're playing here, lady, but if Jeremy really is here, tell him I don't forgive him. Not yet. Maybe not ever. He hurt a lot of people, and I'm tired of cleaning up his messes."

Jeremy looked devastated. I felt bad for both of them.

"This is the detective that was on the case. Give him a call, tell him I referred you, and ask him for the case files. It's fairly cut and dry. Then maybe this asshole will stop following you around."

He scribbled something on a piece of paper and handed it to me. Detective Hartley's name and number.

"Screw you," Jeremy said.

I didn't tell Greg that. When Jeremy realized I wasn't going to pass that sentiment on, he crossed his arms over his chest to sulk.

"Thank you for this. I appreciate the help. He seems adamant that he didn't kill himself. Says he had too much to live for to commit suicide and knew what he was doing in the lab, so it couldn't have been an accident." I said for myself this time, not Jeremy.

"Well, that might be, but I've seen the reports and the security coverage. It's clear that it was at the very least an accident."

At Greg's words, Jeremy had a mix of emotions pass over his face from anger to sad and back again.

At least Greg didn't suspect we were checking him out for murder. I'd need more facts to really be able to judge whether he should stay on the suspect list. He definitely seemed angry. Angry enough to kill was the question. With no real facts and this being an initial conversation, I couldn't say either way.

I thanked him again and got up to leave. Jeremy hesitated, but I didn't care; I was leaving. He could stay here or come with me. He gave his brother a final look and then followed.

On my way out, I thanked Bridget for her help, flashing another of my famous Joanna the Medium smiles. She gave me a half-smile in return.

I wished Jeremy wasn't following me. I really did need to process this new information without him and wanted to call Micah to discuss it. He was always good at helping me work things out. Instead, I was going to be forced to listen to Jeremy's version yet again.

I stood on the sidewalk for a moment, searching for my car keys.

"That sucked. He's a lying prick. I didn't make that type of deal with Hank. I mean, I did but not that Greg had to pay him back. That should have come out of my estate. There was plenty of money for it."

"Are you sure? I've heard that Hank's deals can be pretty... sleazy."

"Yes, I'm sure. I know what I signed up for. I'm a smart businessman or at least, I was."

I fidgeted with my keys. I was ready to go but wanted to be free of Jeremy. The introvert in me was on overload, and I had other things to do today. One being lunch with my mother, which I would need all my energy for.

"I really need to process all this. Can we take a break for today? Maybe start fresh tomorrow?"

"What about the detective? What about Aaron?"

"I probably need to call and make an appointment with the detective before anything else, and I have plans to have lunch with my mother."

"Fine. I will go follow Laney or Cate. Or maybe I'll go back and follow Greg around today. I'll be back in the morning." He started to walk away but turned back after a moment. "And it will be early, so be ready."

My soul groaned at the thought. I needed to figure out my next move, so I could be done with him, but first to get through lunch with my mom.

As I walked to my car, I couldn't stop thinking about what Greg had said. The gambling debt to someone called Hank "the Hammer." If Jeremy didn't know about it, or if he was lying about paying it off, who else was keeping secrets?

Chapter Six

~Clint~

I leaned over the body. It looked like the serial killer had struck again. This was his or her, I supposed, signature. He carved letters, we assumed his initials, into the victims' foreheads. Hands and feet tied together. Throat cut. The victim was left to bleed to death, sadistic, gruesome.

The rookie was currently getting sick in the alley. Poor kid. I understood his feelings, but years had hardened me, though even my stomach was feeling a bit uneasy at the sight. I hated this case and couldn't wait to solve it, and we weren't even close.

This town was usually quiet. Moderate-sized, with roughly two hundred thousand residents. Creekview had its problems, but nothing this serious. Petty crime, vandalism, maybe domestic disputes, and on the rare occasion, there would be a manslaughter case, self-defense case, or accidental death to investigate. Just enough work to keep us busy, challenging enough to keep the job interesting, but nothing as barbaric and evil as this. It made my skin crawl each time we found a body.

The media had arrived and were trying to set up as close to the scene as possible. Each one wanting the prime spot. We had to keep a wide perimeter to keep them out to get our work done and not disturb the crime scene. Since we weren't accustomed to this, we had to call for backup to bring barriers.

"Clint, look at this," my partner, Terry, called from the other side of the room.

We were working in a grid pattern to collect evidence and check the crime scene. We had the two of us, the responding officer, and two other officers who responded to the assistance call.

I crossed the room to join Terry. I studied the floor where he was pointing.

"Footprint? He was a little less careful this time," I observed.

"Yeah. Wonder if he's growing tired. Ready to get caught."

We stared at the footprint, both lost in our own thoughts. This case had been going on for less than a year. This was victim number seven. She was younger than the others but still fit his favored type: dark hair, fair-skinned, and roughly between five feet and five feet six inches tall. He didn't seem to do anything sexual with them, just tortured them and left them to bleed to death, scared and alone. It was such a cruel death.

We found the first three in an empty warehouse. Another was in an abandoned house. The rest were in various places around town. Nothing that gave us a clue as to who was doing this.

"Hartley, Walden?" Officer James had been the responding officer. She wanted to show us some evidence near the entrance of the room.

This time he'd been sloppy, and it looked like this victim put up a fight, more than the others had. She had been a tough one, though I didn't know her, it was the impression I got from the state of this room.

The officers were doing their job of sweeping the room of all fingerprints, DNA, and anything else they could find. I pointed them in the direction of the footprint Terry had shown me as we left the scene.

"Send me your reports as soon as you have them available," I said.

"Will do, Detective Hartley," Officer Harper said.

As the crime scene leads, we had to make a brief statement to the media before heading back to the station. Terry spoke, keeping it brief and answering as few questions as possible. We just didn't know enough to share more, anyway.

Once back at the station, I had a few minor cases to go over and reports to file. Mundane work, but it had to be done, and at least it made the day pass faster.

After a few hours of reports, typing, and phone calls, it was time to call it a day. I stretched, shut down my computer, and said goodbye to Terry.

I had a date tonight, one I wasn't necessarily excited about, as it was something my mother had initially set up. She was worried I was going to die alone. Moms could be a bit melodramatic. I was only thirty-two. Plenty of time left.

Besides, in my line of work, I saw enough of the effects of love gone wrong and the heartbreak of loss. Suicides, murders, or accidents. No, thank you. I didn't want to deal with that.

I had focused mostly on my work. When I did date, it was primarily a casual thing to fulfill a need, be it loneliness or something more physical. I hadn't met a woman yet who I wanted to spend more time with than a few weeks or a couple of months tops. Don't get me wrong, I had the odd relationship that would last longer, but typically nothing serious.

This was my third date with Kelly. She was pretty, sweet, and had a decent sense of humor, but something was missing. I kept asking her out partially out of obligation to my mother and partly to fill my own void for companionship.

Kelly was the daughter of a church friend. Our mothers were already planning our wedding, but honestly, I didn't see the same ending. I just hoped that there was enough of a spark, or the third date was where this ended.

I headed home to get ready. My brain flipped through the day's events as I tried to put together clues about this serial killer. I had nothing concrete yet on it. The only thing I could tell was he had a type.

"Frustrating," I said to the steering wheel, then turned the radio to the sports to try to distract my mind.

I pulled up to my house, a three-bedroom ranch-style in one of the older neighborhoods on the west side of town. I'd lived here for a few years, and still, two bedrooms were completely empty. I could have lived in a one-bedroom apartment, but I loved the freedom of a yard with the deck I built to relax on.

I headed to the kitchen for a beer, then sat on my deck to unwind before my date. I kicked back in my favorite Adirondack chair and watched the clouds, birds, and the breeze blowing through the trees. Even though I tried not to, I thought again about the serial killer and each victim. I could see their faces. They would haunt me until I solved this.

Resolved to the fact I wasn't going to solve it tonight, I drained the beer and headed in to get ready for the date.

Fresh out of the shower, shaved, and dressed, I was a lot more positive about the date. Concert tickets? Check. Flowers? Check. Nobody could say I wasn't at least a good date. I always tried.

An hour later, I pulled up in front of her house. I was suddenly nervous. Why? I took a deep breath, then hopped out of my truck and headed for her door. As I knocked, I thought, "Third time's the charm."

Chapter Seven

~Joanna~

"Jo, you look too thin. Did you even eat on this trip?"

My mother reached over and squeezed my waist, but really it was a fat roll. This was her form of body shaming me. She always said the opposite of what she meant. The slam would come at some point. I was easily fifteen to twenty pounds over my ideal weight.

"Mom, I ate. Look at me. I'm a chunk." I was eating a cheeseburger and fries as we spoke.

Not exactly diet food. She was eating a dainty salad, "dressing on the side, please." I couldn't tell if her insult about my weight was to call attention to my eating habits. Knowing her, it probably was.

"Well, if you really think so, you should eat better. Look at me."

There it was.

I internally chastised myself for playing into her game. She had wanted to bait me.

I knew she disapproved of my food choices. I didn't care and didn't know why I even responded to her at all. Taylor's had the best burgers in town. I couldn't understand coming here to get a salad unless it was the blue cheese steak salad. Yum!

I popped another fry into my mouth and ignored her. She changed the subject, not that she cared, but she liked to give the illusion of a caring mother.

"So, tell me about your travels. Where did you go? How were the shows?"

I reluctantly filled her in, skipping over the part about Jeremy and seeing dead people again.

While I did have powers as a child, when I started doing this medium thing, I assured my family I was faking it for my mom's benefit, and they kept my secret. If she knew my last show was real, she would freak, and she was prone to the dramatics.

As I spoke, she mostly rolled her eyes or looked around the restaurant. She probably didn't want anyone to hear what I was saying, even though half the restaurant already knew me and knew my job, that was, if they recognized me at all.

When I was a child, it worried her that I saw dead people. She was part of the reason I taught myself to block them out. She would get so upset, crying and carrying on. Her reaction scared me more than seeing the dead people. The dead people were always nice to me.

When Ted passed, I had so many questions and no way to get the answers. I wanted that yelling, screaming, ugly cry moment to tell him off.

Desperate to regain my powers, I started going to clubs and conferences for people that believed in the afterlife, mediums, and ghosts. I thought if I hung out with those types of people and in those places, I could regain my ability. That's when I met Micah.

He was in a job he hated, and I didn't make enough money in my previous job to get out of my debt. In a moment of desperation, we started doing the fake readings as a side gig.

He helped with marketing, especially maintaining my social media presence, and I did the scheduling, readings, and bookkeeping. We split what we made evenly, which was minimal at first.

But it slowly grew, and soon we were making some money, and I had become a semi-celebrity. Not long after that, we brought Tessa in to do the bookkeeping and scheduling, jobs neither of us enjoyed.

Mom and I wrapped up our lunch. I paid, as I'd come to expect with her. She didn't even offer or pretend like she might. As we said goodbye in the parking lot, she gave me a lecture about changing jobs if I ever wanted to find another husband.

"No man wants to date or marry a woman who talks to dead people, whether fake or real. What kind of wife would you make? I mean, look at Ted."

"Oh, gee, thanks, Mom."

"You know what I mean." She waved her hands around as she spoke.

No, no, I didn't know what she meant, but I didn't reply. She'd said all of this before, but it never hurt any less.

And what was all that waving anyway? Like trying to wash the mean comment out of the air?

Besides, I didn't want to be with a man who thought my job was weird, so that was all right with me. I wasn't even sure I would ever get married again. Trust issues don't go away, at least easily, and I hadn't met anyone else I trusted.

Overall, I thought I got off easy. Everything she said about me, I had expected and heard before, and she only mentioned three of her supposed illnesses. Plus, I got a yummy Taylor Burger out of the deal, so not a bad lunch.

Before heading home, I sent Micah a text message and asked him to meet me at my house later. He responded he would but asked if he could bring Josh. Sure. I liked Josh. I just hoped he didn't think what we were doing was weird.

I didn't know how much Micah shared with him about our business. They hadn't been dating long. Maybe four or five months. I knew some of Micah's previous boyfriends hated his job, especially the travel. It was one of many reasons I didn't date.

I got home and fired up my computer. I had to answer emails and research some of my upcoming clients. Even though I could see the spirits, I didn't know if those loved ones would show up for the appointments. It made sense to have the information in my back pocket just in case. It was the planner in me to be prepared for any and all scenarios.

There was a knock on the door, then I heard Micah call out as he let himself in. It woke me from my Google coma. I saved my notes and got up to meet them in the foyer.

"Hey, guys," I said.

"Hiya, Boss. You remember Josh?"

"Yeah, of course. Good to see you again."

"Thanks for having me. I'm always curious about my boy's work." He smiled lovingly up at Micah and touched his arm.

Josh was several inches shorter than Micah. He was blond with blue eyes, the opposite of Micah's dark complexion, and not as thin as Micah, but not exactly heavy. They made a cute couple.

"Well, let's get right to it," I said and gestured toward the living room.

I launched right into the new developments in Jeremy's story. From the confrontation with Greg to running into Laney. Micah was on the edge of his seat. Josh was just staring back and forth, but mostly at Micah. He was clearly in love. It was cute. Micah deserved him.

"So, you think they might be dating?" Micah asked.

"Definitely, and if you had seen her face, you'd probably think the same," I replied.

"Doubt it. I'm not so good at picking up on those types of clues the way you are."

"No, he's not. It took him forever to realize I was into him," Josh teased.

"Aw, babe, you weren't good at flirting. You've gotten better, though." They shared a sweet look for a moment before Micah continued our conversation. "Okay, Boss, so it sounds like the next step is to talk to this detective, and as much as I hate to say it, we might need to talk to Hank the Hammer."

I gasped at the second part of his suggestion, though I knew he was right about Hank.

"Hank? Oh my gosh. Maybe, but what would I even say to him? He's so scary!"

"I think we just ask him about the deal he had with Jeremy. You know, confirm what Greg told you. What's the worst that could happen?"

"We end up dead," I said flatly.

Micah laughed. Josh inhaled and grabbed Micah's hand.

"Babe, that doesn't sound like a good plan."

"No, it's fine. Joanna has a charm about her that seems to hypnotize people. I've seen it time after time."

"When I'm Joanna the Medium on the stage, maybe, but not when I'm just plain, everyday Jo."

He nodded. "Yep, even as plain Jo. You don't see the way people look at you. I've seen it. I think it's your calm tone or something, not so much the words. You just have this air about you that people, alive and dead, are drawn to."

I just stared at him. What was he talking about? That couldn't be true, could it? I thought about my most recent interactions, like with Greg. He did seem upset but not with me. He actually took my story at face value, more or less, and with very few questions. But thinking about it, I could see what he was saying. Maybe there was something to what Micah said, even though I always felt so awkward and lacked confidence at times.

"You think we can just walk into Hank's place and talk to him?" I asked.

"Yeah, why not? Doesn't he hang out at that bar? What's it called?"

I thought for a second. "Leo's?"

"Yeah, Leo's. Do you want to go?"

No way was I going to that place, or so I thought.

After much coaxing by Micah, I decided to go. I trusted him, and if he thought I could do this, maybe I could. Plus, there was my own overwhelming curiosity to see this investigation through.

When we walked into Leo's, I recognized Hank's crew immediately. They were well known around town, so, though I hadn't personally "done business" with them, I knew their faces and some of their names. A few were lined up along the bar, and others were playing pool. The man himself was entertaining a busty blonde in a corner booth.

There were other random people dotted around as well. Leo's had good food, and it was a popular hangout, so not exclusively for mobsters and their lackeys. I'd only been hesitant in coming since I knew the plan was for me to talk to Hank. Any other time, I might have jumped at the opportunity.

I glanced toward Hank. A shiver crept up and down my spine at the thought of having to go speak to him.

We took a seat at a booth on the opposite side of the bar. I slid into the side of the booth facing Hank so I could easily see him. Micah and Josh got cozy on the other side. We ordered drinks, and the guys got nachos.

"Okay, so now what, Boss?"

"I'm not sure. I wasn't expecting the woman with him, but it makes sense. I've heard he is a bit of a ladies' man." I eyed him.

At first glance, he looked like my old science teacher. He was a short, stocky older man with slicked-back gray hair that was starting to thin. However, unlike my high school science teacher, Hank was well-dressed and carried himself with confidence. And let's not forget all his power and money. I supposed some women found those things attractive, especially the money part. Rumor was he showered his girlfriends with expensive gifts like jewelry, cars, and fancy trips.

We chatted, sipped our drinks, and tried to act like we were there hanging out and not stalking Hank. But I kept my eyes on him and his companion, looking for an opportunity to talk to him. They were snuggled up in a corner booth, and I was starting to think this was a wasted trip.

As we waited, the boys flirted and made goo-goo eyes at each other. They were still in that lovey, new relationship phase. I felt like a third wheel, but tried to keep my focus on the mission at hand, not on how comfy the couple across from me seemed or how awkward, and possibly a bit jealous, I felt.

"Are you going to go talk to him, Boss?"

"I don't know if I'll get a chance. Look at them. I think he would get mad if I interrupted their snuggle time. Don't you think?"

They both agreed. Hank was known for his temper, among other things.

We finished our drinks, and the guys worked their way through the nachos. I might have helped with a few.

"I'll go up to the bar to order us another round and to get closer to Hank." It also gave me a moment away from the happy couple.

After I ordered, I leaned on the bar, making small talk with the bartender. When the drinks were ready, I turned to go back to my table. That's when I got my chance with Hank the Hammer. His companion excused herself to go to the ladies' room. I took action, leaving the drinks and letting the bartender know I would be right back.

"Excuse me, Mr. Hammer?"

"Yes, can I help you?" he grumbled. His deep, stern voice had me second-guessing my choice to speak to him.

A couple of his guys stepped forward from the bar, eyeing me. Yikes, what had I gotten myself into? Alarm bells went off in my head.

Run, run! My inner voice said, but I stayed to see this through.

"I'm very sorry to disturb you. Let me introduce myself. I'm Joanna. I'm a medium, which means—"

"Oh, you're that 'Medium with a Heart.' The one that sees dead people." He waved his goons back to their spots, but I could see them keeping an eye on us.

"Yes, sir. That's me."

"Who is it that wants to talk to me? My mother?" he asked hopefully.

I looked around, but really couldn't tell if there were any dead people here. To me, they looked like everyone else until they walked through a table, a door, or a living person. On closer examination, there were a few here as I watched one step through the bar and another passing through one of Hank's guys that was playing pool. However, none appeared to be his mother.

"No, not your mother, but I do have a question from someone. He isn't here right now, but Jeremy Landon borrowed money from you before he died, and I was wondering what the terms of the loan were. I think there might be some confusion with his brother, Greg."

His demeanor changed, and his tone became business-like. "You been talking to Jeremy? Or Greg?"

"Both, actually. I got two different stories. I was curious which one to believe."

He eyed me suspiciously. I could hear my heart beating in my ears.

"Greg is a whiny bitch. He owes me money for my help with his construction business and a few other... let's call them business ventures. Jeremy owed me money, too, but he died. I've not gone after his family, not his parents, not Greg, and not his widow. Especially when he left her pregnant. She has enough problems. I might be tough on people, but I have my limits." He paused and eyed me again. My heart hammered against my ribs. He pointed a meaty finger my way. "Don't trust Greg. He has the most to lose at this point. What's Jeremy got to lose? He's dead."

"Thank you. That makes sense."

"Now, if you'll excuse me. My date has returned."

The blonde stepped around me and slid in beside Hank. She gave me the once-over, then cuddled up close to him as if to make sure I knew he was hers and to back off. If she had hissed, I wouldn't have been surprised.

"I'm sorry, of course." I started to walk away.

"Oh, and Ms. Joanna, a warning for you. Don't ever question my deals. I'm nice the first time. After that, I might not be so understanding." He paused to let that sink in. "And if you do hear from my dear mother, please come see me right away." With that, he waved me away, and one of his guys stepped forward to let me know he meant business.

I retreated quickly, joining Micah and Josh. They'd paid our tab while I was with Hank, and we left without drinking our second round. Back in the car, I could breathe again, and my heart returned to a normal beat. My hands trembled as I buckled my seatbelt.

"Holy crap, I can't believe I did that! I was so scared."

"I can't believe you did that, either. You were so brave." Micah declared as he turned the car on and backed out of the parking spot. His voice was tight. He'd been scared, too.

"This was your idea. What do you mean you can't believe I'd do it?"

"Well, I didn't think you actually would. That was Hank the Hammer. Hank the freakin' Hammer!"

I stared at him in disbelief. He'd practically dared me to go in there, calling me a chicken if I didn't do this. Ugh! I let that go and filled them in on what Hank had said. It made sense that Jeremy didn't have anything to lose. He was no longer alive to lose anything. Greg, on the other hand, had everything to lose.

I was also shocked that he told me so much, at least confirmed what Jeremy had said. Hank hadn't exactly given me any details. Was it what Micah had said about people being drawn to me that made them trust me? While there were times I met people who didn't believe that I could talk to dead people, which used to be true, I met just as many that did. However, for Hank to give me even limited details on his business dealings was a huge development and a show of trust.

The guys dropped me off at my house. They were heading to a party. I had big plans myself. I was going to cook a single-serving chicken pot pie and binge watch one of my guilty pleasure reality shows. Exciting evening at home, right? Woohoo!

Chapter Eight

I was sitting up, rubbing my eyes, and cursing the morning when Jeremy arrived the next day.

"Good, you're awake. Now come turn on the news for me, and then get yourself ready. We have to visit the detective today." He turned on his heel and waited for me to join him in the living room.

He seemed a bit snippy this morning. It could be that I hadn't had coffee yet and was projecting my own feelings, so I shrugged it off.

I stumbled in, switched to the news for him, and grumbled that I would be back before heading for the bathroom. Unlike yesterday, I decided to shower and dress before joining him in the living room. I wasn't looking forward to a day with Mr. Chatty.

Once I couldn't stall any longer, I headed straight for the coffee. He seemed to have learned not to talk before I had my coffee because he continued watching the news until I had my second cup in hand.

"Ready to talk?" he asked.

I nodded but didn't say a word, just continued to sip my coffee.

"I watched Greg for most of the day yesterday, and I couldn't believe what I found out. He's seeing my wife! I left before things got heated. I couldn't watch that."

"I'm sorry. I saw her right after I left you yesterday. She told me she was going to have lunch with him, but that was all she said."

He started pacing and stomping around. Stomping might not be the right word, but it was kind of a ghostly marching but without the stomping sound.

"I just can't believe it. It sounds like they might have been dating before I died. I knew they would both move on. Cate has. She's young; I don't blame her. But Laney? And with my brother?" He paused and looked at me. His face was long and pinched with sorrow. "What if that baby isn't mine? I can't live with myself if she isn't mine."

I decided not to point out the obvious, that he wasn't alive now. He started pacing again. I watched him while I sipped my second cup of coffee and let my mind wander, not really listening to his rants. He seemed like he wasn't looking for a response, just wanting to vent his emotions, so that was exactly what I was letting him do.

I was surprised that he only just found out. I thought he had been following Laney for a while now. Perhaps he had just missed the signs.

Finally, his temper fizzled out. He sighed heavily and stood to stare out the window facing the backyard.

"It's too early to go to the police station, so what do you want to do until then?" I asked.

"Beat the crap out of Greg. But since I can't do that, I don't know." He shrugged and sounded defeated.

I felt awful for him in a way. Maybe if I shared some of the information I found out yesterday, it would cheer him up a little bit.

"Well, we can't do that, but I understand. So, I talked to Hank yesterday, and he said..."

"Excuse me, you talked to Hank? As in the Hammer? What were you thinking? He's dangerous if you don't know what you're doing, which I can't imagine you do."

"I was thinking I could get some answers, and I did. Greg owes him money on his own, not from your loan. He also confirmed he wouldn't go after Laney for the money. He's just written it off with your death."

"That's what I already told you. Anything else? Something new, perhaps?"

"Nope." I didn't tell him that Hank told me I could trust him and not Greg, or how he threatened me. Jeremy didn't need to know about the former, and he couldn't help me with the latter, so no point in mentioning either.

"Good. As long as you don't piss him off, you will be fine," he cautioned.

I would keep that in mind and didn't mention that Hank had already warned me to stay out of his business. I fought the cold chill as I remembered Hank's stern tone as he issued said warning.

"When is your appointment with Laney?" he asked.

"Thursday."

"Okay, so we need to figure out a plan for what to say to her. I don't want to tell her everything yet, especially not with this new information. I want to make a list of questions for her."

We spent the next hour making a list and discussing topics that I should cover with Laney. It was a good list, but I knew that Laney would have her own questions. Jeremy wanted to feel in control, and I humored him.

With that done, I called over to the station and asked for Detective Hartley. After listening to their hold music for a minute, the detective picked up.

"This is Detective Hartley."

"Hi, Detective, my name is Joanna Webber. Greg Landon gave me your card."

"Are you that medium?"

"Um, yes?" I wasn't surprised that he knew me, and yet after all this time, it still caught me off guard when people did.

"And you said Greg Landon gave you my card. Why?"

"You investigated the death of his brother, Jeremy Landon, right?"

"That's right. Closed case. Why?"

Oh geez, this guy wasn't going to make things easy for me. Not that he should. I was some random person calling him on the phone. But I just wanted to make an appointment with him and hadn't expected the "whys."

"I'd just like to come in and talk to you about it. It's a little bit complicated. Better to have the conversation in person."

"I'm quite busy and don't have time to spend on a closed case."

"Detective, please, this is important."

He sighed. He was thinking about it. That was good.

"Fine. Come by the station in an hour." He hung up without a goodbye. His phone etiquette could use some work, but we were in.

An hour later, we were standing in the police station waiting for Detective Hartley. The place was hectic. There was yelling, crying, and lots of movement. I also noticed several dead people by the way they didn't interact with objects.

I didn't want to call attention to the fact that I could see them. I didn't need anyone else following me around.

"You can see them, can't you?"

I put my cell phone to my ear, a habit I was getting used to with Jeremy around. I should dig up my Bluetooth and wear it all the time. "Yes, I can, but I don't want them to know. One of you is enough."

He chuckled and went over to talk to a few of them. I sure hoped he didn't blow my cover.

The comings and goings in the police station were chaotic, and before long, things started to blur together. That was when I noticed an incredibly attractive man coming from the back offices. He said something to the officer at the reception desk, who gestured toward me.

Oh, snap, this must be my guy. I shifted in the hard plastic chair as I watched him make his way across the crowded room.

Not to sound unprofessional, but wow. He had that messy, just-out-of-bed styled dark hair, blue eyes, and was dressed in a dark polo shirt with khaki-colored slacks. He had that hot, geeky look about him that I found myself attracted to. I hoped my brain would reengage before he made it to me.

"Joanna? Detective Hartley," he said as a curt introduction. "Please come with me."

I nodded and felt an instant blush. Thankfully he had already turned his back, so he didn't notice.

Jeremy looked over, making eye contact with me. He said something to the gentleman he was talking with before following us.

The detective didn't say a word until he led me into a closet-sized office. Not a plush walk-in closet either, but your Aunt Ida's tiny coat closet. That might be a slight exaggeration. It was a little bigger than that, but not much. There was a chair on each side of a desk and a couple of file cabinets behind. He gestured for me to sit.

"Okay, so Ms. Joanna, you want to know about the Landon suicide."

Jeremy started cursing and "stomping" behind me. He really believed he had been murdered. I wasn't yet convinced, but I was positive he hadn't killed himself, at least not by suicide. Maybe by accident.

"He didn't kill himself," I said.

"Oh, really? Well, accidentally or on purpose, I have proof and years of experience."

"But I have the truth!" Jeremy screamed in his face.

I tried not to laugh at poor Jeremy. I knew he believed this, but seeing him yelling at the unsuspecting detective gave me the giggles.

"And how do you know this?"

"Because I speak to dead people, and Jeremy told me himself."

"Oh, he did, did he?"

Cynical jerk, I thought.

"Yes, and he has told me he had too much to live for to kill himself. He also said..." I paused to hear what Jeremy had to say. "He knew how to handle those chemicals and believes someone tampered with them to murder him."

"Murder, really? That's a serious charge."

"Yes. Murder."

"And who does he think did it?"

"He doesn't know yet. That's why we need your help."

Detective Hartley just stared at me for far too long. It was unsettling, but two could play that game. I sat without saying a word during his staring contest that only he was playing.

He finally broke the silence. "Okay, so let me get this straight. You see dead people, and Jeremy Landon came to you, telling you that he did not, in fact, kill himself either intentionally or by accident. He wants your help to solve his murder, and you now need my help. Did I get that all correct?"

I looked at Jeremy, and we nodded at each other.

"Yes," I said to the detective.

"Is he here now? Is that what you're looking at?"

"Yes, he's right here. He's almost always with me. I can't get rid of him until I solve this to his satisfaction." I hoped that Jeremy caught the annoyance in my tone.

"This is insane. Insane." He stood, pacing the two steps in each direction that the office allowed. "How do I keep getting all the crazies?" he muttered to himself.

I should have been offended by his statement, but I wasn't.

"Let's say for a moment that I decide to believe this and help you. What exactly is in this for me? I have other cases I've moved on to that require my time." He glowered at me.

"You will have solved a murder and get that murderer off the streets."

"And if it's not murder but exactly what I said it was, what then?"

"Well, then I'll apologize on his behalf. Either way, I'm free of him."

Jeremy laughed. Detective Hartley scowled at me.

"This is crazy. Unless you have concrete evidence and not some hallucination, I can't take time away from my other cases to play with you." He muttered something I couldn't make out.

I probably didn't want to know.

He sighed. "Fine, I'll help. It's a closed case anyway, but my involvement will be limited and only to end this."

"Thank you, Detective."

He excused himself. I didn't know how long he was going to be gone or where he was going. Ignoring Jeremy, I checked my emails and social media on my phone. Nothing really exciting was going on, but it passed the time.

"Okay, Ms. Joanna, here is the file." He tapped a brown folder with one hand. "I have a room down the hall where you can review it. You can't take it out of the building. You can't make photocopies or take pictures with your cell phone. You can only review it and then leave it here. Do you understand?"

"Yes, sir." I saluted him.

His flat expression told me he did not find that humorous. He had no sense of humor.

"Don't try anything funny just because you think I'm not watching. There are cameras in the room, and we'll see if you take pictures or try to take anything out of the file." I nodded. "I'll be back in thirty minutes to check on you."

I followed him to the room. He handed me the file and a bottle of water before turning and leaving.

I took a seat and opened the file. It wasn't very thick. I flipped through it once to see what was included. I had never looked at a police file before and didn't know what to expect. It included pictures of Jeremy post-mortem. His body was both covered and uncovered.

"Weird to see myself like that," he said over my shoulder.

"Does it bother you?"

"Nah. It probably should. But it doesn't."

I flipped through the additional pictures that showed the bottles of drugs and ingredients he had been mixing. There were some screen grabs from the video. The toxicology report was clear, at least to my amateur eyes. It stated that the drugs he had been mixing were not compatible, causing a toxic gas to fill the room, which killed him.

"That's bullshit. Those chemicals weren't even supposed to be in those bottles. See this one and this one?" He pointed to one of the pictures. "These two are safe to mix. I've done it hundreds of times. They should have mixed into a powder. It's part of the recipe for Remarpax." He looked at the report. "I don't understand how chemicals I wasn't even using could be in my system. The labels are clearly marked, and we have a robust procedure for ensuring this doesn't happen."

He started pacing the room and muttering to himself. It must have been hard to come to terms with his demise and then learn that you actually did it to yourself.

"I'm so sorry. I can't imagine what you must be feeling seeing all this and finding out that you did actually do it."

"I'm going to stop you right there. I still don't believe this. It's bull. I didn't do it, accidentally or on purpose. Whatever that detective said or believes. Someone must have switched things on me." He went back to talking to himself. "I guess if someone switched them, it was an accident, but gosh darn... I just don't buy that. Our lab techs were smart. We had procedures in place. They wouldn't have made that kind of mistake.

Someone must have done it on purpose. Only a few people had that level of access to our labs and had a motive to kill me."

"Yeah, I get that, but this report seems to be clear, even to my untrained eyes." I tapped the file.

"I know, and who else is adamant it's a clear case?" We locked eyes.

"Greg," we said in unison.

I closed the file and just looked at Jeremy. It made a lot of sense. He wanted the girl and revenge on his brother for the wrong done to the family, the near-death of their grandmother. He knew about the debts to Hank and was trying to use it to further soil Jeremy's name. Granted, I didn't like Jeremy, but he didn't deserve that.

If this were true, I couldn't imagine what Laney would feel if and when she found out.

"And you think Greg had access to the lab?"

"He built the building. His firm is still doing work on the third floor."

"Okay, so he had access." I agreed.

The door opened, and two detectives came in, one of whom was Detective Hartley.

"Done?" he asked.

"Yes. This was quite helpful. Thank you."

"This is my partner, Detective Walden. Terry, this is Joanna the Medium."

"Nice to meet you, Joanna. My mother is a huge fan of yours. She's seen your live show and has your book." He extended his hand, and I shook it.

Detective Terry Walden was tall, dark, and handsome. He was built like a bodybuilder. His size was almost intimidating, but his wide smile and friendly tone put me at ease immediately.

"Oh, that's sweet! If she ever wants a personal consultation, I would be happy to meet with her." I smiled my best Joanna the Medium smile.

"I'll tell her. She'll be thrilled," Terry said warmly.

"So, I assume this has cleared up the murder theory?" Detective Hartley asked.

"Actually, this makes it very clear it was murder. He's sure of it." I looked to where Jeremy was standing, arms crossed with an icy glare on his face.

"Son of a... You can't be serious. You really think, after this report, that it's still murder? You're a nut," Detective Hartley said and stormed out.

I was unfazed by his reaction. Although storming out was a tad unprofessional, I had expected him to be skeptical.

When I have client readings or a show, those people come to me because they believe or at least want to believe that I'm real.

However, going to people with this is new, and I didn't expect it to be believed. Yet both Greg and Hank had. My luck with believers was bound to run out.

"Sorry about my partner. He doesn't believe in this kind of thing. I'll be honest. I'm not sure if I do, but my mom does, and she would kick my butt if I didn't at least hear you out. Hartley filled me in on what's going on, but what else have you come up with?"

I told him our theory about the switched ingredients. He nodded along, asked questions at times, and seemed to be sincerely listening and willing to help. He didn't appear as skeptical as his partner, but perhaps he was just humoring me. I wasn't sure yet.

"Well, I can show you the whole video. Normally we don't show them, but since the case is closed, it has been declassified and left to my discretion to share it if I think you have information that can help. Again, I'm still on the fence about believing you on this, but I can almost hear my mom's voice telling me to help."

"Thanks. That would be helpful. I assume you have already seen the comings and goings of everyone in the lab."

"Yes. We have it for the twenty-four hours leading up to the death and, of course, showing his death, but we might not know who should and shouldn't be in there. We asked others at the lab. They all said nobody out of the ordinary, but Jeremy would know best. If this is real and you are talking to him, he can tell us."

He left the room and came back a few minutes later, pushing a television on a stand. They were still old-school with their technology. Jeremy moved from the window closer to my side, so he could see the screen better.

"Okay, this is the footage. Here is the remote. I need to go catch up with Clint on another case. I'll be back shortly to hear what you find. If you need one of us sooner, here are our phone extensions." He wrote them on a pad next to the phone. He nodded, flashed me a friendly smile, and left.

I pressed play to see where the video started. We watched it on fast forward, but not so quickly that we couldn't see the faces. It was a lot of footage. Jeremy mumbled the various names of people as they came in and out of the lab: Marcus, Ben, Cate, Angie, Elias.

"I didn't know Cate worked for you. You hadn't mentioned that," I pointed out.

"Oh, yeah. She's worked there for a few years now."

"And you didn't think that was an important fact in all the things you told me?"

"No, why would that be important? She's really not a suspect," he said and shrugged.

"What? I thought you first listed her as a suspect. What changed?"

"She's too sweet and innocent. Not bright enough to have planned something like this."

Despite wanting to work with me, seeking me out, he held back. I wondered what else he was holding back from me.

And how had I missed this simple fact in my research? All I'd found was that she was a lab technician. I thought about his assessment of her. I hadn't met her yet, only seen a few things on her social media, so I had no real opinion and had to trust his judgment until I had more evidence. However, considering her job, I figured she had to be smart in some ways, but was she the type to plan a murder? That was the real question.

"Ugh, none of them are Greg. All of them are my employees. Trusted employees," he said through gritted teeth, his tone gruff and hopeless.

He started pacing the room again. I could tell how frustrating this was for him. He might be a jerk, but he deserved answers.

"I'm sorry, Jeremy. I was hoping we would see something."

"Not your fault. I thought we might see who switched the ingredients or something out of the ordinary. This... this is not what I thought." He rubbed his face.

I wanted to help him and give him closure, but I didn't know how. We hadn't seen anyone out of the ordinary, at least according to him. We watched it twice, and some parts more when he asked me to back it up, thinking he saw something.

After an hour of staring at the video and the file, we gave up. I closed it and gathered my things, then stepped into the hallway. I hoped to see one of the detectives. I guess I should have called their extensions, but I was ready to go.

Thankfully, Detective Hartley appeared, walking toward me.

"Done?" he asked.

"Yes, thank you. I left everything on the table as instructed."

"Did you get the information you were hoping for?"

"No, unfortunately."

"Ah, I'm sorry," he said, though he didn't sound sincere. More smug than sympathetic.

He walked me out without a word. Jeremy's shoulders were sagging, and he was hanging his head by the time we got outside. I hadn't realized until now how much he believed he was murdered. I was starting to believe him, too, simply because he believed it so strongly.

"Well, thank you for your time. I appreciate it." I offered my hand to Detective Hartley.

He took it begrudgingly. The brief contact was businesslike, but my body hummed at the slight touch.

Boy, I needed a boyfriend.

"Not a problem," he said with a smirk and nodded before turning back into the building.

I didn't expect to ever see him again.

"So, now what?" I asked Jeremy.

"I'm going to check on Laney. I just hope she isn't with Greg. I'll see you in a day or two or three for her appointment." He shuffled off, head bowed.

Poor guy.

Chapter Nine

Jeremy was true to his word and didn't come back until the day of Laney's appointment. Sadly, I had gotten used to the early wakeups. I cursed him each morning, even though he wasn't there.

Jeremy arrived only an hour before she was scheduled to arrive. "Did you miss me?"

No, but I grinned sweetly when I replied.

"Of course. Getting to sleep to a normal hour is overrated. I'd much rather wake to a start with you smiling down at me."

He chuckled, but I could see some of the shine had gone from his eyes. It made me sad. He might be annoying, and I'd only known him a few days, but I had started to like him.

He wanted to discuss once more the plan for Laney's visit. I had my own ideas about how this would go, but I didn't want to spoil it. I knew how important this was, so I let him talk it out.

"She'll likely want to know why I was with Cate. Honestly, I loved them both. They are such different people. Laney is smart, well-dressed, well-spoken. The perfect wife for an executive. I hate to say trophy wife because she was so much more than that. We were a perfect pair. We complemented each other. She was... is just perfect."

"So why cheat?" I hoped his answer would give me some peace of my own.

"Because Caitlyn was completely different, the total opposite, and it was exciting. She's spunky, bubbly, fun. Like one of those toy dogs that are always happy to see you. Do you know what I mean?"

"Did you seriously just describe your girlfriend as a dog?"

"Yes, but not like a dog, more like a cute, fluffy purse puppy."

My eyes nearly rolled out of my head. This guy. But I had to admit his description did paint a picture.

"So, Laney was your wife, and Caitlyn was what? A fun hobby?" I almost couldn't say the words.

He sighed. "Look, I loved my wife very much, and I didn't mean to hurt her. She has to know that. If nothing else... I loved her... I love her still. Cate was just Cate."

There was a knock at the door. I looked at Jeremy, and he nodded but seemed as nervous as I felt.

"Hi, Laney, please come in," I said as I opened the door for her.

"Thank you, Joanna." She stepped inside and looked around. "You have a lovely home. Not exactly what I pictured but lovely."

"Um, thank you." I looked around, feeling self-conscious. What had she expected? Maybe more like my stage personality: flashy and glamorous.

My house didn't really have a style unless casual is a style. The foyer was plain, with only an abstract floral print on the wall and a throw rug. From the front door, you could see into my office to the right or straight ahead to my living room. My couch was light denim blue with blue and yellow plaid throw pillows. There was artwork throughout the house like the one in the foyer. Some knick-knacks were scattered here and there to make it look homey for my clients. I wasn't home a lot to decorate and had only lived in the house for a little over a year. For much of that time, I had been traveling.

"We can go into my office or the living room if that's more comfortable for you."

"Hmm," she looked around. "How about the living room? Keep it casual."

"Great." We walked on through. "Please, have a seat. Would you like a drink? I have tea or water or..." My mind blanked on what else to offer a pregnant lady. Coffee was out, or at least my sister avoided it during her two pregnancies, and it was 9:00 a.m., so too early for wine, which she couldn't drink anyway.

"Water is fine. Thank you."

I stepped into the kitchen, returning with a glass of ice water for us both.

"Thanks," she said as I handed her the tall glass.

"So, are you ready?"

She took a deep breath and nodded.

"Okay, great. Well, I have been talking to Jeremy and..."

"Wait, what? You have been talking to my husband... er, ex-husband? Dead husband? I thought I was going to have to give you details or something... wow." She appeared flustered as she started to fidget in her seat. She set the glass down and grabbed a tissue from the box on the table.

"Yes, and he has a few things he'd like to tell you."

"Oh, he does, does he?" she said angrily. She pushed herself up from the sofa, which was not easy at nearly seven months pregnant. "I have a few things to say myself. I was left alone to deal with a huge mess. Debt, a baby, and a soiled reputation. This isn't a big town, and not only do we work together, but did you know his girlfriend and I go to the same OB/GYN? We are due within a week of each other. The office staff makes sure our appointments aren't at the same time, so we don't run into each other, but what happens if our girls have the same birthday? How weird would that be? Or what if they end up in the same kindergarten class?" Her hands balled up in tight fists that she waved around as she spoke. Only once done with her speech did she place them on each of her hips.

I didn't know what to say. I tried not to make eye contact with Jeremy at all. He was standing to my right, looking concerned. A mix of emotions played across his face. Sorrow. Anger. Love. Heartache.

"If it wasn't for Greg, I would be in a lot of trouble, money-wise. He has helped me sort out all the debt and get my life reorganized to my new reality."

"I'm sorry to hear that. It must be hard." I looked at Jeremy. I could see his nostrils flare at the mention of Greg.

"Is there anything you want me to say?"

"Me?" asked Laney.

"No, sorry. I was talking to Jeremy," I said and gestured toward where he was standing.

"Oh crap, he's here? I didn't know. I thought... I guess I assumed he would be, but... did he say anything?" She slowly sat back down, cradling her belly.

I felt a pang of jealousy. Where had that feeling come from? I had given up on the idea of having children a long time ago. I brushed it aside to focus on the job at hand.

I listened for a moment before repeating Jeremy's words. "Yes, he says he is very sorry. He didn't mean to hurt you and didn't expect to leave you so suddenly, or else he would have handled things differently."

"That's it?"

"What do you want me to say?" I spoke for Jeremy.

"I don't know, but you left me. You just... died. And I'm left behind to clean up this mess. I'm going to be a single mom, and... I'm scared."

"Laney, I'm so sorry. If I could go back to that day, I wouldn't have gone into the lab." He paused and looked at me. "Wait, do you really want to say that?"

Jeremy nodded. I shook my head. He tried to get me to say it, but I wasn't going to.

"What's going on? What is he saying?"

"Nothing. It's not part of this. He..." I tried pleading with my eyes for him to reconsider, but he gave a confident nod, and I knew he wasn't going to back down on this point.

"He knows about you and Greg, and when things started. He saw you the other day, going to lunch."

She gasped and blushed bright red.

"I'm sorry. I didn't think. I mean, it only started after I found out about his... your girlfriend. At first, Greg was just someone to talk to, but... but then it changed."

"So, you started dating Greg after finding out about Cate?"

"Yes," she said so softly I wasn't sure if she actually spoke the words or I was hearing things.

Jeremy's reaction told me she had. He exploded.

I watched him as he cursed and yelled, stomping all over my living room. Laney just watched me and occasionally followed my gaze. She was trying to see him, too. I wasn't going to be able to say all this. He wouldn't want me to, anyway.

"What is he saying?"

"He isn't happy."

"Jeremy, I'm sorry. I swear nothing really happened until... after. But you were with Cate, what did you care? We didn't have a perfect marriage. I thought we did, but clearly, we didn't. You found love with someone else and got her pregnant. What did you expect me to do?"

"I don't know," he said and hung his head.

"I was lonely. Most of my friends are fake. You know that. They just like me because of my supposed status. Big executive's wife. Ha. Money, country club, fancy parties. I had no one who I felt could really understand or to confide in. Greg, well... he listened to me and seems to care."

Jeremy had no reply. Silence fell as we each processed the conversation and tried to decide what to do or say next. I couldn't think of what could make this better, though I could think of hundreds of things to make it worse.

Laney was the first to break the silence.

"Jeremy, I loved you very much. I was so hurt when I found out about Cate. I just didn't and still don't understand. And now you're gone. Just gone. What am I supposed to do, be alone for the rest of my life?" She wept softly.

I handed her another tissue and shot Jeremy a dirty look.

"I can't explain it. I really can't, but I love you so very much. She has nothing to do with what we had together."

I relayed Jeremy's words.

We sat in silence until Laney shifted and rubbed her stomach, letting out a soft groan. Clearly, she was uncomfortable.

"Are you okay?" I asked.

"Yeah, the baby is moving a lot. I guess she can sense my stress. I had always heard the last few months are the most uncomfortable, and I am finding that to be true." She sipped her water and then winced. "This girl. I guess I should go. I probably need to rest."

"I'm sorry that things got a little... emotional. It happens with some of these connections, and I understand why yours is so tough."

Oh, boy, did I understand.

"Is that you talking or him?"

"Me. He says..." I looked at Jeremy and listened to what he had to say. "He says he loves you, and for what it's worth, he is really sorry."

She nodded and gave a weak smile but didn't reply verbally. Jeremy hung his head and moved to stare out into the back yard.

She paid me for the appointment and thanked me. Before leaving, she asked if she could stay in touch. I agreed. I needed to for several reasons, one being I wanted to. She seemed like she needed a friend as much as Jeremy did.

After she left, Jeremy stormed around, muttering to himself. I didn't try to engage. He needed to process this.

I rinsed Laney's glass, refilled my drink, and headed to my office to check emails while he threw his tantrum. After he settled down, he left, saying he would be back tomorrow or the next day. He was going to go stand in traffic.

I sat alone for a moment, processing what had just happened. That session had been intense, even by my standards.

Then I called Tessa to see where she was. We needed to go through my schedule and start planning for the next tour. It took months to put them together, so we needed to work on it early. She said she would be over shortly.

Before Tessa arrived, Micah showed up with samples of our newest products. We were adding some new shirt designs and tote bags in addition to mugs, keychains, and other trinkets. Everything looked good, so he placed our order with the vendor.

Tessa arrived with green teas and her laptop. That laptop held my whole made-up world of Joanna the Medium. Sure, I could access it on my computer, but Tessa was the key to all of it. I had no idea how to keep the business side of things running without her. Heck, I couldn't do any of this without either of my assistants. They were a godsend. From appointments to show bookings and everything in between, they handled it. I got to meet interesting people and help them with their grief. My job was easy.

"So, how did things go with Mrs. Landon?" Tessa asked.

"Things were... interesting." I gave them a rundown of events, including the video footage we had watched at the police station a few days ago, as I hadn't talked to them about it yet.

"Intense. So, what's the plan, Boss?" Micah jumped in.

"I have no idea. Jeremy said he would come back either tomorrow or the next day to discuss."

They nodded. Then we shifted back to medium work and the tour planning. Tessa had a few checks for me to sign. She then printed out my schedule for the week before they both left.

No quiet evening for me. I had plans to go to a friend's house for dinner. Lindsey and I had met our first year in college and were on the same degree path.

She was an accountant and had recently gotten a big promotion at work. It was a super cool corporate title: Senior Staff Accountant. I could make an educated guess on what that meant, but not having worked in the corporate world as she does, I would only be guessing. All I knew was that my friend was excited, so I would raise a glass and celebrate with her.

I wouldn't think about Jeremy or Laney, or how unprepared I felt in this new role I had taken on, or how I was starting to see dead people more and more everywhere I looked. I would just enjoy the time with friends.

I arrived with a bottle of wine. Lindsey squealed when she opened the door. We hugged hello. A few people were already there, so I got through intros and hellos, then got a drink and a plate full of the appetizers she had laid out.

I knew a few of the people, but quickly learned those I didn't know were her co-workers. Small talk was difficult for me as an introvert, but I managed.

I didn't always take an active role in social events. I was more of an observer, so I watched my friend laugh and chat and enjoy herself. She looked like she was having a wonderful evening, and that made me happy. It was fun to watch her interact with work people like this, not a side of her I got to see.

After the party ended, I stayed to help Lindsey clean up, and we got to talk one-on-one. It was nice to catch up without the distraction of the party. We promised to get together soon.

I didn't know if it would happen or if it was just a polite thing to say when goodbye alone didn't seem enough. Like when guys say they will call but never do. I would be okay either way, and I was glad I came.

Lindsey lived roughly fifteen minutes away in a neighborhood closer to my sister. Driving home, I let my mind wander. Mostly about Jeremy's murder, the suspects, and the limited facts I had learned so far. I really wanted to figure this out and quickly, but I had only met with a few people, and my research hadn't given me much to go on. As Greg said, it seemed pretty clear cut.

I was so caught up in my thinking that I didn't notice at what point the car got behind me, but I had a strange feeling I was being followed. I tried to tell myself that I was just paranoid. It was dark out, so I couldn't see the car well enough to know for sure.

The same car stayed with me nearly the entire drive. My nerves fired up to near panic levels. I fumbled for my phone, ready to call 911.

Two streets from my house, the car turned.

I breathed a sigh of relief, then chastised myself for being paranoid. I was just letting my mind get the better of me for no reason.

But as I pulled into my driveway, I couldn't shake the feeling that someone had been watching me.

Chapter Ten

I stared at the crime scene photos spread across my desk. Another victim. The second one this month.

I was writing up a report on the latest details in the serial killer murders. Twice in the same month was odd for him. The others had been spaced much farther apart, two months, sometimes three. But this time? Only three weeks between victims.

The change in pattern worried me. Serial killers don't usually accelerate like this unless something's changed. Stress? Getting bolder? Or maybe he wanted to get caught.

I didn't have experience with serial killers. This was my first. I had studied cases online, Bundy, Dahmer, the Zodiac, to see if there were any similar patterns or if I could determine a motive. My thinking was, if I could pinpoint his motive, I could find and stop him. No luck so far.

Each moment that I didn't find this guy, the town was at risk. Especially the women. All the victims fit the same profile: dark hair, fair skin, petite. Between five and five-six. Always found bound and bleeding out from a slashed throat, his initials carved into their foreheads.

The thought made my stomach turn.

My phone chimed. I checked the text. Kelly.

Can't wait for tonight! I'm making reservations at that Italian place you mentioned. 7:00?

The third date had been the charm, so to speak. I guess the concert was the perfect way to loosen us both up and let our guard down. We had been out every night since. I smiled as I typed out a reply.

Sounds perfect. See you then.

While I wouldn't say she was the one, I enjoyed my time with her and wanted to keep seeing her, at least for now. I wasn't thinking long term by any means. She was just the one for however long this thing lasted, which, given my history, would be another few weeks at the most.

The thought should have bothered me more than it did. Kelly was sweet. Smart. Funny. Pretty. Everything a guy should want. But I'd been down this road before. I'd start pulling away in a week or two, and she'd get the hint. They always did.

Maybe I was broken. Or maybe I just wasn't built for the whole commitment thing.

Terry knocked on my door. "Hey, we just got a call. Looks like a murder-suicide on the south side."

I stood and followed him out. In the car, we talked through the facts we had been given. The house was a regular for domestic disturbance calls. Neighbors had heard fighting and then gunshots. The wife made it next door to get help but passed away on the way to the hospital. There wasn't much to investigate, but we had to write up the report and probably give a statement to the media.

My phone chimed. I wasn't driving, so I was able to read. Kelly again. She let me know she was looking forward to dinner tonight.

"Who's that?"

"Kelly."

"Ah. Things getting serious?"

"Nah, but I do like spending time with her."

"I've heard that before. Well, good luck to her." Terry chuckled.

"What's that mean?"

"You know exactly what that means, Mr. Non-Commitment."

"Gee, thanks, bud." I thought for a second. "But yeah, you're right."

We arrived at the scene. Yellow tape cordoned off a small ranch house with peeling paint and an overgrown lawn. Neighbors clustered on the sidewalk, watching. A few were crying.

I ducked under the tape and followed Terry inside.

It was a typical murder-suicide. The living room showed signs of a struggle. Overturned coffee table, broken lamp, a smear of blood on the wall. The wife had been stabbed several times and then shot. Defensive wounds on her hands and arms. She'd fought hard.

The husband lay in the bedroom, self-inflicted gunshot wound to the head. A bottle of whiskey on the nightstand, mostly empty. Neighbors said they'd heard screaming, then gunshots. The wife had made it next door before collapsing. Died on the way to the hospital.

I surveyed the scene with a familiar numbness. This house had been on our radar for months. Domestic disturbance calls every few weeks. Screaming matches. Once, she'd called 911 but refused to press charges. Said she'd fallen down the stairs. We all knew that was a lie.

And now she was dead.

"Such a waste," Terry muttered beside me.

I nodded. There wasn't much to investigate. The facts were clear. But we had to document everything, write up the report, and probably give a statement to the media.

This was the kind of stuff that made me not want to get into a serious relationship and solidified my resolve to keep things brief, fun, and casual with Kelly. While I wasn't the violent type and knew I wouldn't snap, I understood how fragile life was. How quickly love could turn dark. And I didn't want to put myself through that.

Yes, my job had made me cynical and jaded about life and love.

After we wrapped up and gave a statement to the media, Terry and I headed to our favorite coffee shop. I needed something to get through the long afternoon of reports. Inside the shop, the robust scent of bitter coffee and sweet baked goods hit me. I could almost feel my energy level surge from the smell alone.

"Hey, isn't that the medium, Joanna?" Terry gestured toward the other side of the coffee shop.

Damn, I forgot how cute she was.

"We should say hi," he suggested.

I shrugged in reply and pretended to study the menu while waiting for our turn to order.

"Hey, Joanna," Terry called out to her.

She looked over, and I could see the moment she recognized us. Her whole face brightened with her beautiful smile. It went right to her honey-brown eyes. She waved and walked over.

"Hey, detectives. Keeping the town safe?"

"Yes, ma'am. How're you doing?" Terry beamed at her.

Whoa, boy. You're married, I thought.

"Wonderful. Did you get the box I sent over for your mom, Detective Walden?"

"Yes, she loved it. And, please, call me Terry."

She smiled at Terry while I tried to ignore them both. I didn't want to engage in a conversation with her and risk liking her.

"So, anything new with Jeremy's case?" Terry asked her.

My ears perked up.

"Unfortunately, no. Brick walls." She sounded disappointed.

I chuckled. She shot me a death look. Whoops. I hadn't meant to react at all.

"I still believe he was murdered. I just haven't figured out yet how to prove it."

She smiled and nodded to Terry before walking out with her coffee. I watched her until I couldn't see her any longer.

"Why do you push her buttons? Even if it isn't true, why not just humor her? We have worked with crazier. Besides, she is super cute."

"Dude, you're married."

"I can still think a girl is hot, and that one is. I can tell you think so too."

I shrugged. "I'm dating Kelly."

"That's not a denial."

"Drop it, Terry."

"I'm just saying, you could be nicer to her. She's not hurting anyone with this Jeremy thing. And who knows? Maybe she's onto something."

I snorted. "You don't actually believe she talks to dead people."

"My mom does. And my mom's not stupid."

"Your mom also thinks crystals can heal chakras."

Terry laughed. "Fair point." He paused. "But Joanna seems genuine. I don't think she's a con artist. I think she really believes it."

That was the problem. I couldn't shake the feeling that Joanna actually believed the things she was saying. Which made her either delusional or...

No. There was no "or." Dead people don't talk. It's that simple.

Thankfully, it was our turn to order, so I didn't have to continue this conversation.

But as I waited for my coffee, I found myself thinking about those honey-brown eyes and that bright smile.

And I hated that I was.

We grabbed our coffees and headed back to the station. Terry chatted about his mom's latest attempt to get him to try meditation classes. I only half-listened.

My mind kept drifting back to two things: the serial killer case sitting on my desk and the medium who'd just walked out of the coffee shop.

Both were mysteries I couldn't solve.

One was a murderer I needed to catch before he killed again.

The other was a woman who claimed to talk to ghosts and somehow made me want to believe her.

I wasn't sure which one unsettled me more.

Chapter Eleven

I couldn't stop thinking about Detective Hartley's smug face at the coffee shop. That little chuckle when I mentioned hitting brick walls. Like he was just waiting for me to give up and admit Jeremy's death was exactly what it looked like.

Which made me more determined than ever to prove him wrong.

I pulled out my notebook and reviewed my suspect list. I'd talked to Greg, Laney, and Hank. That left Aaron Novak and Cate, Jeremy's girlfriend. Each one would be tricky to approach for different reasons.

Aaron would be the toughest. Jeremy didn't think the "message from the other side" approach would work with him. After our first awkward meeting, I wasn't sure what angle to try next.

Cate would be second hardest. What was I supposed to say to the pregnant girlfriend? Hi, your dead baby daddy wants to chat? And Jeremy's description of her as a "fluffy purse puppy" didn't exactly give me useful intel. At least I knew she worked at the lab, which might give me an opening.

I needed a new strategy. Or maybe I needed Jeremy to actually be helpful for once.

As if summoned by my thoughts, Jeremy appeared in my living room.

"You look stressed," he observed.

"I am stressed. I have no idea how to approach Aaron or Cate. You've been zero help with strategies."

"What do you want me to say? Aaron's impossible. He's too cynical, too logical. He'd see right through the ghost message thing."

"Then what do you suggest?"

He was quiet for a long moment. "I don't know. Maybe you could say you're investigating on behalf of another client? Someone who knew me?"

"That's lying."

"You lie for a living."

"That's different." I wasn't sure why, but it felt different. "What about Cate?"

His expression softened. "Cate's easy. She's sweet. Trusting. Just tell her you have a message from me. She'll believe you."

"And what message do you want me to deliver?"

"I don't know yet." He rubbed his face. "I need to think about it. I don't want to hurt her more than I already have."

At least that showed some growth.

"Fine. But I need you to start being more helpful. I can't solve this if you keep holding back information."

"I'm not holding back."

"You didn't tell me Cate worked at your lab until we were watching the security footage. What else haven't you told me?"

"Nothing important."

"Let me be the judge of that."

He vanished without responding. Typical.

I needed to clear my head. Gardening always helped me think.

I headed to the backyard to putter around in my garden. I still had a few days before seeing clients again, so I would give my neglected yard a good weeding and some of the plants a prune. I had a lawn service that kept things mowed for me, but I liked to do this part myself when I was home.

It was a beautiful day. The sun was warm and felt good on my face. I worked for an hour or so and had a decent pile of weeds and debris to throw out by the end of it. I was nice and relaxed for my quiet evening at home.

I gathered up the bag of trash and took it around to the front of the house. Since tomorrow was trash day, I collected the other bags to take to the curb.

When I rounded the corner with my trash bags, I froze.

A dark sedan sat across the street, a few houses down. Just like the one that had followed me home from Lindsey's party.

My heart kicked into overdrive.

There was nothing inherently suspicious about it. Just a car parked on a public street. But something about it felt wrong. The way it was positioned. The tinted windows. The fact that I'd never seen it in the neighborhood before.

I forced myself to keep walking, trying to appear casual as I deposited the bags at the curb. My hands shook slightly.

It's probably nothing. A visitor. Someone waiting to pick up a friend.

But I didn't believe it.

I turned and walked back toward my house, fighting the urge to run. The moment I was out of sight, I bolted for the back door, locked it behind me, and rushed through to check the front door. Locked.

From my office window, I could see the car more clearly. Dark blue or black sedan, maybe a Honda or Toyota. Pennsylvania plates, though I couldn't make out the number from this distance. The windows were too tinted to see if anyone was inside.

It was parked between the Tompkins' and Smiths' houses. Could be visiting either family. Mrs. Tompkins had a son who visited sometimes. The Smiths were always having people over.

I watched for five minutes. Ten. Fifteen.

The car didn't move. No one got in or out.

My rational brain said I was being paranoid. My gut said otherwise.

Hank had mentioned someone was following me. He'd said his guys would keep an eye on me, but this didn't feel like protection. This felt like surveillance.

But who? And why?

Finally, I forced myself to step away from the window. Standing here watching wouldn't accomplish anything except making me more anxious. I needed to act normal. Get dinner started.

In the kitchen, I washed the garden dirt from my hands and pulled out ingredients for a simple pasta dish. But every few minutes, I found myself drifting back to peek out the window.

After about thirty minutes, the car was gone.

I let out a breath I didn't know I'd been holding. Relief and embarrassment washed over me in equal measure.

You're losing it, Jo. Getting paranoid over nothing.

But I couldn't shake the uneasy feeling that had settled in my stomach.

I ate dinner in front of the TV, some mindless reality show I'd recorded. But I couldn't focus on it. My mind kept circling back to the car. To Hank's warning. To the investigation.

Maybe I was in over my head. I was a fake medium pretending to solve a real murder. What did I know about detective work? About dangerous people?

Jeremy thought Greg killed him. Greg thought Jeremy committed suicide. The police agreed with Greg. I had no evidence, no proof, just the word of a ghost.

A ghost only I could see.

My phone buzzed. A text from Laney.

Hi Joanna. Thank you again for yesterday. It helped more than you know. Would love to stay in touch if that's okay.

I smiled and typed back.

Of course. Anytime you need to talk, I'm here.

At least something good had come from this mess. Laney needed a friend, and honestly, so did I.

Another text came through. This time from Micah.

Boss, just checking in. You okay? You seemed off earlier.

I hadn't realized he'd noticed.

I'm fine. Just tired. Too much going on.

Want me to come over? Josh and I can bring takeout.

I considered it, then declined. I needed to be alone tonight. To think.

Thanks, but I'm good. See you tomorrow.

I turned off the TV and headed to bed early. But sleep didn't come easy.

Every sound made me jump. Every car passing on the street made me peek through the curtains.

Tomorrow, I decided, I would figure out my next move. I'd find a way to talk to Aaron and Cate. I'd piece together what really happened to Jeremy.

Tonight, I would just try to survive my own paranoia.

And hope that the dark car didn't come back.

Chapter Twelve

~Joanna~

After a few days, Jeremy finally showed up again. When I opened my eyes and his face was inches from mine, I nearly jumped out of my skin.

"Good morning, sunshine."

I shot him a dirty look in reply and slipped out of bed without saying a word, just giving him the one-finger salute as I headed straight for the television in the living room. I passed him on my way back to the bathroom. He nodded his thank you and looked like he might be stifling a laugh at my expense.

An hour later, showered, dressed, and partially caffeinated, I felt a lot more human and willing to talk. I took another sip of coffee. I could almost feel it working magic on me.

"Ah, that's better."

"Does that mean you're ready to talk?" he quipped.

"Sure," I said, though I really would have rather been sleeping.

"You need to talk to Aaron today. I'm starting to think it was him. I found out a few things over the last few days."

"Okay, what did you learn?" I pulled my legs into the chair, tucking them under me.

"He's started another company to compete with mine. He actually founded it before I died and was trying to recruit my employees. He likely paid one of them to take me out. So, one of those lab techs we saw that is actually authorized to be there was up to no good. There's more, but that's the gist of it."

"How am I going to get near him? What do you expect me to say? I can't just accuse him of murdering you."

He stared at me like I had grown a second head.

"Why not?" he asked.

Now it was my turn to stare.

"Seriously? Because people don't say that to other people, at least, those still alive."

"It worked with Greg."

"I didn't accuse Greg of killing you. I passed on a message from you. You said with Greg that would work. This is coming out and accusing Aaron of murder. Very different." I paused, waiting for a reply. When none came, I continued. "Plus, if he did do it, wouldn't that put me in danger? You wouldn't be able to help me. Nobody else can see you." I stood and started pacing.

"What is wrong with you? PMS?"

I stopped my pacing long enough to give him a death stare. It would have worked if he wasn't already dead.

And why did a lot of guys use PMS as a reason for women to have a strong reaction to things? Could it be that you were just an idiot?

"Okay, okay, not PMS. What's the deal, then? You seem on edge. More than usual."

"I just have to think. I can't go up to everyone and say we suspect them of murdering you. Do you know how crazy that sounds?"

I paced, thought, stopped to look at him, and then paced some more. The strange car had gotten me thinking about how dangerous this was. Granted, it was likely all in my head that the car was stalking me.

But it had gotten me thinking about the danger. If someone he knew had murdered him, someone he trusted, then what would stop them from killing me?

Not to mention that I didn't have a good, solid plan. With Greg, I had just walked into his office, but the reception hadn't been welcoming, and it was a stroke of luck that I got to talk to him at all.

I chastised myself for getting involved with Jeremy and this case. It had been my first instinct to tell him no, but I'd given into my curious nature and well, here I was in too deep and wanting to see it through. I just might not like what it took to get there.

This whole thing had already pushed me out of my comfort zone. Now Jeremy wanted me to go to his business partner to ask if he murdered him? Aaron would think I was a crazy person.

Then again, I grew up looking like a crazy person, so what else did I have to lose?

Knowing I had to talk to him, I needed to develop a solid plan, better than my previous meetings. Then, I had a spark of an idea. It wasn't a good plan, but it was all I had at the moment.

"Okay, I got it."

I told him my idea, and he agreed that it could work. Now I just had to get in to see Aaron.

A couple of hours later, standing in Novak Industries' lobby, my confidence level was substantially lower than it had been on the drive over. I hoped this would work. Without knowing enough about Aaron, I didn't know if he would go for it. Though Jeremy had assured me he would.

"You can do this."

I nodded and walked over to the reception desk.

"Hello, I'm here to see Aaron Novak. I have an appointment. Joanna Webber."

The receptionist typed into her computer, then dialed the phone and gestured for me to have a seat in the waiting area.

I sat near a window facing a grand staircase. Everything was glass, seamless, modern. The building screamed money, but as far as I knew, Aaron hadn't made any yet, or not much. Jeremy looked around with an expression that said he was thinking the same.

"Joanna, he's ready for you now."

I stood to follow the receptionist. She knocked, then entered without waiting for an answer.

"Mr. Novak, this is Ms. Webber." She motioned for me to move into the room.

"Have a seat," Aaron said without looking up from his computer.

The receptionist retreated quickly. So quickly that it made me nervous. Alarm bells sounded, and I had an urge to go with her. There was no real reason for this. I just had a sense of uneasiness.

"It's fine. Just be calm. He won't bite," I guessed Jeremy sensed my unease.

I gave a slight smile and took a seat.

Aaron kept typing for several minutes without so much as a word or glance. Was this some form of intimidation? If so, it was working. I almost forgot what I was here for.

Deep breaths, I reminded myself.

It gave me a chance to look around. Like the rest of the building, his office was modern, seamless, with almost a sterile feeling. He had no family pictures on the walls or his desk, no personal touches. Nothing that would tell me about his personality or lifestyle.

Glass and steel, black leather chairs. Maybe that was him. Cold, unyielding, intimidating.

I felt a cold chill running up my spine, but I focused on Jeremy's face. He seemed calm and relaxed.

Finally, Aaron stopped and turned to me. His next move was to stare at me without saying a word. It was probably just a split second, but it felt longer. I tried to look comfortable and confident, smiling in a friendly way at him, but I was about to come out of my skin. He was creepy.

"So, Ms. Webber, what can I do for you?"

"Joanna. You can call me Joanna."

"Joanna then. Please tell me what I can do for you?"

Condescending much?

"I'm a medium, which means I can talk to spirits. Dead people. Your ex-business partner, Jeremy Landon, has been talking to me and has a message for you."

"Oh, really?" he said and sat back with an unreadable expression. His fingers formed a steeple, which he pressed to his lips, his eyes studying me. "Let's say I believe this. What could that scheming bastard have to say to me?"

"He wants to apologize for making that deal without you. He was caught up in a life that wasn't healthy or right. He realizes now that it hurt others." My twist on the Charles Dickens classic story. It had worked for Scrooge.

"Bah! That doesn't even sound like him. What do you want? Money? Are you trying to blackmail me with something?" He sat forward.

I started to panic. I looked at Jeremy.

He shrugged. "I told you he might not buy it."

"You agreed to this plan, though."

"Who the hell are you talking to?" Aaron asked.

"Jeremy."

"Are you serious?" He stared at me, then looked at the empty spot on my right. Well, it wasn't empty for me, but he couldn't see Jeremy.

I could see his gears working as he tried to decide if he believed it.

"Yes, I'm serious."

He jumped to his feet.

"Jeremy, you backstabbing bastard! How could you do that to me after all we had been through? You can rot in hell for all I care. I don't know what you hope to gain by coming here."

"I just want to make amends for my wrongs. I have two little girls about to enter the world, and they made me realize how precious life is, and losing mine, I realize how short it is."

"That's rich. This doesn't even sound like him. I still don't know if I'm buying this, but okay. You said what you want. Now what?"

"Well, I hope you will forgive me." I again spoke for Jeremy.

"You think I could forgive you? Millions of dollars were more important to you than our partnership, our friendship. And you think some apology from the grave will wash that away? You're an idiot."

"I know, and for that, I'm a dick." I stopped speaking for Jeremy and added my own thoughts, "I definitely agree with him on that. He is a huge dick. He is always waking me early, and I'm not a morning person. At. All."

Aaron laughed. "He was always a morning person. I'm not either. He was so annoying. Always wanting to chit-chat at 6:00 a.m."

"He wants me to get back on topic. Was he always this bossy?"

Aaron laughed again and relaxed back into his chair. Okay, this was a good sign. I had to get him to talk freely with us and trust me.

"Oh yeah, he always had to be in charge. When we were kids, he was always the one in control of the games. Normally he got us into trouble with his antics. This one time, I thought for sure we would get arrested, just stupid teen boy stuff, toilet papering, and egging a house, but somehow, he talked our way out of it. That was Jeremy." He had a faraway look in his eyes and a faint smile like he was reliving a moment. His face suddenly hardened, and the moment was over. "But he threw it all away. Years of friendship, and for what? Money."

"You were my best friend. I wasn't going to leave you out. I just had to make the deal, and they didn't want to work with both of us, just me. As you said, I can talk my way out of or, in this case, into anything. That is all that happened here. I had to get the deal. Once I had it, I was going to pull you in, but I never got the chance."

"Yeah, right. You had no plans to share with me. You said so yourself, and I have the paperwork that you sent over to prove it. Your signature is on all of it. Now you want something, I can tell. That's all this little show is. Well, as you can see, I have a thriving business now without you. I have a new product that will compete with and be better than Remarpax. I'm close to a deal. We're just waiting on the FDA. So, you can take your apology and shove it."

"Aaron, please. Greed got me killed, and I just want to ensure your safety." I paused for effect, then added, "He thinks you might be in danger."

That stopped Aaron's anger. He looked from me to the empty space where Jeremy was standing. This might work.

"Do you know something? Is it Hank? He's been impatient for the money, but I swear I'm close to closing this deal. You know how the FDA is. They have to do all their tests and ensure it is safe, which I understand, but it takes time. Hank has to know that."

I wasn't sure why he was almost begging us for mercy. We didn't work for Hank. And does everyone in this town owe Hank money? Am I missing something by not borrowing from him? The terms didn't sound reasonable, from what I have heard.

"Jeremy's heard some things around but nothing solid. He's worried that you might fall the same way he did," I said.

"He was murdered? By who?"

Aaron's look of shock told me we could probably cross him off the suspect list. Every time I hoped we were getting close to solving this case, we got further away from it.

"He isn't clear. It was a good cover-up, whoever did it."

"And he thinks whoever did it will come after me too?" Aaron had gone from arrogant and creepy to almost scared.

"That's a possibility. Since we don't know who did it or why, we thought it best to at least warn you."

He looked like he was considering what I had said. "What do you need from me?"

"We need help figuring out who the killer was. You have connections that I don't have access to."

He stared blankly at me. "Are you serious?"

"Yes, and until we figure out who killed Jeremy, he's going to keep following me around. From one non-morning person to another, I'm asking for your help." I had hoped to appeal to our common ground. Any little connection could mean gaining his trust.

"Okay, okay, but I don't know how to help."

"Well, if you could just ask around, find out if anyone heard or saw anything, but try not to draw suspicion. Be discreet. We have to be careful since we don't know who the murderer is."

He seemed to be receptive to it and agreed to let me know what he found out. We wrapped up and said goodbye.

"I think that went well." I beamed. I was mostly relieved to have it all over with.

"I don't know. I know Aaron. Known him for years. That seemed too easy."

We were quiet as we drove back to my house. I had appointments this afternoon, the first since returning from the tour, excluding the one with Laney. I didn't know if Jeremy planned to stick around or go haunt someone else, but I hoped for the latter.

As we turned right at a crossroads, I noticed a dark car following us. I wasn't sure if it was a coincidence again or if I was truly being tailed. It looked like the car from across the street the other day.

Jeremy chattered as I drove. It took my mind off the car, but as we got closer to home, I decided to take a detour.

"Why are you going this way?"

"I think there's a car following us. Second time this week. Plus, there was one parked across the street from my house. It looks similar to this one."

"What do you mean, the second time? And at your house?" His head snapped around to stare at me.

I nodded while keeping watch on the rearview mirror and taking a random route. The car stayed behind me, but not close enough for me to tell who it was. I think I could have given a rough description of the car this time, at least.

"It's definitely following us." Jeremy had turned around to watch it.

"What should I do?"

"Maybe drive to the police station."

I whipped my head around to look at him this time.

"Don't look so surprised. If I weren't dead, I'd pull over and confront the driver, but I can't help you."

After considering it for a nanosecond, I agreed that it was probably the smartest thing to do. I turned up Scott Street to head toward the police station. We got within a block of it before the car turned right, and that was it. They were gone. I parked in the lot next door to the station in case the driver came back.

"That was a bit scary. But it was probably just a coincidence, right?"

"Um, yeah. Probably." He didn't sound any more convinced than I was. "Darn, I should have gone to see who was in the car."

"Oh, we should have thought of that while it was still behind us."

"Next time."

After waiting several minutes to ensure it didn't come back around, I put the car in drive and headed home. I had appointments and other work waiting. I didn't have time to be stalked.

Luckily, we made it home without any further pursuit that either of us saw. I put the car in the garage today. Usually, I left it in the driveway, but I felt extra paranoid.

Since it was connected to the house, there was no chance of being caught outside alone. I felt vulnerable and wanted to be in my safe place.

"Do you want me to stick around?" He sounded sincere.

"You can, but I have appointments, and then Micah and Tessa will be here. There isn't much you can do."

"But I can keep you company at least?"

I smiled and nodded. "Yes, that would be nice, actually. At least until someone alive that can call for help gets here."

I flipped the television on for him, then moved into my office to ensure that I had everything set up for my first appointment. This would be my first appointment since seeing real dead people. It was a widower who recently lost his wife of 50 years to cancer. I wondered if thinking about her hard enough would make her show up. I could do this.

I sat at my desk, eyes closed, and meditated, focusing on her name over and over. Several minutes went by before I heard a soft voice.

"Hello, dearie."

I opened my eyes. "Hi. Are you Claire Marshall?"

"I am. You can see me?"

It worked! "Yes, ma'am. I have an appointment soon with your husband, and I was hoping you would come to talk to him."

"Yes, yes, I know. I came ahead to see if maybe you could actually see me. The rumor is you're a fake."

Damn, I guess the meditating hadn't worked after all, or not exactly in the way I had hoped, but she was here, nonetheless.

"Well, yeah, that was sort of true, but I have learned how to see the dead again."

She smiled. "Oh, I'm so glad. I have a lot I want to say to him. Even though I knew the end was near, there never seemed to be enough time, and what seems important in the moment... isn't." She turned and looked toward the front door. "He's here."

There was a knock at the door. I smiled at her and then walked to the door.

"Hello, Mr. Marshall. Come in."

He stepped inside.

"Would you like a drink?"

"Water would be nice. Thank you."

I showed him to my office, then went to the kitchen to get him a glass of water. I came back in, setting the water on the table in front of him. He took a sip, then smiled.

I made small talk with him to relax him, then explained how the session would go.

"I will speak to you as if your wife is speaking, so feel free to speak as if to her, if you are comfortable with it. She is here waiting to talk with you."

Claire stood nearby, hands clasped, waiting anxiously, and looking at him with love in her eyes.

I wanted someone who looked at me like that. I thought it was Ted, but that didn't work out. I didn't know if I would try again, but with my luck, I'll end up alone, and the only one looking at me like that will be a cat or two or twenty as I open a can of kibble for them.

Once we were both comfortable, I began translating his wife's messages. There were tears from both of them and a few from me. Moments of love, sharing of memories. She let him know she was no longer in pain, and he let her know he missed her. She promised to be close by as long as he needed her. With that, they said their goodbyes and thanked me.

At some point during Mr. Marshall's appointment, my assistants showed up, and Jeremy left. Micah knew I had an appointment, so he got to work in our second office space. It was one of the secondary bedrooms that we'd turned into an office for him and Tessa. The other spare bedroom was our storage space for products. It was floor-to-ceiling shelves for easy access to everything.

Once my reading with Mr. Marshall was over, I joined them both. We quickly went over the invoices and bills. I signed everywhere Tessa had marked for my signature. By then my next appointment arrived.

I didn't have time to tell them about my meeting with Aaron or the suspicious car that followed me. I was on the fence about whether I'd even share that with them or anyone else.

Chapter Thirteen

Finally, the appointments were over, all the bills were paid, decisions made, and my assistants gone. I was alone.

I sat to process my day and recharge my batteries. After today, all I wanted to do this evening was watch mindless television shows and do nothing. However, my phone chimed before I could get too comfortable. A text from Laney. That was odd.

She asked me to meet for dinner. I groaned. I really wanted to hide in my house but replied with "sure." Her reply was instant. She gave me the name of a restaurant and asked if 6:00 p.m. would work. I agreed. But first, one more minute of being a slug on the couch before I pushed myself up and went to freshen up.

Twenty minutes later, I was on my way to the restaurant and doing the paranoid thing. Every car was following me, at least in my mind. I was a nervous wreck by the time I pulled into the lot but calmed when I saw Laney park next to me.

"Hey, Jo. I'm so glad you could meet me." She waddled over, her belly leading the way. She had that cute pregnant look going on.

"I'm glad you asked."

We headed inside, where the hostess greeted us and walked us to an available table. I opened the menu but was too busy looking around to see if Jeremy had joined us. I didn't see him. He must be following Cate or maybe Aaron or Greg.

"Is he here?" She looked around.

I guessed she was hoping he would come along.

"No, I don't see him." I gave her a smile. It was meant to be supportive but probably came out on the sad side, given her disappointed reaction. "So, what is good here?" I asked, changing the subject.

She offered a few of her favorites. We discussed a few other options, but both settled on the same thing: a pasta dish that was creamy, buttery, and lemony, with grilled chicken and vegetables. It sounded delicious and comforting, perfect for my mood.

After we ordered, the waiter brought us a basket of fresh bread and glasses of water infused with a variety of fruit that tasted so refreshing. I'd had water with lemon, cucumber water, and cucumber mint water, but this was amazing.

Taking my first sip, I sighed. Laney gave me a knowing smile.

"This is why I come here. I can't have wine, can't have caffeine, and try to limit sugars, so fruity water is one of the few things I have left."

I nodded and took another sip of the heavenly water.

"Have you talked to Jeremy recently? I miss him so much." She lightly touched her stomach.

"Um, not really," I said. He wasn't there, and I wasn't sure what to say. "I've been busy with appointments and planning my next tour. They take a few months to plan."

"I bet. I just hate that I was so mad at him the last time. With Aspen coming soon, I am missing him more and more."

"I'm sure." I reached over and squeezed her hand. I wanted to tell her how much I could relate, but I wasn't ready to share that part of my life yet.

She looked up and smiled.

"Thanks. I already told you about my fake friends. Here for my money and staying for the drama. It would be nice to have at least one that wasn't here for the money. I don't know who to trust half the time."

"I can relate. Imagine being the kid that sees dead people. I didn't have a lot of friends growing up."

It was her turn to squeeze my hand. I hadn't shared that aspect of my childhood with anyone before and wasn't sure why I had now. There was something about her that made me feel an instant connection, like we were long-lost best friends.

"That couldn't have been easy. But look at all the good you are doing with it now. You give people hope."

We didn't have time to talk more about that, as our food arrived. Instead, she changed the subject, asking how I got into being a medium, which I answered vaguely, then steered the conversation back to her by asking how she and Jeremy met.

"Oh, wow, I haven't thought about that in a while. We were in college. We were lab partners in chemistry."

"Oh, same class? Do you have the same degree?"

"Yes, similar. He ended up taking more of a business route while I stayed on the chemistry and biomed track."

I knew that she worked at the lab with Jeremy, but I wrongly assumed she did an office job or something. It was an interesting bit of information to store for later.

She then told me about the preparations she was making for Aspen and how she had picked the name. Jeremy hadn't been alive when she decided. They had discussed a few before he passed but never settled on one. They had a top-five list, so she felt she had to pick one from it.

"Her middle name will be Marie after my favorite aunt."

"Aspen Marie. That's pretty."

"Do you think he'd like it?"

"I honestly don't know. Do you want me to ask?" I wasn't sure if that was my place, but I could offer.

"Oh, I would love to know what he thinks, but that seems too personal to ask a new friend." She tried to seem casual about it, but I could tell she really wanted to know.

"I'll ask him. It's no problem at all."

She smiled her appreciation. I had gotten wrapped up in this whole thing for her anyway, so anything I could do to give her peace, closure, and answers, I was going to try.

We ate until we were both too full to move. Of course, Laney had a baby taking up some of the space. I didn't have the same excuse. We asked for boxes for the leftovers, and on Laney's suggestion, we ordered desserts to go.

"Trust me. Best in town."

"I'll enjoy it with a good book later," I said and smiled as the waitress handed us each our bagged orders.

"So, do you think he follows her around?" I had been hoping Laney wouldn't ask. "Oh, I'm sorry, I shouldn't expect you to know. I just mean it more rhetorically. I wasn't really looking for you to answer..."

But I knew she really did want to know.

It was something I had wondered about Ted. If he was a spirit somewhere, were he and his girlfriend together, living happily in the afterlife? Was that why he wasn't coming around me? He never knew I had powers, though. It hadn't been something I shared. It didn't seem important at the time. Could that be another reason he never visited? Not knowing I could see him.

Refocusing on Laney, I needed to give her some comfort.

"I know he loved you and still loves you. He talks about you all the time. I can see the love in his face."

"You talk to him often?"

"Some. But like I said, lately, I have gotten busy." I didn't know why I kept letting it slip about how much I talked to him. I didn't want her to know what we were up to.

"I really wish I could hear his voice one more time. I still have a few voicemails from him. I play them sometimes." She touched her belly. "Have you met her?"

"Cate? No, why?"

"I thought he might ask you to talk to her. I just happened to find you, but I wondered if he might have asked had that not happened."

"No, he hasn't. He was happy that I ran into you because he had wanted us to meet."

She brightened.

"Really? He asked you to find me?"

"Not until after I met you, but then he was excited and asked me to stay in touch."

"And you saw Greg and Aaron because Jeremy asked?"

Crap! I figured that might come out. At least with Greg, but how did she know about Aaron? Did they still talk too?

"Yes. He thought he could get all his unfinished business done."

"But not with her." She said it more to herself than to me, so I just took a sip of water. "Do you want to meet her?"

"Really? Um, I'm not sure..." This could be my in, but I didn't want to seem too eager and give away my intentions.

"Oh, come on, she is... interesting." She kind of snickered. "No, but seriously, it might help you understand our whole weird situation a bit: the husband, the wife, the girlfriend."

"Um, okay, then. Sure."

"Oh, great. I'll talk to her and set something up for the three of us."

Would I have been so casual about meeting Ted's girlfriend? Laney seemed accepting of it. Here I was about six years later, and I still wasn't over the idea of his betrayal. Maybe because Laney and Cate worked together, it was easier. I might never know.

We wrapped up our meal, split the tab, and agreed to do this again soon. As we were about to walk out, I noticed a familiar face near the door: Detective Hartley. His hand rested on the lower back of a stunning brunette.

We were going to have to walk right past them on the way out. This could be interesting and a bit uncomfortable once he put two and two together and realized I just had dinner with Jeremy's widow.

"Oh, Detective, hi. Do you remember me? Laney Landon."

"Yes, good evening, Laney," he said. His eyes were on me. "Good evening, Joanna."

Laney gave me side-eye but didn't say anything. I acknowledged the detective. Thankfully, his name was called, signaling his table was ready before more conversation could happen.

"Enjoy your evening, ladies." He nodded to us and guided his date toward their table. He looked over his shoulder once but didn't say another word.

"So, you know Detective Hartley? How?"

"Oh, just from around. How do you know him?" I already knew but tried to keep my voice calm and even. I was the master of faking it, after all.

"He was one of the detectives on Jeremy's case."

"Oh, really? Huh. That's interesting." I rifled through my purse for my keys as a distraction. "Well, this was fun. Thank you so much for asking me."

"I know it was a last-minute invite, but I'm happy you were available." Her voice still held a hint of caution, like maybe she wasn't buying my act, but I had built my brand on acting. "I'll call you when I can set something up with Caitlyn."

"Great. I'm interested in meeting her." We hugged, and each got into our cars.

I was relieved when I drove away. While I had fun with Laney overall, there were moments of uncomfortable questioning. This was a complicated relationship.

On the one hand, I didn't want to let anything out that Jeremy didn't want. On the other hand, I liked Laney, and I wanted to be friends with her separate from Jeremy. I needed more friends.

I did have family nearby, like my sister, whom I'd hang out with on occasion, but nothing beats having friends.

With those distractions, I drove home without worrying about being followed. I didn't even think about it until I got home and remembered.

Oh, well, too late to worry about it now.

Chapter Fourteen

~Clint~

What had Laney and Joanna been doing together? It was a shock to see them.

I couldn't stop replaying the moment in my mind. The way they'd been laughing together. The easy comfort between them. Like old friends, not two women connected only by a dead man.

Was she hanging out with the widow to get more information? That had to be it. There was no way those two would be friends by chance. Joanna was investigating Jeremy's death, convinced it was murder despite all evidence to the contrary. Of course she'd befriend the widow. Get close to her. Gain her trust.

Smart, actually. Manipulative, but smart.

Except the look on Joanna's face when she saw me hadn't been calculating. It had been genuine surprise. Maybe even a flash of guilt, like she'd been caught doing something she shouldn't.

And why did I care?

I tried to focus on whatever Kelly was saying, but I couldn't quite manage it.

"You seem distracted. Is everything okay?" She gently caressed my hand.

"Yeah, oh yeah, I'm sorry. I was just thinking about a case. It's nothing." I smiled and tried to reengage in our date.

"Are you sure it doesn't have something to do with the two ladies we just saw?"

Perceptive. That's what I'd always liked about Kelly. She paid attention.

"Who?"

"The ones leaving as we came in." She wasn't accusing. Just curious. "The pregnant one seemed to recognize you. And you got this look on your face when you saw the other woman. The one with the brown hair."

Damn. I thought I'd hidden it better.

"Oh, them. Just people from an old case."

She watched me for a moment, like she was deciding whether to push. Then she nodded and let it go.

"Okay. I trust you."

The words made my chest tight. She shouldn't. Not when I was sitting here thinking about another woman.

She seemed satisfied with that answer and began telling me about work. Thankfully, I was good with names and details, so I could follow her story about people I didn't know and events I had never experienced.

She got a text and looked down at her phone, laughed, and gave me the "one-minute" sign with her finger. With her distracted, I glanced around the restaurant.

At this hour, it was mostly filled with couples and groups of adults, but I got the impression that this was a nice family place. There were stacks of high chairs in one corner, and they had a basket of crayons and kids' menus by the hostess's station.

"Sorry about that. Jamie is having a major crisis with her boyfriend and needed to vent. She doesn't have one as amazing as I do." She smiled at me.

I wasn't feeling it tonight. Not after seeing Joanna and Laney. Mostly Joanna. What was it about this woman that threw me off? I smiled at Kelly instead of overthinking Joanna, someone who was basically a stranger to me.

She continued with her previous anecdote. It was like it would never end. I faked interest, inserting comments or questions as needed. But this wasn't fair to her.

I really did like her. She was sweet, funny, easy to be around. The kind of woman most guys would be thrilled to date. Hell, most guys would be thinking about rings by now.

But not me.

I kept waiting to feel more. Kept thinking that if I gave it enough time, the spark would turn into something real. Something lasting. But here we were, three weeks of daily dates, and all I felt was comfortable.

Comfortable wasn't enough.

She deserved someone who looked at her the way my dad still looked at my mom after thirty-five years of marriage. With that mix of affection and partnership. Someone who couldn't imagine life without her.

I wasn't that person. And I never would be.

The worst part? I knew exactly why. Because the only time my pulse had jumped tonight was when I'd seen Joanna. A woman I barely knew. A woman who drove me crazy with her ghost stories and stubborn insistence that she could talk to dead people.

A woman I had absolutely no business thinking about while on a date with someone else.

I needed to end things with Kelly. Tonight, if possible. It wasn't fair to string her along when my head was clearly somewhere else.

But not here in the restaurant. It would have to wait until we had some privacy.

Unfortunately, I wouldn't get the chance. My phone rang. It was work.

"Sorry, I have to take this."

I answered the phone and stepped outside to talk. Terry's voice was tense.

"We got another body. Female, mid-twenties, same M.O. as the others."

My stomach dropped. "Where?"

"Warehouse district. Off Morrison Street."

"I'll be there in fifteen."

I hung up and stood there for a moment, letting the cool evening air clear my head. Another victim. Another woman who'd never go home to her family. Another set of parents I'd have to notify.

A murder. Not sure if it was connected to the serial killings or not. What happened to my town? We used to be safe. Boring, even. Now we had bodies piling up and a killer who seemed to strike at random.

And here I was, worried about relationship drama and a medium who may or may not be conning people.

Priorities, Hartley. Get your head in the game.

I stepped back into the restaurant, signaled to the waiter to bring our check, and apologized to Kelly. The breakup talk would have to wait. I couldn't decide if I was relieved or disappointed.

"Sorry to do this. I really am."

"No, no, it's fine. Jamie needs me anyway." She grabbed her stuff while texting.

I dropped her off at Jamie's apartment with just a quick kiss, and then I was off to see what fresh hell awaited me at the crime scene.

As I drove, my mind churned through everything. The serial killer. Kelly. Joanna and Laney having dinner together. The closed case that maybe wasn't as closed as I thought.

I pushed thoughts of Joanna aside. I had a murder to investigate. Real police work with real evidence, not ghost stories and hunches.

But as I pulled up to the warehouse and saw the flashing lights, I couldn't quite shake the image of those honey-brown eyes looking at me across the restaurant.

Focus, I told myself. Lives depended on it.

Chapter Fifteen

It was a few days before Laney called me to let me know she'd made arrangements with Cate. We were meeting for brunch at a bistro, Poppy's Table. It was one of those cool, hip places that were always packed that I typically avoided like the plague.

Jeremy wasn't thrilled with the idea but did agree not to hang around. He said he would follow his parents for a while. He seemed worried about his mom.

"She's not dealing with my death well and seems to be drowning her sorrows in booze. My dad is really concerned, but also isn't helping her or getting her professional help," he said.

"I'm sorry to hear that. I'm sure that's hard to watch."

As I drove, I felt my nerves kicking in. I didn't know what to expect. Jeremy said Cate was basically a fluffy toy dog in a person's body. Not a flattering description. I hoped I wouldn't let it cloud my judgment. I wanted to be fair when I met her, but to be honest, from what I had seen on social media, the description fit.

The bistro was packed. I knew I avoided it for a good reason. I pulled into the only open spot I could find at the back of the lot. I saw Laney's car parked not far from mine. I didn't know what Cate drove, so I wasn't sure if she was here yet.

When I stepped inside, I saw Laney immediately. She was seated alone near a window facing the street. I made my way through the tables to join her.

"Oh, hi, Jo, so glad you could make it."

"Me too. I hope you didn't have to wait long."

"Not at all. Just got here."

I looked around as I sat and placed the napkin in my lap. "This place is nice."

"Yeah, one of my favorites. Obviously, Cate isn't here yet." She checked her phone. "Running late like always. She's such a poodle."

I smiled, not knowing the right reaction, but I guess Jeremy wasn't the only one who thought Cate was a toy dog.

While we waited, we ordered drinks, then chatted like old friends. We talked about everything except Jeremy.

Finally, after we'd been waiting about twenty minutes, Cate, the toy poodle, arrived. I had seen pictures of her on social media and then the video from the security footage, but she had been dressed for the laboratory and was a blip on a grainy screen. This was Cate in full living color.

Blonde, shiny, bubbly, and bouncy. Perfectly manicured and primped. She had a much smaller baby bump than Laney. I was surprised since they were only a week or so apart. She looked more like a few months behind.

"Laney, helllooo!" she gushed as she came to the table. Her voice was shrill and piercing above the murmur of the packed restaurant. She leaned over to hug her and then turned to me. "You're Joanna the Medium with a Heart. Wow, I never thought I would have an opportunity to meet you." She leaned in and hugged me.

I noticed a few heads turn to look. Was it Cate mentioning my job, or was it her loud personality? I hoped for the latter. While I loved my job, I hated the attention that came with it.

"Oh, yes, hi." I also didn't like the invasion of my personal space by a stranger.

"I am so sorry. I'm late. It's getting so hard to move with little Oakley here in the way." She rubbed her tiny belly. She slowly lowered herself into an empty seat and looked around for the waitress. "Which one is our waitress?"

Luckily, ours saw Cate join us and was there in seconds. She got Cate's drink order and returned quickly.

They had an incredible brunch buffet, so we hit the line. I overloaded my plate. Lots of fruit, yummy maple bacon, a poached egg, and a cucumber-tomato salad, plus a couple of other things that looked good and smelled heavenly.

Once we were all seated again, Cate monopolized the conversation about celebrity gossip. Who was dating whom, or which couple had broken up. This one was in a new movie, and that one was arrested for DUI. I didn't really follow celebrity culture, so what she said was news to me.

Laney would look at me on occasion as if to say, "I told you." She clearly found Cate's airhead routine entertaining.

"So how do you know each other? Seems like an odd friendship," Cate observed, finally off of the latest celeb love triangle.

"I ran into her at the grocery store and then made an appointment to see if she could contact Jeremy."

I looked at Cate to see how she would react to that. Her eyebrows moved slightly, but she quickly controlled her emotions. If I hadn't been looking right at her, I would have missed her shock.

"And did you?"

"Yes," Laney said flatly.

"Oh." Cate sounded a little sad. "Do you think he would talk to me?"

I looked at Laney, and she nodded to me. I took that as her way of giving me her blessing.

"He might." I smiled at her.

Cate brightened. I could see that she loved and missed Jeremy as much as Laney did. I felt terrible for them both being in love with the same man.

"I would love to try. Sorry, Laney, but I just miss him so much. And I am sure you feel like me: the closer it gets to this little girl's arrival, the more I miss him being here."

They shared a look. This was a strange bonding moment for them tinged with sadness and drama.

Seeing the hope in Cate's face, my mind went to Ted's girlfriend, Sienna. I hadn't thought of her name in forever. She almost didn't seem like a real person to me.

What if this was us sitting here missing Ted? I shook off the thought. It was all hypothetical since she had passed with him. No point in hurting myself more with impossible scenarios.

We continued our meal with the mothers-to-be discussing baby stuff, birthing plans, and why they picked the names. I had already heard about Aspen's name but was interested in Oakley's.

It wasn't as interesting as I thought it would be. She had heard a celebrity mention the name in an interview and thought it was cute. She seemed to idolize Hollywood and that lifestyle. It almost seemed like she wanted her life to mirror that of the celebrities she worshipped.

I mostly listened, only adding to the conversation when spoken to directly. Cate liked to be the center of attention, and I liked to be an observer. I got to take her in and get a feel for her.

During lunch, I finally understood why they called her a fluffy toy dog. She yapped a lot but was no real threat. Her appearance was polished and perfectly groomed. She had that pampered pooch look for sure.

We wrapped up our meal, split the check, then walked out together to say our goodbyes. We were all parked relatively close together.

"Oh, Laney, your car!" Cate exclaimed.

"Oh my, how did that happen?" Laney stared down at two flat tires. They looked like they had been slashed.

"How did someone do this without being seen? There are a lot of people coming and going from the restaurant."

"Someone had to have seen something, or maybe the restaurant has cameras?" I looked up at the building but didn't see anything. "We should go in and speak to the manager and probably call the police."

We went back inside. The manager listened to us, came out to look at the car, and unfortunately said they didn't have cameras on this part of the parking lot. He suggested we call the cops to make a report. He would call someone to come fix her tires.

Chapter Sixteen

~Clint~

Terry and I had just finished researching a lead on the serial killer case and were heading back to the station. It hadn't given us much information we didn't already know. Another dead end.

I wanted this guy caught before he had a chance to kill again. I didn't want to look at another one of this guy's victims and feel that sick, helpless feeling. The kind that made you question why you became a cop in the first place.

The cases were piling up. The serial killer. Jeremy Landon's "accident" that kept circling back into my life. And now my personal mess with Kelly, who I still hadn't broken up with.

I needed a win. Badly.

We sat in silence, both reflecting on the facts we had when the call from dispatch came over our radios.

"All units. Any available near the corner of Elm and Market Street. We have vandalism of a vehicle at Poppy's Table. The victim is Delaney Landon. Please respond if you are in the area."

"We're close." I looked at Terry.

"You want to take a vandalism case?"

"You heard who it is? Laney Landon. Why do I keep hearing her name?" I also wondered if she might be with Joanna. I had a gut feeling.

"Fine."

Terry turned the car toward Poppy's Table while I called dispatch.

"This is Detective Hartley. Walden and I are around the corner. We'll take the call."

Dispatch acknowledged.

When we pulled into the parking lot a short time later, I instantly noticed Joanna. Of course she was here. But I also saw Laney and Caitlyn Fitzpatrick. What kind of weird group was this? I could only guess it had to do with Jeremy Landon.

Three women. One dead man connecting them all. The widow, the mistress, and the medium who thought she could talk to ghosts.

"Hello, ladies." Terry was the first out of the car.

"Oh, Detectives, I'm glad they called you," Laney said and smiled at us. "We were having brunch and then came out to this."

We looked at her car. Two slashed tires on the driver's side. Clean cuts, deliberate. Not random punctures from road debris.

I crouched down to examine them more closely. The cuts were deep, made with something sharp. A knife, probably. Someone had taken their time with this. This wasn't a crime of opportunity. This was targeted.

"Any security cameras?" I asked the manager, who was hovering nearby.

"We couldn't find any witnesses, and we don't have cameras on this part of the parking lot. They cut off just at the edge here." He gestured to a section just to the side of her car.

Either someone knew about the camera blind spot and saw an opportunity, or Laney had horrible luck. Given everything else surrounding Jeremy Landon's death, I was leaning toward the former.

"Not much to go on," I said.

A tow truck from the local auto repair shop pulled into the lot. I assumed to change her tires.

"For you?"

Laney nodded. Terry and I pulled out a kit so we could check for prints and take pictures of the scene. I didn't expect us to get anything from it. Then we gave the okay to the mechanics to change the tires.

As everyone started to break into groups or move away, I took the chance to speak to Joanna in relative privacy.

"Interesting running into you again, and with Mrs. Landon and the mistress. Anything to do with Jeremy's accident?"

"More like clients of my medium service. Just coincidence on the murder part." She emphasized the word murder.

Oh, she wasn't going to let that go.

"You don't think this has anything to do with that?" she asked.

"Well, I admit this looks a little... suspicious." It could be random, but in my line of work, I questioned almost everything. And this? Two tires slashed in a busy parking lot in broad daylight? Someone was either very bold or very desperate.

"Glad you finally see things my way," she said with that mischievous smile.

She touched my arm lightly, then went to stand with Laney as the tow truck driver finished changing her tires.

The touch lingered longer than it should have. My arm felt warm where her fingers had been.

Oh, she was good. And that smile hit my soul.

I watched her walk away, then caught Terry giving me a knowing look.

"Don't," I warned.

"I didn't say anything." But his grin said plenty.

Terry looked at me and nodded toward the car. There really was no reason for us to take this call, but it did feed my curiosity about the Landon case. Maybe there was more to it than I had first thought.

We said a quick goodbye to the ladies, got in the squad car, and drove off.

After a few moments of thought, I said, "What if we were wrong about the Landon case?"

"What the hell, man? Seriously?" Terry stared wide-eyed at me.

"Yeah, I'm serious. I know it sounds crazy, but that Joanna is persistent. And what about the tires being slashed? Do you think that was random?"

"Probably not. These things rarely are. But you know as well as I do, it's hard to find the perp in a case like this."

"I know, but what if Landon was murdered, and now they're coming after her? How could we be that wrong?"

Terry was quiet for a moment. "You really think there's something there?"

"I don't know. But I think I need to look at it again. With fresh eyes."

"And this has nothing to do with a certain brown-haired medium?"

"It has everything to do with making sure we didn't miss something. If there's even a chance someone got away with murder..." I trailed off.

Terry shook his head but didn't argue further.

I would have to do some investigating into this closed case because I couldn't shake the feeling. What if she was right? I couldn't live with myself knowing I had let a killer go, especially if that killer struck again.

And maybe, just maybe, I wanted an excuse to see Joanna again.

Not that I'd admit that to Terry. Or myself.

Chapter Seventeen

I had seen the look of doubt in Detective Hartley's eyes. He was starting to believe Jeremy's death was no accident. This was a positive turn of events, and Jeremy would be happy to hear it.

Though oddly enough, I would miss him a tiny bit. He'd started spending more time in other places. He wasn't annoying me as much. He had also stopped doing the early morning wake-up calls, which I appreciated. Still, I was ready to be done with him.

Most of my days were full of appointments, so I didn't have a lot of time to think about him when he wasn't there. The most recent tour had been my best so far, which meant our website was selling out of products, and my schedule was booked solid for months.

However, the job wasn't as enjoyable as it used to be. The more stories I heard firsthand, rather than through online research, the more real it was, and the more depressed I became about my own life. It brought Ted's death back to the front of my mind, and I felt I was reliving that first year.

Don't get me wrong, I loved hearing stories full of adventure and love. There were tales of dream jobs and dream homes, families and friends, celebrations, and holidays. I learned so much about people that you just can't learn from online searches, but it was also full of pain, loss, and heartbreak. Some gone too soon, some with things left unsaid, and all wished they had had more time.

It made me want to hide in my closet with my great-grandmother's quilt over my head. It was my security blanket and made me feel loved and safe. I'd had it since I was a baby, and it was always proudly displayed over the back of my couch.

She was the first dead person I could see. She had died right before I was born but used to visit me daily and would tell me stories, make me laugh, and in many ways, was my best friend.

When I first started talking about Grams around my mom, she brushed it off as something I had seen in family pictures or stories I had overheard. However, one day Grams introduced me to my Uncle Peter. He had died when he was young. Mom had never mentioned him.

Along with learning I had an uncle, I found out a huge family secret that hurt my mother so much. At ten years old, it was too much for me to handle, so I taught myself how to block the spirits, and I had to say goodbye to my Grams and Uncle Peter forever.

There were so many moments in my life since she left when I could've used her guidance. This was one of those times. But I didn't know how to get her back. No cell phones or mail service in the afterlife.

Each day, I saw more and more dead people. Word had gotten out that I wasn't faking it any longer and could actually see them. They flocked to me. Thankfully, they all respected rule number one: privacy. They would wait in the public areas of my house, like the living room and kitchen, and never came into my bedroom or bathroom. I already felt like my life was being violated, so that bit of respect and privacy was appreciated.

As I walked from my office to the kitchen to get my second cup of coffee, I greeted a few of the regulars by name and continued to the coffee pot. I tried not to think about how weird my job was. If I thought too long about it, I would get depressed again.

It would make my mother proud if I went back to my previous work in accounting since she hated this job. On the other hand, my father loved the perks he got from being my dad, like free coffee at his favorite diner. Anything to help my dad live his best life.

My phone rang, shaking me from my daydream. It was Laney.

"Hello."

"Hey, Jo. Are you busy?" Laney said, her voice rushed and breathless.

"Not at all. I don't have any appointments today."

"Do you mind if I come over? I just need... a friend."

"Sure." I tried to keep my voice casual, but my mind started running possible scenarios about what she could need.

Thirty minutes later, she was sitting on my couch. She alternated between fiddling with a seam on her shirt and sipping the water I brought her. I could tell she was upset about something, but she was having a hard time getting started.

"So, what's going on? You okay?"

"I'm worried about Greg."

"Why?"

"He's been acting... erratic. Not himself at all. Hank's guys seem to really be putting on the pressure for the money he owes. I think it's making him a little crazy."

"I don't understand. I thought his business was pretty successful."

"It is. Very." She picked at her nail and didn't make eye contact with me for a moment. "I don't know how much to share, but... I feel like I can trust you." She hesitated then looked me straight in the eyes. "He has a gambling problem and keeps spending more than he takes in. If he would just stop, he would be fine."

"He gambles that much?" I've only been to Vegas a few times, played a few slots, but never anything substantial. Usually, no more than $40. I would typically get bored with it and would end up people-watching instead, which I found much more fun.

"Oh, yes, it's a huge problem. Hank runs some underground poker tournaments, and Greg takes part. Jeremy used to gamble, too, but not this bad. Hank loans out money if people are short. That's how Greg racked up so much debt."

I nodded. That made a lot of sense, and now I understood how so many people owed Hank money. Although Jeremy had never mentioned that he gambled. I wondered if any of this could be related to his murder.

We sat for a moment, lost in our own thoughts. I could hear the various conversations around my living room, and by the set of her mouth, she looked pained.

I wanted to ask her more about Jeremy's gambling but didn't want to call attention to it or have her question my motives. She needed a friend right now, and that's what I was determined to be. I would figure out the gambling thing later.

"Do you think one of Hank's guys slashed your tires to send a message to Greg? Or maybe someone else from the gambling thing? Do you know if he owes other people?"

"I don't know. I hadn't thought of that. Maybe," she paused. "I tried to give Greg some of the money from Jeremy's estate. He left me plenty. But he wouldn't take it. Said he would figure it out on his own. But he looks awful. He doesn't seem to be eating or sleeping much lately. He might end up losing everything if he doesn't get that money soon."

"I'm sorry."

"Yeah. I think I might cut ties with him for my own happiness... and safety. I feel like I'm always looking over my shoulder, especially if you are right about the tires."

We both looked toward the door out of paranoia. We then turned back to face each other, giggling nervously at our awkward moment.

"I know why I'm so jumpy, but why are you?" she asked.

"Well, I didn't tell you, but after I spoke to Aaron, I was followed most of the way home. I ended up driving toward the police station, and thankfully whoever it was turned off about a block before I got there."

I didn't mention the time after Lindsey's party, hoping that might have been a coincidence rather than someone following me. Nor did I mention the car that had parked across the street. It hadn't been back again, so I chalked it up to my paranoia.

"Did you see the driver?"

"No. I figured it might be someone from Aaron's office. He wasn't thrilled to hear from Jeremy. Or maybe one of Hank's guys after he saw me at either Greg's or Aaron's." I stopped short of mentioning that I had talked to Hank, and he warned me not to get involved in his business. He might see my conversations with Greg and Aaron as getting involved.

"Either is possible. Aaron was always a little... off. I never understood why he and Jeremy were friends." She must have seen something in Jeremy that I didn't because I could see why they were friends. "He was always arrogant and so... creepy."

Okay, she had me on the creepy part. Jeremy wasn't creepy, but Aaron was. My short meeting with him had sent shivers running down my spine.

"I don't know that there's much we can do right now," Laney said. "There's been no crime, other than my tires, but fat chance the police will find out who did it, and they know about Hank, and he isn't doing anything criminal. Exactly. Stretching the boundaries of the law, perhaps, but nothing criminal."

We changed the subject to small talk, the type new friends shared. It was nice. She started to get tired and uncomfortable, so she said her goodbyes. I wished her well and told her to call me anytime she needed to talk.

After she left, I cleaned up her glass, puttered around for a few minutes straightening up, and then walked into my office to look out the front window. I felt a bit paranoid after talking with Laney.

That's when I noticed the dark car was back. I eyed it suspiciously and tried to see into the windows, but it was too far away, and besides, they were tinted. It looked like the same one that had been following me and the one parked there the other day.

Unfortunately, the license plates were those temporary paper plates. Not a good identifier.

I looked around to ensure my cell phone was nearby. Micah and Tessa were coming over, and I hoped they would arrive soon. I didn't want to be alone.

I watched the street, and more specifically, that car for a moment before stepping away and getting back to my computer work. I had a lot of work to do, so I didn't have time to worry about what may or may not be a threat. If this was the same car, they had never tried to interact with me, so I felt relatively safe.

From my desk, I had a limited view of the front yard, so I wouldn't be able to see if or when the car left. I was just going to have to put it out of my mind.

I heard a car door shut. My head snapped up. I had been so focused on my work that I had completely forgotten about the car across the street, until that moment.

I checked the time and hoped it was one of my assistants. I grabbed my cell phone, just in case, and moved slowly toward the window to peek out. Thankfully, the dark car was gone, and Micah was strolling up the sidewalk toward the door.

I was so relieved it was him that I met him at the door. He greeted me happily and then headed straight to the kitchen to help himself to a drink and a snack.

We worked separately until Tessa arrived later. Once she was settled, we went over a few items for the next tour. I had questions about the schedule and the new opening act we'd need to find, but we wrapped up quickly.

After they left, I made myself a grilled chicken breast and tossed it with some greens for a quick salad. I ate it in front of the television.

After I finished my salad, I set the bowl on the coffee table, not wanting to move right now, and just settled in to mindlessly watch TV.

I must have dozed off because I woke to darkness and a strange noise at my back door. I was a little disoriented from sleeping, so I wasn't sure if I had heard something or not, but when I heard it again, I shot up.

It sounded like someone shaking the doorknob. The door was only feet away from me. At least the curtains were pulled shut so they couldn't see me.

I grabbed my cell phone and headed toward the office. Since it was in the front of the house and right by the front door, I thought I could get out if need be. I called 911.

"9-1-1, what's your emergency?"

"Yes, someone is trying to break into my house," I whispered.

The responder asked my name and address, then stayed on the phone with me while waiting for the police to arrive. The sound moved from the back door to the side of my house like they were trying some of the windows. Thankfully, I never left them unlocked.

I let the operator know that I could hear them on the side of the house. She kept talking to me, trying to keep me calm. I tried to peek out of the front window without moving the curtains too much. I could see a car parked across the street. It looked like it could be that same dark car, but it was hard to tell in the dim light.

Dang it. Who was this person?

"Joanna, the police are almost there."

"Okay, thank you."

"Do you still hear them?"

I listened. "No." I peeked out again. The dark car was gone.

Damn. As I looked out, the police cruiser pulled up in front of my house. I let the operator know, thanked her, and disconnected, then went out to greet the police officers.

As I walked out of my house to greet the officers, all I could think was that my life was no longer boring.

The officers took my statement, walked around the house, took some prints, and ensured everything was secure. They offered me some tips, like keeping my porch lights on and maybe getting a dog.

I thanked them for their time. I hoped I would be able to sleep tonight.

Chapter Eighteen

The next day was Saturday. I had no appointments, and no medium work of any kind planned. I was spending the day with my sister and her boys at the zoo.

When I arrived at Audrey's house, it was full-on chaos. I forgot how much energy my nephews had. Audrey was wrestling Dylan into shorts, and Harris was running around, climbing on furniture, and jumping off again.

Oy! I was already exhausted, and I had been there less than two minutes. Granted, I hadn't slept well the night before as I had listened for any sound of an intruder, but the boys quickly drained what remnants of energy I had saved for the day.

I stood back and watched my sister and nephews while wondering what I would be like as a parent. I'd never been much of a kid person, but I did rock the cool aunt thing. I bought fun gifts, and the few times I babysat them, I brought pizza and cookies. They loved me.

"Harris, stop that. Dylan, let me finish getting you dressed," Audrey called out. "Boys, we need to get going."

Stanley came out from the master bedroom. He looked relaxed and calm. Audrey, on the other hand, was frazzled and stressed. Men got off so easily. Here she was struggling while he was cool as can be without a worry.

A prime example of why I didn't know if I really wanted another husband or to have children of my own.

"Hey, Jo. I hope you all have fun today."

"Thanks. What are your plans?"

"Golf." He kissed Audrey.

He grabbed Harris off the table, set him on the floor with a gentle scolding, and then scooped Dylan up and placed him back in Audrey's arms. She smiled at him and mouthed, "thank you," then Stanley saluted her and left. Okay, so I take back my earlier thoughts about him. He was one of the good ones.

With the kids now under control, we got them into Audrey's car and headed to the zoo. The boys alternated between singing and cheering. It was too loud for Audrey and me to talk much, but that was okay. It was nice to be with them.

I hadn't been to the Creekview Zoo and Botanical Gardens in a few years. They had made quite a few improvements by expanding some enclosures, adding a few others, and in general, making everything look more natural and less prison-like. They'd also added beautiful, lush plant life and gardens. It was wonderfully done.

Audrey had a wagon to pull the boys in, so they could jump out when we stopped at various exhibits or sit back and admire the animals while riding along.

It was a warm day, but not too hot. We were still in spring, so the weather was mild. It would almost be unbearable out here in a month or two, with higher humidity levels and temperatures near the upper nineties.

We headed toward the children's area, following the line of other wagons and strollers. The boys were getting excited. They wanted to pet the various farm animals.

"Cows! Goats! Chickens!" they sang out.

Audrey smiled and lovingly rolled her eyes. "They're silly but cute, right?"

I smiled and nodded.

We got to the children's section. They jumped out of the wagon and ran toward the petting area. Audrey parked it outside in a stroller area, then we tagged along behind them as they went from petting this animal or saying "hello" to that one.

Dylan was a bit timid at first, but he followed Harris' lead and soon was petting anything that would stand still long enough for him to touch them. Their giggles were precious.

After petting the animals, we moved on to watch a zookeeper talk about birds of prey. The boys enjoyed watching the birds fly overhead and land on the keeper's gloved hand. When the keeper asked for volunteers, they both got called to the stage and had the opportunity to pet an owl.

Overall, it was a good distraction from everything else that was going on in my life. I hadn't even thought about Jeremy or his murder or the mysterious person that was following me.

Both boys fell asleep in the car. Dylan almost immediately and Harris just minutes before we pulled into the driveway.

"They always do this." Audrey turned in her seat to peek at them once we were in the driveway. "I hope you can carry a sleeping boy."

"I guess we'll find out." I laughed quietly.

She took Harris and asked me to get Dylan. We got them in the house and into their beds. Harris mumbled but then settled in to finish his nap.

"Want tea?"

"Sounds great."

She put the kettle on, grabbed mugs and tea bags. I took a seat at her kitchen island. We talked about how well the day had gone and shared the various pictures we had taken.

"So, how's work going? Are you still seeing dead people?"

"Yes, all over the place. It seems like I see more and more each day. I wish Grams would come back, though."

"Me too. I hated Mom's reaction. I loved Grams being around, even though I couldn't see her. She told the best stories."

"She did."

We both sat for a moment, remembering, then Audrey stood and filled each mug with hot water, then brought them back to the island, placing one in front of each of us.

"So, anything new with the murder mystery?"

I thought about her question. How much did I want to share with her? She would be worried if I told her about the potential break-in last night or the car following me.

"Not really. It might be a wild-goose chase." I fiddled with the teabag, dunking it a few times in the hot water.

"That's a shame. I thought it had potential."

"Me too, but it's just random bits of information."

"Nothing you can put together?" Audrey asked.

"No. I did learn that the guy was involved in some gambling that Hank the Hammer does. I thought I might try to find out more about that. His brother is involved with it, too."

"Hmm, it could be worth checking out. Have you talked to Jeremy about it?"

I shook my head. "He hasn't been around since I found out, and obviously, I can't just call him up. But I do plan to ask him next time he's around."

Our dad's birthday was coming up soon, and we were going to throw a surprise party for him. We had to finalize the plans, so we started discussing that instead. It would take place at Audrey's with caterers, cake, decorations, and games. The works.

His brother would be flying in from out of town. He was our only relative who didn't live in Creekview. Dad would be so surprised.

Once we'd finished our tea and our plans were solidified for the party, I left her house. On my way home, I made a quick stop at the grocery store, looking over my shoulder the entire time.

The coast seemed clear, and I was ready to breathe a sigh of relief until I pulled onto my street and saw a strange truck in the driveway with a man leaning against it.

Oh crap, it was Aaron.

What did he want? I almost continued driving by my house but decided instead to see what he wanted. I pulled in next to his truck, giving him a friendly smile and a wave.

"I need to talk to you," he grunted.

I nodded and grabbed my groceries. He sighed and came over, grabbing a few bags to help me. What a gentleman. Maybe not quite the creep I initially thought. He followed me into the house to the kitchen.

"Do you mind if I put this stuff away while you talk?" I asked.

"That's fine," he grumbled.

"Would you like a drink? Bottle of water or soda?"

"Water is fine. Thanks," he said. He sounded less gruff and less mad with each hospitality I offered.

I handed him a bottle of water, then started unloading my groceries into the refrigerator and pantry. He took a big gulp while watching me.

"I talked to Hank."

A cold chill ran through my body. This was not the plan. Well, okay, I had asked him to find out more information, but I didn't think he would ask Hank directly.

"You talked to Hank?" I squeaked out.

"Yeah, and I told him what you said. He did not seem happy about that."

No, I imagine he would take that as me getting in his business. The exact thing he warned me not to do.

"Did he say anything?" I said as I tried to remember to breathe.

"Not to me, but I could tell he was less than thrilled with you." He looked at me suspiciously. "What game are you playing with me? What do you want?"

"I told you before. Jeremy wants to figure out who murdered him. He thought someone might be after you. We weren't sure who, so it was stupid of you to go to Hank. Now you've put me in danger over a hunch."

"Well, little miss, I have to cover my own ass here. You don't know Hank like I do. I've worked with him for a while now." He paused. "Do you know how I got involved with Hank? How my deal with him came about?"

"No. Do you want to tell me about it?"

He took another drink of water, looked at me like maybe he wouldn't tell me, then exhaled heavily.

"After I found out that Jeremy was in the process of making the sale of Remarpax without me, I was at Leo's, drinking. I got plastered and started spilling my guts to Al, you know, Hank's right-hand man? He brought me over to Hank, who put the idea in my head that I should start my own company. He had some ties with the building I'm in now and loaned me money to get started. And, bam, I was in business."

"Did you try to recruit lab techs from Landon Labs?"

"No, there are plenty of lab techs coming out of Creekview College. They get stuck working in hospitals and are desperate for something else. It's easy to get employees."

"So, do you have any ideas on who might have wanted to murder him?"

"Well, if you're asking if I did it... I mean, I wanted to in theory, but I didn't. I figured my revenge on him was better served by competing with him. He hated to lose, and I thought I could at least give him some strong competition." He took another sip of water and eyed me. "It really could have been several people. I always thought the police were too quick to rule it as an accident. He wasn't well-liked and stepped on a lot of toes. I will say this: the way it was done, it's not Hank's style. If he was going to do it, it would have been less of an accident." He formed a gun with his hand and stuck it to his head.

"Ah, got it. I'll scratch Hank and his guys off the list for sure. I wasn't really leading with them, anyway. It seemed too obvious. Although, I did hear recently that Jeremy was involved in some of Hank's gambling. Do you know anything about that?"

"Of course. I sometimes participate myself. A lot of people in town gamble with Hank."

I felt so naïve. I knew nothing about my own hometown. Who else was involved in this gambling thing?

"Anyone else you can think of that might have information?" I asked. "Maybe someone who didn't like him?"

"A few for sure. They all thought he cheated. Not long before he died, there was a fight between him and some guy named Butch. I wasn't there that night, so not sure what happened. Also, there was something with a woman named Nina. Again, I don't know many details. Just heard their names together. Not sure how they were involved, but you asked for names. There are some names."

"Thanks. I'll look into them."

"Have you talked to Frank and Priscilla Landon yet?"

"His parents? No, but I thought about it." I remembered their names from my research.

"Could be worth a visit to see if they know anything."

I had been thinking about talking with them, so hearing someone suggest it solidified it in my mind that I needed to. I would have to speak with Jeremy to see how he felt about it.

Aaron drained the rest of the water bottle, crushed it, and handed it to me. "Thanks for the water. If you have any more questions about this, please give me a call. I'm sorry for going to Hank. I'm sure it will be okay. He's a fair guy, despite what people say, just does his business, and as long as people stay out of his way, he leaves them alone."

I swallowed hard and thanked him as I walked him to the front door. We shook hands, and I looked for the dark car, but it wasn't there. I was relieved not to see it. I hoped it stayed away.

What was I going to do about Hank? Aaron had thrown me under the bus for sure, and I felt in real danger now. I had to figure out what I would say to Hank if he came asking questions. Hopefully, Jeremy would have some ideas.

Chapter Nineteen

After Aaron left, I was just relaxing on my couch, reading, when there was a knock at my door. Instinctively, I grabbed my cell phone and went quietly to peek out the front. I didn't see the dark car across the street. Nope, it was Detectives Hartley and Walden. My reaction was mixed. Somewhere between a sigh of relief and "oh crap, what did I do?"

I opened the door with a smile. "Hello, detectives. Here for a reading?"

"Hmm, what? No..." Clint's eyes widened with surprise at my question. "I heard you had a little bit of trouble lately. Someone following you and trying to break in? We wanted to talk to you about it."

Ah, word got around.

"Yes. Come in."

They followed me inside. I gestured for them to sit once we reached the living room.

"Would you like something to drink? Water? Soda?" I asked.

"Water for me. Thanks, Joanna." Terry smiled politely.

"Same. Thanks." Clint grunted.

I came back with two bottles of water. "You have questions?"

"Yes, when did all of this start happening?" Clint asked.

"Um, about a week or so ago. I'm not actually sure. The first time I noticed the car, I thought it must just be a coincidence. They turned off on Masters, so they didn't follow me all the way home, but I drove toward the police station the next time I spotted them. I got to Filmore before they stopped."

"Just the two times?" Terry asked, pen and notebook ready to take notes.

"No, possibly a few other times, but they always turn just before I get to my destination. It looks like the same car, though, a dark blue sedan. I can't quite see what type. They keep too much distance, and I honestly don't know much about cars. Maybe BMW? Four doors with dark windows. I can't see into the windows at all, so not sure if it is a male or female driver. The license plate is one of those temporary tags, so I can't even give you a number to trace. They sometimes park across the street," I half gestured toward the front of my house. "I mean this could all just be a coincidence, and I'm just being silly."

Both detectives looked at me, then followed my gesture down the hall toward my front door.

"Where? Show us," Terry said.

We walked to the office with the front window. I pointed out the house across the street and two houses down. The car wasn't parked there now. They probably saw the detectives' car.

"I'll call dispatch and see if we can get extra patrol out here." Terry stepped out of the room to make the call.

"You think this is serious?" I guess I did too, but I was only just realizing it.

"Yes, very serious, especially the attempted break-in part. This has never happened with a fan?" He did the air-quotes thing around the word fan.

"No, never. This is the first time."

"Do you think it could be related to the Landon murder case?"

"I guess it could be. I mean, I thought about it, but..." I paused to gather my thoughts on how much to share. "As far as potential suspects and who I've talked to so far. Aaron was here earlier, so I don't think it was him. I have gotten to know Laney, and if she had a problem with me, I hope she would just say it to my face. I only met Cate once, but she seems like an airhead. That really just leaves Greg and Hank the Hammer."

"Who gave you these names as potential suspects?" He didn't do the air-quotes thing this time, but the way he said potential suspects sounded sarcastic to me.

"Jeremy."

"Okay. If not them, then as you've been talking to people about this, the wrong person heard?"

"I guess that's possible, but I haven't really talked to anyone else."

"Okay, good. Please be sure you report any suspicious activities and call me if anything new happens, especially regarding the Landons. You still have my card, right?"

I nodded, even though I wasn't completely sure where it was. It was probably on my hot mess of a desk. I'd look once they left.

Terry returned and stated that extra patrols would start immediately. They thanked me for my time, making me promise again that I would not let things build up but would report immediately if something happened. I agreed.

With those promises, I walked them out.

What had happened to my life? My existence used to be so plain, at least when I wasn't on stage. I hung out at home, spent time with my family, and maybe the odd night out for dinner with friends. Nothing exciting.

My phone rang. I checked the display. My mother.

"Hello, Mom."

"What is going on over there? Marcy Dalton just called. She said there were police officers at your house again. Again? Twice in two days."

"It's nothing, Mom. Nothing. Just some... issues with work stuff. Nothing serious."

"Oh, why couldn't you just stay in accounts receivable? Something normal. Dead people? I thought you had outgrown all this when you were a child... with your imaginary friends."

I heard shuffling and bumping sounds on the other end.

"Hello?" said the familiar voice.

"Hi, Dad. I guess Mom isn't talking to me again."

He sighed. "Oh, yeah, I don't know what's up with her. She has been working herself up over here for the past 15-20 minutes. I think she might have gone to bed." I heard him walking through the house. "I guess I'm on my own for dinner. Want to meet me at Reggie's?"

"Sure. At five?"

We disconnected, and I called my sister to warn her about Mom as I knew Mom would try to get Audrey on her side at some point.

Before I headed over to meet my dad, I peeked out the front window again. No dark car. Good.

I was extra vigilant as I drove, watching for anything out of the ordinary. No car followed me to the diner that I could tell. I was looking forward to seeing my dad. We didn't get a lot of one-on-one time.

As I pulled into the parking lot at Reggie's Diner, I saw him standing by the front entrance. He smiled when he saw me and came over to open my door. My dad was always a gentleman.

"Hiya, Jo."

"Hey, Dad."

We headed inside and got seated almost immediately. This was my dad's favorite place, and they loved him here. He was greeted by nearly every server.

"Hey, Mr. Webber. Hi, Jo." Lisa and I had gone to high school together. "What can I get you to drink?"

We ordered iced teas. I hadn't been here in a while, so I scanned the menu quickly. Typical diner food, deli sandwiches, salads, and blue-plate specials that included meatloaf, roast chicken, or turkey dinner. I settled on a BLT with avocado. Dad ordered the meatloaf.

"So, tell me about what's going on? Are you safe?" His voice was laced with concern.

"Yes, I'm fine. It's nothing serious. I promise."

"Okay, good. I know your mother overreacts, but you've been through a lot. We... I just want to make sure you are okay."

"Thanks, Dad. I'm okay."

Our drinks arrived, and we changed the subject. I told him about taking Harris and Dylan to the zoo and showed him the pictures.

Overall, we had a pleasant dinner with good conversation and better food. He just wanted to check on me and told me to call if there were any problems, then we parted ways.

Today had not been what I had expected. It started out as I planned, but the afternoon had been one unexpected visit after another. I just hoped I could get through the night without any further drama.

Chapter Twenty

I was working in my office before my appointments and hoping Jeremy would show up so I could ask him about the gambling and see what he thought about me meeting with his parents. He hadn't mentioned me speaking to them for him, but I also thought it would help the case.

Since yesterday when Aaron suggested I talk to them, I had been thinking about it more seriously. It made sense. If there had been a family feud, wouldn't they have some information about that?

After answering a few emails and reviewing a few invoices that Tessa had left for me, I stared out my window, daydreaming and hoping Jeremy would show up. Since the dead didn't have cell phones, I didn't know how to contact him. Maybe if I shut my eyes and thought about him, I could make him appear. It worked for that one widow... sort of.

Focus on Jeremy. I thought to myself. *Earth to, Jeremy.*

"Hello, sunshine."

"Jeremy! It worked."

"What worked?"

"Nothing. Never mind." Suddenly too embarrassed to share, in case It hadn't really worked. "I was just hoping you would show up."

"Why? What's going on?"

"I had a visit from Aaron. He talked to Hank about me asking questions."

"He did what? That could put you in danger. Why did he do that?"

"He said because he wanted to know if Hank was after him."

"Hank does not like to be questioned."

"Yeah, I got that impression myself." I didn't elaborate on the fact I had gotten a warning already.

"So, what did he say about Hank?"

"Not much, just that he talked to him, but he suggested I talk to your parents."

"My parents? Why?" He crossed his arms across his chest.

I took this to mean he didn't want me speaking to them. Maybe I should ask him something else and come back to his parents.

"I guess first, I wanted to ask you about the gambling at Hank's. You were involved in that, right?"

"Yeah, most everyone I knew was. That's how a lot of Creekview's business owners got our money to open our companies. We gambled."

I stared at him for a second. "You didn't think that was an important part of your life to share?"

"No, and honestly, how do you not know about it?"

"Because I don't make my money that way."

"Ah, right, you just trick people. Got it." His voice was sharp and cutting.

I ignored his jab. "Anyone in that elite gang that might have felt you wronged them? Perhaps someone accused you of cheating or something? I heard the name Butch. And who is Nina?

"Butch is a nobody. He sucks at cards, so he thought I was cheating. I'm just a damn good poker player. And Nina? She had a crush on me and claims I'm the father of her baby."

Another girlfriend and another baby?

"How old is this baby?"

"Not born yet. I don't even know exactly how far along she is."

"Were you dating her? Could you be the father?"

"No, it was just a fling. It meant nothing. A couple of times. Not my fault she got attached. It probably isn't mine, and I'm not claiming it."

He didn't sound as callous about his other two children. Why did this one draw such dismissal? Did he not understand how babies were made? A fling could still make a baby.

"I guess I need to talk to this other woman, too, huh?"

"Why? She's nobody."

"What if she killed you?"

"How would she get into my lab? She doesn't have access."

"She could have conspired with someone that worked there, right? I mean, that isn't outside of the realm of possibility, is it?"

He agreed that it was possible and that maybe I should try to meet with her. He said she hung out at Leo's often. He also suggested that I ask Laney to introduce me to his parents.

We didn't talk more about Butch. This new woman seemed far more important, only because of the baby situation, and our conversation had centered around her. I would have to figure out a game plan for talking to Nina and, of course, Jeremy's parents. A text message to Laney would take care of that.

I still got the feeling he wasn't telling me everything. He either didn't think it was necessary, like Nina, or he was hiding something. Since

I didn't know what was missing, I wasn't sure what questions to ask. I would just wait and see what information I got from others.

For now, I had my first work appointment of the day and a full schedule to get through. We couldn't continue to discuss this, but Jeremy agreed to come back later.

After my first appointment, I texted Laney, asking her if she could introduce me to Mr. and Mrs. Landon.

Why?

I shouldn't have been surprised that she questioned me. My request was a bit out of the blue.

Jeremy wants me to pass on a message

Ah, got it. I'll let you know

That was easy. I hoped they would be receptive.

During a break between appointments, I filled Micah and Tessa in on the new developments, specifically the third baby mama. They both agreed this was something we should check out.

"So, nachos at Leo's again?" said Micah. "I'll call Josh!"

A few hours later, after picking up Josh, the four of us walked into Leo's. Several of Hank's guys eyed us but didn't approach. I didn't see Hank. Hopefully, he wasn't here. I didn't want to appear like I was questioning him again. Today was about finding Nina.

I looked around the bar. I wasn't sure exactly who I was looking for, but I didn't think there would be many pregnant women in Leo's.

"Any ideas?" Micah asked, looking around.

"No. I guess I could ask at the bar."

As if on cue, a waitress came up to wait on us. We ordered drinks, nachos, and fried pickles. Tessa's suggestion.

"Do you happen to know Nina?" I asked as casually as I could.

"Um, yeah."

"Is she here?"

"Yeah, she's over there." She pointed to a redhead near the bar. I hadn't noticed her before. "Does she owe you money, too?"

"Oh, hmm, no. We just have a mutual friend, and I was going to introduce myself and say hello." That sounded believable, right? I smiled confidently.

She shrugged, then said she would put our order in, and then walked away.

I watched Nina for a moment. She was laughing and flirting with one of Hank's guys. She had a beer in one hand, which I thought was odd if she was pregnant, but who was I to judge other people's choices? She turned slightly, and I could see her pregnant belly.

"Are you going to talk to her?" Tessa asked.

"I should, but I really don't know how to start that conversation. Plus, I don't want to interrupt her."

"Should she be drinking?" Josh said with a frown.

"Yeah, that can't be good for the baby," Micah added.

Tessa and I just nodded. I'm glad I wasn't the only one that caught that. I had to make a move soon, or the waitress might become suspicious that I hadn't gone over.

"Alright, I'm going to just say 'hi.'" I walked over to the bar. "Nina?"

"Yes? Do I know you?" Hank's guy gave me the stink eye at having his date's attention taken from him, but he stayed quiet.

"No, no. I'm Joanna, and I'm a medium. I was recently —"

"Oh, you're *that* medium. Oh, oh!" She got animated and flapped her hands around. "Does someone want to talk to me? Is it my Auntie Trudy? She raised me and passed last year. I really wish she was here to meet this little one." She touched her belly much more roughly than I had seen Laney do.

"Um …" I looked around. No spirits stepped forward to say they were Auntie Trudy. "Sorry, not her. But if I hear from her, I will definitely let you know. No, it's Jeremy Landon, who I've been talking with."

She winced and pursed her lips. "That lying bastard can rot for all I care. I have nothing to say to him *or you*."

She turned her back and took a long drink of her beer. Why didn't anyone in here stop her?

"Is that good for the baby?" *Crap,* I didn't mean to say that out loud.

"Mind your own *damn* business." Nina snapped.

Hank's guy, I didn't know this one, stood and took a step toward me. Nina put her hand on his chest to stop him. He didn't move past her.

"I'm sorry. I shouldn't have said that. I just wanted to introduce myself. If you want to talk about Jeremy, please call or email me. Sorry to bother you." I slid her my card, then turned on my heel and walked as quickly as I could back to my friends.

"How did it go, Boss?"

"Not good. Not good at all. I thought what's-his-name was going to snap me in two."

Our drinks and food arrived at the table, so we ate and chatted. I kept my head down and tried not to watch the redhead at the bar. The nachos were good, but the pickles were better. I'm so glad Tessa ordered those.

As we were wrapping up our snack and finishing our drinks, Nina came over.

"Okay, fine, I'll talk to you. But you can't tell me what to do with my body. If I want a beer, I can drink one or two. My doctor is fine with it." She wagged her finger at me.

My companions made surprised faces.

"I'm sorry about that." I tried to offer a genuine smile.

She gave me a tight-lipped smile in reply.

"Do you want to join us or go somewhere private to talk?" I asked.

"I don't care. It depends on what you are going to say?"

"I just have some questions about Jeremy."

"What could you possibly have to ask about him? The fact that he denied this kid or something else?"

More surprised expressions around my table.

"Um, yes, that, and also, what can you tell me about the gambling club? What was Jeremy's involvement in it?"

"That bastard. He played in the weekly game. He was good. Could have done professional tournaments, like legit stuff. Not this illegal shit Hank runs. He won more than he lost. A lot of people thought he cheated, but he had skills. That's what first attracted me to him. He's also quick-witted, smart, sexy, and in bed ... oh, he is gifted." She had a slightly dazed look. I didn't really need to or want to know about his skills in bed. "When I told him I was pregnant, he ended things. He denied my baby and wouldn't help me with anything. I can't prove it's his until it's born, so I was going to get a paternity test once this little guy pops out. Of course, now that dick is gone, I'm just stuck."

"He said you were only together a couple of times. Was it more than that?" I know I was getting personal, but I was trying to find out the truth.

She stared at me for a moment. When she finally spoke, her tone was harsh. "We were sleeping together for months. I didn't count how many times, but it was probably a few dozen times."

"Sorry, just letting you know what he had said."

"Yeah, well, nobody really knew about us. A few people, maybe. I didn't want others to know I was like that ... ya know? Sleeping with a married man. I have never done that before. I'm really not that kind of person, ya know?"

I nodded and looked around my table. Everyone was looking so intently at Nina. They loved the drama. Nina looked at them with a frown causing them to quickly look away.

"Well, I really appreciate your time. Was there anyone else in these games that might have it in for Jeremy? Have a motive to kill him?"

"What? You think I killed him?" she said way too loud. We all looked around. Nobody else seemed to flinch, but she lowered her voice to ask, "You think someone killed him? I thought it was an accident."

"He thinks it's possible. I don't know what I think yet. Still fact-finding."

She nodded and said if she thought of anything new, she would let me know, and added, "Sure, I was mad at him, but what good is he dead? I need child support, and he was loaded."

That made sense. I thanked her again. We paid and quickly left. I didn't need Hank thinking we were butting into his business when I wasn't.

In the car, we all let out a nervous laugh. It was always nerve-racking to be near Hank's men, and I kept expecting him to show up with a goon on each side and follow through on his threat. Thankfully, he hadn't so far.

Once we pulled away, I remembered I had wanted to ask Nina about Butch. Damn, missed opportunity.

Micah was the first to break the silence. "Do you think she'll call with anything, Boss?"

"Nah, I doubt it," I said.

"That was crazy! I am so glad you guys picked me up," Josh gushed from the back seat. "I wish I could work with you guys all the time."

"It isn't always like this, babe."

I don't think Josh believed Micah. Our job probably did look glamorous to him, since the few times he had been with us, we got nachos and adult beverages with a side of drama and danger. That probably looked like fun to an outsider.

On the drive back to my house, I got a text from Laney. The Landons could see me tomorrow morning, but Laney couldn't go with me. My nerves kicked in. I wasn't sure what I would say to them, but I'm sure I'd figure it out by morning. I was relieved that Laney couldn't be there; it saved me from having to reveal too much in front of her.

"I'm meeting with Jeremy's parents tomorrow. Can we change my schedule a bit tomorrow?" I directed to Tessa.

"Absolutely."

"Do you think they'll have anything new to share, Boss?" Micah asked from the backseat.

"I really hope so. But if nothing else, maybe I can at least get a better picture of who Jeremy was. Several weeks into this thing, and I feel like he's still a huge mystery. He's not telling me everything. I mean, we just learned about a new mistress and possibly a third baby. Crazy!"

I'm not sure at what point the car started following us. Tessa was driving and didn't know to look for it, but I caught it in the side view mirror. They stayed behind us nearly all the way home. If anyone else in the car noticed, they didn't let on. They just chatted and sang along with the radio. All I could think was at least I wasn't alone if something happened.

Luckily, they turned off before getting all the way back to the house and didn't engage us in any way. I was glad I didn't have to explain to the others or answer questions about who it could be. I wouldn't have many answers or ideas to give anyway. But I had plenty of my own questions, like who was driving, why were they following me, and what did they want?

The guys left, while Tessa joined me inside to help me change my schedule. She made some calls and tapped away at the computer while I mostly watched her work. She was a quiet and reserved person, but she was an excellent assistant. She could remember my schedule, people, and places as easily as she did her own name.

"All done. That was the last appointment that needed to be changed," she said, pushing back from the desk.

"Wonderful. Thank you so much."

"Do you want me to stay a little while with you? I know things have been … stressful lately. The attempted break in and that car following you."

"Yes, stressful and scary. Wait. I don't remember telling you about the car, did I?" Was I losing my mind?

"No, I noticed it today, and it has been parked out front too. Any ideas who it is?"

"None. I'm not sure if it's related to this thing with Jeremy or maybe a crazed fan. Until they show themselves, I won't know."

"So, do you want me to stay? I'm happy to."

"Nah, I think I'll be okay."

She nodded, gathered her things, and left. I appreciated her offer, but I was tired and wanted to have a quiet night. I needed time to think about how to handle tomorrow. I had no idea what to expect from the Landons, but I just knew they lived in the posh part of town, and from what I had read, they were the epitome of Creekview elite.

I was used to interacting with people from all walks of life, but for some reason, this meeting terrified me.

Chapter Twenty-One

The next day, I dressed with extra care in cream-colored slacks and a navy-blue button-down shirt, finished up with matching heels. I put my hair up in a loose bun. I stepped back and looked at my reflection. I thought I looked good enough for the Acre Meadows neighborhood, or at least as a guest.

Driving over to their house, I tried to calm my nerves. The landscape changed as I got closer. It was oak-tree-lined streets and perfectly manicured lawns in front of McMansions full of rooms I could only imagine.

They lived in the exclusive part of Acre Meadows. There were maybe a couple dozen homes in their gated estate.

I'd been here once before for a personal reading. The wife of a CEO. He had died of a heart attack, and she wanted to ask him about their accounts. It was a business-like session, no love or feelings. Unfortunately, this was back when I was faking it, and she was not thrilled because "he" didn't have the answers she wanted.

Driving up to the gatehouse, I gave my name to the guard. He called the house. There was a brief discussion. The guard eyed me a few times, then got off the phone and opened the gate, gesturing for me to go ahead.

The Landons lived in a gorgeous Victorian-inspired house with a turret, gables, and all the trimmings. It was stunning, and my nerves went into overdrive as I parked and walked up to the front door.

An older version of Jeremy opened the door to greet me. He had wavy gray hair and a neatly trimmed mustache. His blue eyes popped against his dark, tanned skin. He was dressed in khakis with a maroon polo.

"Hello, Mr. Landon?"

"Yes."

"I'm Joanna Webber, the medium." I extended my hand to shake his.

He stared at me with an unreadable expression. For a moment, I thought I had offended him with my offer of a handshake, but after his brief hesitation, he shook my hand.

Awkward.

"Yes, Ms. Webber. Please come in."

I followed him into the marbled foyer.

Every decoration and architectural detail screamed money. Moldings, spindles, gold, and marble. Mr. Landon led me through a living room and into a sunroom. Mrs. Landon was seated by one of the many windows, martini in hand and a phone pressed to her ear.

"Oh, Martha, darlin', I need to go. We have company... Yes, I'll call you later." She put the phone down and took a long sip from her drink before acknowledging me. "My, Ms. Joanna, so good of you to come to visit us. Would you like a drink? Martini, perhaps?"

While I enjoyed a martini now and then, it was 9:00 a.m. I could see why Jeremy was worried about her.

"No, thank you, I'm fine. Your home is lovely."

"Oh, thank you, dear." She took another sip, finishing the drink, then held the empty glass toward her husband. "Frank, could you fix me another, please?"

He sighed heavily as he took her glass and walked out of the room. I sat in a chair across from her. We didn't speak as we waited for him to return, which was only a minute later with her full glass. Handing it to her, he then took the chair opposite her.

"I know you both must be wondering why I'm here," I took a deep, slow breath. "I have been speaking with your son, Jeremy."

Mrs. Landon gasped and took a long sip of her drink.

"I'm sorry. I know that sometimes it's shocking when I first say it."

"She believes in all this." Mr. Landon gestured dismissively at his wife. "I'm not sure that I do, but I'm willing to listen," he said bluntly. He shifted in his chair as if he didn't want to be here.

I nodded. I was used to getting mixed reactions to my job.

"Is he here now?" Mrs. Landon looked around the room, hopeful.

"No, he isn't. I'm sorry. I haven't spoken to him in a few days. He seemed sad the last time we spoke, and I thought I could do some research without him."

"Research? About what?" Frank asked with a suspicious tone. "Don't mediums give answers, not ask questions?"

"That's true, but Jeremy asked me to investigate his death for him. He doesn't believe that it was an accident."

"Oh my. Oh my! Oh my!" Priscilla Landon finished her drink, stood, swayed, and then sat back down. She began frantically fanning herself with her hand.

"So, what does he think happened? We've seen the reports and video. Well, I have. It was clear what happened," Frank firmly stated.

"I know it seems like that, but he is convinced someone sabotaged him."

"Someone? Like who?" Priscilla slumped slightly in her chair, looking into her empty glass with a sigh.

"He isn't sure. I've done what I can, checked a few leads, but I was hoping you could help me. Is there anyone you can think of that would want to hurt him?"

"Oh, no, dear. People loved Jeremy. Ever since he was a tiny baby, he charmed everyone around him." She put her glass to her mouth and looked disappointed when she realized it was still empty.

Frank stood and took her glass. He left the room only to return a moment or two later with it filled.

"Thank you, honey." She beamed at him through glassy eyes.

Frank looked at me and nodded to the side as if he wanted to speak privately or ask me to leave. Either way, I could see that Priscilla was not going to be helpful. She was just going to drink herself into a stupor.

"I'm sorry. He seems like a good person. I can't imagine who wouldn't like him, but I thought it was worth a shot to ask. Thank you for your time." I directed toward Priscilla.

I followed Mr. Landon out to the front yard. On the lawn, he turned back to look at the house.

"Sorry about her. She always had a slight... problem. But since Jeremy's death, it has only gotten worse. And yes, yes, I'm enabling it by giving her drinks, but I don't know what else to do. She gets... um... insane without a drink. I know it isn't right, but for now, it's all I know to do." He sighed, looking back at the house. "I thought having her mother back and healthy, well, mostly healthy, would help, but she just couldn't handle losing her favorite son."

"I'm sorry. That can't be easy."

"So, to answer your question, I was always suspicious of those gambling people he hung around with. Do you know them? I was especially concerned about a character named Butch. I think Jeremy was sleeping with his girlfriend, Nina."

Wow, why hadn't Nina mentioned her boyfriend, Butch? I wish I had remembered to ask about him.

"Did they threaten him or anything that you know of?"

"There was a pushing and shouting match once after a night at Hank's. Butch or Royce, maybe, accused Jeremy of cheating. Nina defended him, then Butch accused them of sleeping together. It was rough."

This was the first I'd heard of Royce. I assumed he was another gambling patron.

"Were you there?"

"Yes, but I didn't see the start. I just heard the yelling once they started shoving each other."

"Just Butch and Jeremy, or was Royce involved? Or anyone else?"

"No, it was just Butch and Jeremy at that point."

"Do you know if either of them would have access to Jeremy's lab?"

"Butch might have. He works for Greg. He is part of the construction crew working on Jeremy's building. Royce is not relevant in this. He's nearly eighty years old and rarely leaves home. Only for the poker games."

"So, you think Butch?"

"If you believe the murder theory, then yes, I'd suggest looking at Butch. Possibly assisted by Nina."

I nodded and took this in. I didn't know how easy it was to move around undetected or what the security measures were like in a laboratory, but I imagined if Butch was there working, not many people would think twice about where he went.

"I really appreciate your time, Mr. Landon."

"Thank you. Oh, um, how does this medium thing work? I mean, what does he look like?"

"From the pictures I have seen of him, he looks the same. He says he misses you, and he's sorry for everything."

He smiled sadly. "Thank you. That means a lot. True or not, it helps."

I nodded and turned toward my car. As I pulled away, I saw Frank Landon standing in the yard looking at the house. By his slumped posture, he looked like he had the weight of the world on his shoulders. He sighed and went back inside.

Another person was suggesting Nina. I found that interesting. I didn't mention to Mr. Landon that I had met her already. She was staying on the suspect list, and I would have to look into this Butch character. I was pretty sure that was not who she was getting cozy with at Leo's the other day. I couldn't remember his name, but I knew it wasn't Butch. He was Mike or Matt or something with an "M."

I arrived home long before my first appointment for the day, having overestimated how long my meeting with the Landons would take. I decided to do some laundry while I waited. After my laundry was going, I got a fresh cup of coffee and sat outside to enjoy this beautiful day.

I loved working from home. It gave me a lot of freedom like this. I couldn't imagine many accounting jobs where you got the chance to leisurely sit outside with a cup of coffee. I browsed social media on my phone until Micah arrived for the day.

"So how did things go this morning with the Landons?"

"Um, interesting. His mom is lost in her grief, but Mr. Landon was helpful. He gave me some good information and confirmed that Nina is someone we should be looking at. Along with, get this, her boyfriend, Butch."

"Butch? She was hanging all over Mitch yesterday."

Mitch! That was it. I knew it started with an "M."

"Yeah, she was."

I gave him the full rundown on my conversation with Mr. Landon. We were discussing what to do next when Tessa showed up, and I recounted the story again for her. She didn't offer much more that would help.

We sat in silence for a few minutes before getting to work. It was a busy day, so I didn't have much time after that to think. However, as the day ended and my last clients left, I was once again thinking of Jeremy and his parents.

Maybe I should check out this Butch guy. The problem was, I didn't know much about him. I guessed I could go ask Nina, but I didn't want to go back to Leo's, especially alone.

I felt stuck until I could talk to Jeremy. I had no way to get in touch with him.

My phone chimed as I was thinking about it. It was Laney asking how the meeting with the Landons went. I replied it was fine. They were happy to hear from Jeremy. We messaged back and forth a bit before saying good night.

I had really wanted to ask her about Butch and Nina, or any other gamblers she might know of, but it was a conversation best had in person. And I would have to be careful about it. I really didn't want her to know what I was doing as I didn't want her to think I was only friends with her for the information she could give me.

In the short time I'd spent with her, I truly enjoyed her as a person and wanted to be friends. Until she trusted me, I couldn't tell her what I was up to.

Chapter Twenty-Two

~Joanna~

The next few days were uneventful. Thank goodness. I needed my life to get back to some kind of normal. I didn't have any contact with Jeremy, nor did I investigate any of the leads. I felt stuck.

There was all this new information about the gambling and new suspects, but I didn't know what to do with it. Not to mention, I was booked solid, and after shuffling my schedule the other day, I was even busier, so I didn't have time for Jeremy.

Micah and Tessa would be here soon, and my first appointment was set for 9:00 a.m. I was in my office working when I heard a car pull into the driveway. I rolled my chair to the window, expecting to see one of my assistants. Instead, what I saw made my blood run cold. It was Hank's right-hand man, Al, stepping out of a black SUV.

"Shit!"

I looked around for the card with Clint's phone number but couldn't find it. I should have saved it in my cell phone. Peeking out the window again, I saw that Al was opening the back door.

Oh, double shit. It was Hank. Aaron had gotten me in trouble. It had just taken a while for trouble to come calling.

I did the back-and-forth dance one does when they can't decide which direction to go. Should I hide? Should I open the door? If I chose to hide, where?

Okay, let me pull myself together and think.

I quickly sent Micah and Tessa a text message saying that Hank and Al were at my house. I needed someone to know in case something happened. I then put my phone on silent so that it wouldn't go off while I talked with Hank. He seemed like the type that wouldn't like the focus taken off him.

There was a knock at the door. I toyed with my indecision a moment more, still thinking maybe I should hide, but then resolved to answer it. I forced a bright, warm smile onto my face and tried to remember to breathe.

"Mr. Hank, hello. What a surprise. Please, come in," I said as I opened the door.

"Thank you." He stepped inside, and I showed them to my living room.

"May I get you a drink?"

"Nothing for me. Al?" He looked at his lackey. Al shook his head and stood behind Hank. "Let me get right to the point, Ms. Joanna. Aaron Novak has come to me. He said you told him that I was looking to kill him and that I killed Jeremy."

"No, I didn't. I would never—"

Hank put up his hands. I stopped talking.

"I'm a fair man, and I already gave you one warning, but since you are new to this, I'm giving you one more, and only one more. Do not take me on, Ms. Joanna; you won't win."

"Yes, sir."

"Now, let me be very clear with you, so there is no misunderstanding after I leave. I did not murder Jeremy. Yes, he owed me money, but many people in town do. He didn't owe me so much that it was worth killing him over, though. There are bigger fish that owe me much more. Second, Aaron pays me regularly, and while he still owes me a lot, so far, he's been a good investment. I wouldn't kill him, either. It doesn't make good business sense." He looked at me for a long second. "Now, Ms. Medium, you stick to the things you know, and I will stick to the things I know."

"I'm sorry. Yes, of course." I paused. "You wouldn't happen to have any ideas on who could have murdered Jeremy, do you? I got word that maybe someone from your gambling club might have."

"Did you now?" He looked me up and down, sending chills down my spine. "He wasn't murdered. There was an accident at the lab. I'm not sure if anyone of the club members could have accessed the lab. Why do you think he was murdered?"

"He told me he was, and I believe him." I left off the part about Butch having access. I didn't know how much I should say, especially without any proof. Plus, it was just hearsay at this point.

"And he doesn't know who did it?"

"No. It was made to look like a lab accident, and of course, that's what it was ruled to be." I hesitated as I chose my next words carefully. "My job is to help people have peace and closure, both alive and dead. That is what I want to help Jeremy with."

"I understand. Well, I will keep my ears open. I should also tell you that you're being followed, in case you didn't already know. I had my guys keeping an eye on you, and they noticed the car. I don't know yet who it is. We've traced the tags, no match, which is odd, even for temporary tags. They would lead to someone." He paused and looked at me again with an intense stare that made my blood run cold. "Despite you sticking your nose in places it shouldn't be, I like you. So, we will continue to keep an eye on you."

"Thank you. I appreciate it." Some relief in knowing I wasn't alone, but a little scared because I had only noticed the one car. I didn't realize Hank's guys were following me as well. "Are your guys in the dark sedan or another car?"

"Oh, Ms. Joanna, you would never notice my guys. That dark car is the stranger that is following you."

"Ah, okay." That didn't make me feel better.

"No matter what you think, I do take care of the people in this town. That's why the police leave me alone, for the most part. I know I have a reputation, but I'm a good guy." He stood, and the two started to walk out. "Oh, and have you heard anything from my dear mother yet?"

I wondered for a moment if maybe I should make something up to further stay on his good side. I was great at the fake medium stuff, but I thought better of it.

"Not yet, but I promise if I do, I will call you right away."

He nodded, then stepped out the door. I shut it behind them and melted to the floor. I felt like I could finally breathe normally.

I grabbed my phone. I had several missed calls and texts from both my assistants, so I called Micah while sending a text to Tessa.

"Boss! What the hell?" Micah yelled into the phone.

"I know, I'm sorry. I'll fill you in when you get here. I just messaged Tessa, too, so she would know I am okay."

"I'm almost there. Stay out of trouble until I get there."

Oh, funny boy, I thought.

"I'll try."

I paced around, trying to decide what to do while I waited for them to arrive. Watching the road, I noticed a patrol car drive by. It slowed as it got in front of my house and then continued down the road. That was good.

I wondered if they had driven by while Hank and Al were here. Would they recognize their car? I always had random cars from clients in my driveway. What did the officers think of that? How would they know the difference: client or foe?

Walking through the living room, I straightened a few things that didn't really need straightening. I took my mug to the sink, rinsed it, and placed it in the dishwasher. I wiped up a few stray crumbs from my morning toast.

Anything to keep my brain busy and my body moving. I felt like a bundle of nerves ready to come unglued. Thankfully, Micah soon arrived, letting himself in, and came straight to me for a hug.

"I wish I hadn't pushed you into this Jeremy mystery thing. It's put you in danger, but especially my suggestion to talk to Hank the Hammer." His voice was heavy with guilt.

"No, it's not your fault. I could have said 'no.' I wouldn't worry too much, though. Detectives Hartley and Walden know and have asked for patrols in front of my house. I just saw one a few minutes ago."

He nodded and gave me another hug before starting his usual work routine, which always started with getting a snack from the kitchen before heading to the back office. Tessa arrived, lectured me, hugged me, lectured me a little more, then joined Micah in the back office.

I didn't have time to think about all the dangers. I had a fully booked day, plus a house full of spirits waiting on their loved ones, and more that were optimistic, hanging out with high hopes of an afterlife reunion.

They wanted me to start contacting their loved ones to schedule with them directly. I was busy enough with the appointments I already had and planning our upcoming tour. I didn't know how to fit in contacting all these other people, but I was thinking about it just to empty my house out.

Hours later, my appointments were over. Micah left, but Tessa stayed behind. They had agreed one of them should be with me, and this time she wasn't taking no for an answer. Micah had plans with Josh. It was an anniversary of sorts.

Unfortunately, I didn't have a guest room as we used both secondary bedrooms for work, but I had a pull-out couch.

"What's the plan for the evening, Ms. Tessa?"

"Want to order a pizza and watch a movie?"

"Sure."

I called the pizza place down the street and gave them our order while Tessa scrolled through the list of movies to watch.

"Pizza will be here in about twenty. What did you find?"

She pointed out the ones she had shortlisted. I hadn't seen a movie in a while, so all of them looked good to me. We made our selection, then got drinks and talked about the day while waiting for our food.

When it arrived, I grabbed some plates and napkins, and she set the pizza on the coffee table. We helped ourselves to a slice or two, then turned on the movie.

The rom-com made us laugh, cry, and laugh some more. It was a great distraction from Jeremy's case. I didn't think about Hank or Jeremy or the dark car. The fact that Hank and his guys couldn't figure out who was following me should have worried me, but since I knew they were also watching, I felt less alone. Plus, I had the cops looking out for me, as well, so lots of eyes on me.

After the movie, we cleaned up dinner, and then I grabbed some extra sheets for the sleeper sofa. Together we made up the bed for Tessa. Her mother dropped off an overnight bag. Ms. Ruby, Tessa's mom, was an interesting lady.

She had a big personality, much bigger than her tiny frame would suggest. Knowing Tessa, with her quiet demeanor and dark style, you wouldn't think she came from someone so bright and bubbly. It wasn't just her personality but also her clothing choices.

Her favorites were bright, flashy colors and prints. Tonight, she was sporting a purple and teal leopard-print top over orange leggings. Her normally jet-black hair was hot pink. This all might seem odd on some people, but with her dynamic personality and bright smile, it worked on Ms. Ruby.

She stayed for tea and conversation.

"How's business, Jo? I hear so many good things online about you and from Tessa." She smiled at her daughter lovingly.

It sent a spark of jealousy through me. I didn't have that type of relationship with my mother. With my mother, I always felt like I was tiptoeing around a giant toddler on the verge of a tantrum.

"Things are going well. We're booked solid for months, right up until our next tour."

"That's great. I'm hoping to travel out to see one of your shows."

"We would love to have you."

"Now, Micah and I just have to talk Jo into getting on a plane for this next one." Tessa snarked.

I shot her a dirty look that was mostly a bluff with no real anger behind it.

"Oh, I remember the story of the last plane ride." Ms. Ruby chuckled.

I was never going to live that story down. I had to really think long and hard about overcoming my fear so I could rewrite my plane story.

After Ms. Ruby left, Tessa and I both changed for bed. It was finally a quiet night at home. It just took Tessa babysitting me to make it happen.

Chapter Twenty-Three

~Clint~

"Earth to Clint, are you there?" Kelly cooed.

"Oh, I'm sorry. I've been so distracted lately. Work." From the serial killer to this Jeremy Landon case, I felt like I had a lot to deal with right now.

"It must be some case. You've had your mind somewhere else all week."

She knew about the case. It was only the biggest news story in our town right now. Was she being coy or just shallow? I shrugged it off as typical Kelly.

"Yeah, I'm sorry." But if I was honest, I wasn't sorry. I knew this relationship had about run its course, but for some odd reason, neither of us would end it. At times, she seemed almost as disinterested in me as I was in her, or perhaps I was projecting my feelings onto her. "I promise I'll try to be more in the moment."

We were out playing mini-golf. This had been her suggestion and wasn't my idea of a fun activity. I guess with the right person, it could be fun. But this was not the right person, and I couldn't figure out why I was trying at all. To not disappoint my mother, I supposed, or to fill some void in my life.

We finished the hole and moved to the next. I tried to focus on her, laughing at the things she said, telling her stories, and not thinking of other things. This wasn't as bad as I thought it was. I think I was just in a bad mood from everything going on at work. I chastised myself for having such negative thoughts.

As we were finishing up the last hole, Kelly got a text message and became really animated.

"Oh, some of my friends are over at Spades. Want to join them?"

"Sure." I didn't know if I was a Spades type of person.

It was more club than bar. People drank martinis and white wine in slacks and ties, rather than beer and whiskey while wearing jeans and ball caps. I'd go along since I wasn't quite ready to have "the talk." Besides, I didn't have anything else to do.

We pulled into the parking lot at Spades. Not a pickup truck in the lot. Mine was the only one. Before I could get around to open the passenger door, Kelly hopped out, so excited to be here.

She barely waited for me before she was at the door of the club, and she squealed when she found her friends. I felt like a discard.

I leaned over to ask her what she wanted to drink, then headed to the bar for her chocolate martini. I ordered the only type of beer they had. It wasn't my usual drink, but I figured they couldn't ruin beer. I was wrong.

I delivered her drink and stood nearby. She giggled and chatted happily with her friends. I tried to engage with the guys in the group, but they weren't into sports, rock music, or even cars. They wanted to talk about stock options and politics. I listened instead, which wasn't an easy task considering the volume in here. My head was spinning between the techno music and the numerous people talking at louder than normal levels.

After I got tired of listening, I let my mind and eyes wander around the club. I took in the many faces. They were all dressed more or less the same in, I guess, what would be called "business casual." Guys in slacks and button-down shirts, some with ties, others with jackets. The girls were comparably dressed in skirts, dresses, or slacks. I was underdressed, but Kelly wore a beautiful sundress with a cardigan over the top, and she seemed to fit in.

My eyes locked on a familiar face, Greg Landon. He noticed me and nodded a greeting. I nodded back before continuing my scan of the room. I tried to casually glance back at him, not wanting to appear like I was staring or keeping an eye on him. He was with people I didn't recognize.

"Clint, honey, could you get me another drink?" Kelly cooed in my ear.

I nodded and headed back to the bar to do her bidding. I ordered her a drink and myself water. I assumed they couldn't mess that up.

While I waited, a familiar figure came up on my right side.

"Hey, Detective."

"Mr. Landon."

"I haven't seen you here before. I wouldn't have imagined you in a place like this."

"Girlfriend." I nodded toward Kelly.

"Ah. The things we do for the ladies." He chuckled.

"So, how's it going?"

"Not bad. Business is good," he confirmed.

"Good."

"Did that medium come talk to you? I gave her your card."

"She did."

"I assume you gave her the information she was looking for."

"I let her look at the report and video."

"So, case closed."

"Case closed?"

"Yes. She's over the whole 'Jeremy was murdered' theory, yes?"

I wasn't sure how I should answer this. He sounded like he was fishing. Maybe I needed to look closer at Greg's alibi for that day.

"Honestly, I'm not sure what she believes or doesn't. I gave her the information, and she thanked me. That's all I know."

He nodded. My order came up, so I grabbed our drinks and went back to Kelly. Setting the drink in front of her won me a thank you kiss on the cheek for my efforts, and then she went right back to her friends.

I kept one eye on Greg. His posture changed. He seemed to be brooding and bounced his leg as he sat. I had tried to keep my tone casual and give limited information. Had I done that? If he was a murderer, there was no telling what he was thinking. At the very least, he was a loose cannon, and I'd never had a high opinion of him.

I sipped my water while half paying attention to Kelly and her friends as they continued their conversation about people and things that I didn't know or have an interest in. I was losing my patience and wished I had a good excuse to leave.

About the time that thought formed, I saw Greg say his goodbyes to his table. He looked over his shoulder as he stood. Our eyes locked. The expression on his face made the hairs on the back of my neck stand up. I had a bad feeling about him. He continued with his rushed exit.

I leaned toward Kelly, letting her know something for work had come up, and asked if she could find a ride home. Her friends agreed they could. She gave me a kiss and a hug. I was only half in it, resenting losing precious time.

I darted toward the door and out into the parking lot just in time to catch the headlights of a dark car leaving the lot. I couldn't be sure if it was him or not, and even as I stood there, several more cars came and went. Any of them could have been him.

"Damn." I kicked at the ground. "Lost him."

I stared out into the night, but the silver lining here was I was free to go home and have a real beer.

Chapter Twenty-Four

~Joanna~

It was the day of Dad's surprise party. Audrey and I had been planning it for a while and had every detail figured out. Mom was the only factor that had us worried. If things weren't about her or her idea, she sometimes didn't cooperate.

Having experience with toddlers, and Mom was like a giant toddler at times, Audrey tried to make it seem like her role was the biggest and most important. We just had to cross our fingers that Mom didn't blow it for us but had a back-up plan if she decided she was "sick" or some other Mom drama.

I'd be picking our Uncle Dennis up from the airport later. Dad would be so surprised to see him. They had been close growing up but hadn't seen each other in a few years. I knew they missed each other. Uncle Dennis moved away about ten years ago for a job and hoped to move back once he retired in a couple of years.

I loaded some party supplies into my car and headed to Audrey's. We would decorate and get everything set up before I left for the airport. If all our planning worked out, I would have just enough time.

I pulled into the driveway just as Stan was loading the boys in the car. Harris came running to me. He was taking the boys to his parents' house to keep them out of the way and ensure they didn't undo anything. They would all rejoin us at party time.

"Auntie Jo! Auntie Jo!" He threw himself in my arms.

"Hey, sweetie. Are you going to Gigi and Papa's?" I asked him.

"Yep! We can't be in the way."

Kids were honest. Maybe I didn't want kids.

"Come on, sport, we need to get going," Stan called. "Hey, Jo."

"Good morning. Have fun!" I grabbed my bags and headed into the house. "Hello?"

"Hey. Back here!"

I headed toward the kitchen to find my sister standing on a stool, trying to hang a banner. She had balloons already filled and waiting to be scattered around.

"Someone is a hard worker." I chuckled at her.

"Yeah, you know me! If I'm awake, I'm working and always working through my many to-do lists." She finished with the banner and stepped off the stool. "Coffee?"

"You read my mind."

She got a mug for me and poured us both a cup. I added some flavored creamer and sipped. We did a quick run-through of what needed to be done. Having a planner for a sister was a good thing. She had most everything under control.

"...and the catering will be dropped off at 1:00. You'll be getting Uncle Dennis, and then everyone else should start arriving around 2:00," she confirmed.

"Any word from Mom this morning?"

"She texted. I gave her a code name. She seems to be enjoying that part."

"Seriously? What did you call her?"

"Miss Kitty! You know, like the character in Gunsmoke." Audrey almost couldn't keep a straight face saying it.

"What? And she went along with it?"

"She loved it."

"Well, whatever works." I shrugged.

We finished our coffee and got to work decorating the house. Streamers in blue and red adorned every available surface. Helium balloons with long curly ribbons floated through the air. We had rented tables and chairs which were placed outside, and we added colorful tablecloths to each.

Once everything was set up, I headed to the airport for Uncle Dennis while Audrey stayed behind to direct the caterers. I got to the airport in record time and parked in the cell-phone lot to wait. I skimmed through emails and social media to keep busy while I waited.

Once I got bored with my phone, I watched the comings and goings of the cars around me. Some spirits were hanging around, but I didn't react to them, not wanting to call attention to the fact that I could see them. They didn't notice me or seem to know who I was, which was good. I had enough on my plate.

I then watched a few planes take off and others land. I checked the time and realized that one of the arriving planes would be carrying my uncle. As if on cue, my phone rang, and I headed out of the lot to the terminal.

Minutes later, he was in my car, and we were heading back to Audrey's. By the time we pulled up at Audrey's, guests had started to arrive. Audrey came running out.

"Uncle Dennis! So good to see you." She gave him a hug. "I have our guest room all ready for you. Let me show you the way. Oh, and Jo,

Miss Kitty is still good." She winked and showed a confused Uncle Dennis into the house.

We got the last details together. The rest of the guests arrived, and then we had to wait for Miss Kitty to bring the man of honor.

With all the people around and other children, Harris and Dylan were on cloud nine. They were running around, laughing, squealing, and reveling in the joys of being a kid. I was back on team "I want a kid."

"I got a text. They're pulling into the neighborhood." Audrey called out and then flashed me the text.

I burst out laughing. Mom had really gotten into the role of Miss Kitty and secret spy.

A minute later, we saw their car pull up outside. Through a space in the curtains, I could see my dad looking around. He noticed all the cars that we hadn't bothered to hide. He was talking to Mom about something, and she shrugged as she got out of the vehicle.

She hustled up the driveway, giggling the whole way, and to the front door, with Dad close on her heels, still looking confused at the cars. She knocked and opened the door.

"Hello? Audrey?" Dad said as he stepped into the house.

"Surprise! Happy birthday, Charlie." Everyone yelled, followed by clapping, laughs, and cheers.

"Oh, my goodness! What is all this? Oh, girls. Dennis! Oh, wow." He and his brother hugged. He moved on to greet everyone else who had come to celebrate him.

Food was served. People mingled and ate. The kids ran and played. Dad loved the attention even though he always claimed to not like being at the center of it. He secretly did. Miss Kitty hadn't given up her role either.

"So, did I do well, girls?"

"Yes, Mom. You did great," Audrey said.

"He didn't have a clue," I added.

"Well, Miss Kitty knows a thing or two." She shook her hips.

Audrey and I shared a look. Did she know what she was saying? The hip shakes made me think she did.

Hours later, people started to leave. Dad, Stan, and Uncle Dennis, along with a few other close friends, were drinking beer and playing cards. The kids had settled in front of the television with a movie. They were exhausted from the day of activity. The remaining ladies chatted while cleaning up.

"It was a nice party, girls." Aunt Sue complimented us.

"It really was," my parents' close friend, Cindy, chimed in.

"I thought I did my part nicely." Mom had to bring the attention back to her. "It wouldn't have been much of a surprise had I not kept it a secret or gotten him over here. Right?"

"Yes, Mom, you did wonderfully. Thank you." Audrey commented.

I just nodded.

Dylan came to Audrey, arms held high. She scooped him up, and all the ladies started gushing over him. He still had that toddler look to him: chubby little cheeks, cute little hands, and the sweetest smile.

"When are you going to start a family, Jo?" Aunt Sue questioned.

Mom rolled her eyes.

It was a question I got often. I was desensitized to it.

"She's too busy with this crazy dead people business. No man is going to want to marry her, I mean, look at Ted."

"Gee, thanks, Mom."

"Babs, that's uncalled for. She wasn't at fault for Ted's poor choices," Aunt Sue chided.

Mom rolled her eyes again. I could see the storm clouds rolling in.

"But yeah, I do need to find a husband first, right?" I said, trying to stay breezy and defuse the situation.

"Nah, you're a modern woman. No man needed. Well, sort of." Aunt Sue said with a wink.

"Um, I guess." I was stunned.

Was my aunt really suggesting a sperm bank? She was so different from Mom. How were they raised in the same house?

"Bah, Joanna as a single mom? Sue, I can't believe you would suggest such a thing." Mom put her hand to her head. Here came a mom "headache," but at least Aunt Sue was here to deal with it.

"Oh, Babs, don't start with the dramatics. Jo would be fine. She can do anything she puts her mind to. I mean, look at all she has gone through to get here. Ted's death, all the issues with the girlfriend's family, building this business." My aunt smiled at me.

I mouthed a "thank you" to her. She truly was a gem.

"Hmph, you don't know about what I put up with. The stares. The judgment. People look at me like I failed at parenting her."

The three of us stared at my mother. She was crazy.

"Nobody has ever judged you, Mom. People love Jo. I've never heard anything negative about her. Oh, sure, there is some negative stuff sometimes online, but that's normal for anyone with an internet presence." Gotta love my sister for sticking up for me.

My mom grabbed a tissue and wiped her eyes.

"You just don't know. You just don't get it. You have dreams for your kids, and this..." She started to sob.

Dad looked over from the card game and came over.

"What's wrong?" His voice was soft with concern.

"I just want to go. These girls just... don't know what I go through for them." She was full-on, ugly crying now.

Poor Dad looked so confused, but he knew it was just Mom. He never blamed us for upsetting her.

He got her purse and walked her out to the car. Once she was settled in the front seat, he came back in to gather his gifts and say his goodbyes.

"I'm sorry for that. She must be over-tired or something. Thank you, everyone. This was a lovely party. I was so surprised." He hugged us all in turn. "Dennis, I'll see you tomorrow."

With that, Dad left, and the party wrapped up. Aunt Sue and I stayed to help Audrey and Stan finish cleaning up. I would have hated for them to have to deal with all of this tomorrow. We didn't talk about Mom. What could we say? She was like this all the time, and sadly, we were all used to it.

An hour later, I was exhausted and headed home. My brain was distracted by the good, the bad, and the ugly of the day. I pulled in the driveway so ready for bed after the long day.

But I wasn't ready for the mess that I walked into when I got home.

Chapter Twenty-Five

~Clint~

I settled down with a beer and college football. I had spent the day fishing with Dad. We had released most but kept some and had a nice fish fry this afternoon.

I hadn't seen Kelly since the night at Spades. I thought things were over, but neither of us was ready to make it official. My mother asked what Kelly was up to and why she wasn't with me. I just said she was busy. It was a partial lie; I really didn't know what she was up to.

My phone rang, waking me from my daydream. It was Terry.

"Hey, what's up, man?"

"Break-in at Joanna's. Do you want to meet me there?"

"Shit. Do you know anything? Is she okay?"

"Yeah, she's safe. She wasn't home. I don't know much else yet." He gave me the limited details he knew before we hung up, agreeing to meet there.

I grabbed a shirt and shoes, then found my wallet and keys as I sprinted out the door. Joanna lived across town from me, so it would take longer than I wanted to get there.

I knew I should wait until I had facts before trying to figure out a suspect, but I ran through a list of potential names in my head. Only one came to mind: Greg Landon.

He had seemed way too interested in her the other night and in wanting to know what she knew. If he thought she kept any records about the investigation she was making into Jeremy's death, he might have hoped to find them and maybe scare her a little bit.

Finally, I pulled up at her house. Terry was already there, talking to a couple of uniformed officers. I joined them.

"Where is she?" I asked.

"In the house with Smith. She's trying to keep Joanna calm."

I nodded and went to check on her.

Our eyes locked when I came into the room; her face was red and her eyes puffy, as if she'd been crying. She rushed toward me. We barely knew each other, so it caught me off guard, but I instinctively wrapped my arms around her and mumbled comforting words. I hated to see her scared.

Something inside me woke up. I wanted to protect this woman.

"Thank you for coming," she finally whispered.

"Of course."

She let go of me and smiled.

"Sorry about that." She gave a half-laugh as she wiped her eyes. "So embarrassing. I just... look at this mess."

As she gestured around, I finally took in the scene. Wow, this bastard had done a number on her home. She had a simple but classy house decorated with thoughtful items. A person should feel safe in their home, but as a detective, I knew that wasn't always realistic.

"They smashed her televisions, various knick-knacks, and the offices are both trashed," Officer Smith shared.

"Have you been able to determine yet if anything is missing?"

"I can't tell, but it doesn't look like it. I called my assistants, Micah and Tessa, to come over and help me. They should be here any second."

Terry and another officer came in to start taking forensic evidence. They had two other officers interviewing neighbors. Hopefully, someone saw something, heard something, or possibly had a security camera that caught something.

Micah and some guy, apparently his boyfriend, showed up. He went straight to comfort Joanna. I couldn't hear what they were saying, but they were visibly shaken. I stepped closer to listen.

"Do you have any idea who would do this? A disgruntled fan? Or maybe one of Hank's guys?" Micah said.

"Hank? Hank the Hammer?" I snapped.

How was she involved with Hank? She didn't seem like the gambling type.

"He came by the other day and threatened her," Micah informed me.

"It wasn't a threat, exactly, just a business meeting," she argued.

"What the hell? Why are you involved with Hank?" I could almost feel steam coming out of my ears.

"It has to do with Jeremy. I was asking questions, and he got wind of it and told me to stay out of his business."

"You can't be playing around with this. He can be very dangerous." I turned to see where Terry was. We needed to go talk to Hank. Before stepping away, I turned back to Joanna. "You need to be very careful. I'll let you know if we hear anything new. The other officers will be here for a bit to continue gathering information and secure your property. Do you have somewhere safe to stay tonight?"

"She can stay with us," Micah's boyfriend chimed in.

"Great. Give the officers the address and contact number. I'll check on you later." After directing the other officers on the remaining investigation, I stepped outside to meet up with Terry. We needed to speak with Hank.

"Do we take one car or drive separately?" I asked when I caught up to Terry in the yard.

We didn't have time to decide before a dark SUV pulled up. It was Hank and his man, Al. Terry and I walked over to meet them as they both stepped out.

"Hello, Hank. We were just coming to talk to you."

"Me? Why?"

"Just some questions about your dealings with Joanna."

"That's why I'm here. I heard what happened and wanted to check on her. Is she okay?"

"She's shaken up by the whole thing, but overall she's fine."

"Good. I like her," Hank said.

"So, you had nothing to do with this? We heard you made some threats."

"Hartley, you know me. We go back a long way. Yes? Have I ever shown up at the scene?" He said flatly.

I had to admit that was odd for him. "No, you haven't. So, what're you doing here?"

"Checking on her. My men have been keeping an eye on Ms. Webber to ensure she's safe. You know she's being followed daily, right?"

I didn't know that was still happening and had thought it was random.

"I can tell by your face you didn't. Despite her sticking her nose in my business, I like her and don't want to see her harmed. She's good people, Detective Hartley."

"I agree," I said.

Terry's head snapped to look at me. I mentally told him to shut up. He looked away, apparently receiving the unspoken message.

"So, we have the same mission. Find the asshole that did this to Joanna," Hank said firmly.

"Yes, but I'm sure we have different methods of punishment once we've found him."

Hank just grinned his response.

"May I go speak to her? I want to ensure she's okay and let her know I'm here for her."

I stepped aside and gestured for him to head on in, but I didn't try to follow.

"What do you think? Guilty, not guilty?" Terry asked once they were inside.

"I don't think he did it or had his guys do it."

"I have to ask, though: when did your opinion on Joanna change?" He winked at me.

I threw him a "go to hell" look, and even though I had planned to leave, I headed back into the house. There was no reason to go looking for Hank with him here now, and I wanted to ensure that Hank wasn't upsetting her further.

When we walked in, she seemed fine and was laughing softly at something Hank was saying to her. Her body language was more relaxed, shoulders loose, and some of the redness from crying had faded.

Her other assistant, Tessa, had shown up while we had been talking to Hank. The girl was a frazzled mess. She and Micah were going through the merchandise and computers to determine if anything was missing while Joanna was in charge of her household items like televisions and jewelry.

After Hank and Al left, Joanna got back to the task of inventorying.

Then the officers wrapped up gathering evidence. They had found some prints and would compare them to the database to see if we could find a match.

"Well, we have all the evidence we need for now. You'll be okay for the night?" I asked her.

"Yes, I'm fine, or I will be."

"Okay, are you going to stick around here a little bit? Do you want me to stay?"

"You don't have to. We're going to clean up a little before calling it a night. We have clients tomorrow and don't have time to cancel before morning. We have to make this place as presentable as possible."

"Are you sure you don't need help?" I looked around.

There was still so much thrown around. Couch cushions, artwork, and all her kitchen cabinets looked to have been emptied out onto the floor. It was a lot of work, and I had nothing else to do tonight.

"I'll only turn down help once to be polite," she said playfully. "If you are willing, we would be happy for the help."

I suddenly had a lot of respect for her. She had spunk even when faced with something serious.

I let Terry know I was staying behind. He smirked as he turned to leave. I ignored him and got to work following Joanna's instructions.

A few hours later, longer than I had planned to stay, we had the house looking presentable. Everything was put back in its place. Though some of her knick-knacks and artwork had been broken, and some of her glasses and plates smashed, at least it no longer looked like a tornado ripped through the middle of her house.

I had a new respect for all of them. My first impressions of them had been dead wrong. I thought their jobs were cushy and that they were eccentric, non-conforming weirdos. However, they were hard-working, caring, and down-to-earth people.

Micah was a funny, interesting guy. Tessa came off as shy and introverted, but when you got her talking, she had a sarcastic sense of humor that I enjoyed and a creative mind. Josh liked the same music as me and was a football guy. We discussed all things college football while cleaning the kitchen.

It wasn't the evening I had planned, but I was glad that I had stayed behind. Joanna thanked me several times.

I drove away thinking about her smile and was glad she had a safe place to go and people that cared about her. We had to find this son of a bitch. If and when we did, I might forget some of my training and use some of Hank's less-than-ethical practices, even if it got me demoted or terminated.

Chapter Twenty-Six

Today was the day I had been dreading: my appointment with Cate. It didn't help that I had such a stressful evening and slept horribly. I couldn't stop thinking about my house. Who could have trashed it?

Nothing seemed to be missing, so what was the motive? To scare me, perhaps? Were they looking for something specific? Without some clue like missing items or a note telling us what they had done, I may never know.

Micah and I drove over to my house early, as I planned to get ready for clients and ensure nothing else had happened.

I was thankful to Micah for joining me this morning because walking in, I felt odd. A rush of vulnerability washed over me. The house was my home, my sanctuary, a symbol of freedom from my old life. But it felt different now, almost wrong. Would I ever feel safe here again?

"You okay, Boss?"

"Yeah, yeah. I'm okay." But I wasn't.

"Is there anything you want help with here?"

"Um..." I looked around. "I'm just going to straighten up a little and make sure I have everything ready for clients."

We had gotten so much done last night, so there wasn't much to do this morning. However, being here early would give me time to straighten up and rearrange things. I liked it to look a certain way, and right now, it just felt empty.

All night, I lay awake trying to come up with a motive. They were either trying to scare me or find something in my files. Perhaps evidence of what I knew about the Landon case, but I didn't have anything, not even a scrap of paper with a note scribbled on it.

I was so grateful that we didn't keep any evidence of the fake medium stuff. No electronic files or paper copies. If that leaked, I would have no business left. Not to mention the heartbreak I know it would cause my clients. My goal has always been to help people.

Jeremy arrived early. He looked like a bundle of nerves, but then he saw the house. Even though we had straightened it up, it wasn't quite right.

"Holy shit! What happened here?"

"Someone broke in last night. Trashed everything."

"Are you okay?" He seemed genuinely concerned.

"Yeah, just a little shocked. I don't know who would have done this. We got most of it cleaned up already. You should have seen it last night."

"Your TV is busted. Some of your artwork. I actually liked some of that."

"Um, thanks?" Was that a compliment to my artwork or an insult? Doesn't matter. "So, are you ready for today?"

"Not really. I'm nervous about what she'll say or what she'll want to know. Cate is less mature than Laney, less worldly. I don't know, just more innocent and naïve. Everything to her was a big adventure and new."

I smiled at him. He walked to the window. I guess our conversation was over, so I went back to work with the last bit of cleanup. Jeremy stared out the window for a bit but then started pacing around, grumbling to himself. I could understand his anxiety.

I had the same concerns and thoughts he had about what she might say or might want to know about and was anxious about this appointment. She seemed like a wild card as far as how she would react.

While Jeremy was here, I hoped I could find time to talk to him about the gambling and meeting his parents. Right now, he didn't seem to be in the mood.

I had a few appointments before Cate's, and with everything on my mind between dreading her appointment and the break-in, I was distracted from being fully involved with my other clients. I had always prided myself on my professionalism and personal touch, even when I faked things. These were special moments, and now that they were genuine, I realized just how special the appointments were. I didn't want to give them a bad experience.

As it grew closer to her appointment time, Micah and Tessa started arguing over which one of them would get to answer the door for her. They usually just worked in the back office, and unless a follow-up appointment was requested, neither of them saw the clients. However, they were both so curious about Caitlyn.

It was finally settled rock-paper-scissors style while I was with another client. Tessa won.

Once again, Cate was fashionably late. But as the minutes ticked by, she was so late, I started to wonder if she was going to show up at all.

"Where is she?" Micah paced between the front window in my office and the living room.

Unbeknownst to Micah, Jeremy was doing the same in reverse. I tried not to laugh at the sight of them.

Way past the "acceptably late" point, Caitlyn finally showed up. She bounced in like a fancy toy poodle. Each time I saw her, I had to fight back a giggle as I thought of the description. I just couldn't get that thought out of my head. Micah and Tessa shared a look, and I wondered if they were thinking the same thing.

Tessa offered Cate a drink while Micah hovered nearby, pretending this was the normal routine. Once Tessa delivered the water to Cate, she and Micah retreated to the back office, giggling the entire time. I'd have to scold them for that later.

"So, Cate, are you ready for this?"

"Yes, very much. I have so many questions for him. Is he here?" She looked around, hopeful.

People always looked. I knew there was hope that they would see their loved one once again. I understood, and I tried to do the visit justice.

"Yes, yes, he is." I motioned to her right.

She jumped slightly and looked, but of course, she couldn't see him like I could.

"I miss you." She reached a hand toward him but then touched her stomach as tears started to form in the corners of her eyes.

I grabbed the tissue box that I kept on the side table and offered them to her. She grabbed a few and gave me a weak smile, mouthing her thanks.

"He says he misses you, too, and he's sorry. He didn't mean for this to happen. He thought he would be here for you."

"I wish he... you were here too. I'm scared to do this alone." She paused. "Do you like the baby's name? It's Oakley."

"I do. It's beautiful. She'll be beautiful, just like you." I spoke for Jeremy.

Cate smiled.

"I really don't know what I want out of this. I just want to know he loves me and misses me, and he knows what I am going to name our daughter."

"I love you. I definitely miss you, and I can't wait to see our daughter."

She choked up when I passed on his message, dabbing at her eyes.

We had a few more moments of small talk. She told Jeremy, through me, about her preparations for Oakley, and he mostly listened, adding words of encouragement and validation.

I was starting to feel guilty for thinking of her as just a toy poodle. She seemed like more than that. Not much more, but she was the typical mother-to-be and woman in love.

"Well, unfortunately, it's the end of our appointment time, and I have another client shortly. Did you have any final questions for him before we wrap up?" I didn't remind her that she had been so late and that was the reason for the short visit.

"I guess just one: do you know what happened that day? You weren't scheduled to work. Marcus was supposed to be working. Jeremy, you were my everything, and now you're... gone. I don't understand."

Her chin quivered as she appeared to fight fresh tears, though a few broke loose.

"I know, but we had a deadline, so I went to help get us caught up. I took over from Marcus, so he could focus on other things. I didn't want to leave you. Never."

"I know." She wiped her eyes, put on a friendly smile, and looked at me. "Thank you so much for your time. I appreciate this."

She handed me her credit card, which I ran through my card reader.

"Your house is very sparse. You need a decorator. And maybe a maid," she commented as we waited for the confirmation on her payment.

"Oh, um, yeah. I'll look into that." I decided not to mention the break-in. She wasn't someone I wanted pity from.

I walked her out and then turned to see Jeremy standing hopelessly in the hallway.

"You okay?" I fought the urge to touch his hand as a sign of comfort, but it would have gone right through him.

"I know this sounds crazy, but I loved them both. I'm still heartbroken to have lost them, to have left them both alone to be single mothers." He sighed heavily. "Well, I guess Laney is with Greg now, and Cate is young. She'll be fine, but..." He shrugged.

"I'm sorry. I can only imagine how you must feel." I wondered if Ted felt the same way or if he was more selfish. Jeremy seemed genuine in his feelings. "So, now what?"

"I don't know. I thought it would be easier than this to find my killer, but it feels like we aren't any closer than we were on day one."

"I hate to ask this now, but what can you tell me more about this gambling club that Hank runs?"

"What more do you want to know?"

"Well, I got some information that a few people there may not like you too much."

He laughed. "Yes, we went through this already."

"I know, but after speaking with a few people, I think we should discuss it again."

"They think I cheated because I was good. It wasn't that difficult; they were awful players. Couldn't bluff their way out of a paper sack."

"What about Nina?"

"Nina? No way. Like I said before, she's just some trashy woman who hung around the bar. She got pregnant and saw my money and thought it was an opportunity. Is she your source?"

"No. Well, not just her, but I did talk to her. She seemed angry."

"You talked to her? Ha. That probably dropped your IQ several points. I don't know why I even gave her the time of day."

"What about her boyfriend, Butch?"

"A drunk with a bad temper. He's nothing. They deserve each other."

"So, you don't think he could have done it? I know he has access to the lab. He works for Greg."

Jeremy didn't flinch at this news. His face remained unchanged and unfazed.

"No, he couldn't have gotten to that part of the lab. Plus, he isn't smart enough to understand those drugs and that mixing them would cause a gas. Someone with a chemistry degree or a similar degree would."

"Okay, so can you think of anyone else? Even if you think they're irrelevant."

"No. I've given you the names I thought were relevant. At this point, I'm just ready to throw in the towel and move on with my... ha! I was going to say life, but afterlife, it is." He made a half-sigh, half-laugh sound.

I nodded. He was probably right. All the people we had on the suspect list were now off it. I guess the police had this one right. It was just an accident. I didn't want to verbalize that to Jeremy directly; he already seemed down enough.

"Thanks for trying to help. I think I'm just going to head out."

"Okay. When do you think you'll be back?"

"Honestly? I'm not sure if I will. This thing might have run its course." His shoulders fell, and he let out another long, pained sigh.

"You sure?"

"No, but I'm just feeling... lost." He gave me a weak smile. "I wish I could hug you. I do appreciate you putting up with me all this time and trying to help me. It isn't your fault we didn't find the killer. It was just an unlucky day in the lab. But I just have this gut feeling. Something doesn't feel right."

"I'm sorry I couldn't be of more help, but you know where to find me if you think of anything new."

He nodded, smiled again, and disappeared through the door. I stared at it, feeling oddly empty. This was all I had wanted, to be free of him and this strange case. But I really had thought we would solve it or at least give him peace of mind. This felt wrong.

Micah came to join me in the foyer. "What's wrong, boss?"

"Jeremy left. He doesn't think he's coming back. He's given up on this whole thing."

"Really? Why?"

"He's starting to believe that it must have been an accident. I also think he's heartbroken about his daughters. The closer it gets to their births... it's getting more real how much he will miss. At least, that's my impression."

"I can see that."

"But honestly, I don't have time to worry about it. I have bigger things to think about. Like who is stalking me? The car, the break-in... thank goodness I wasn't here."

"Yes, thank goodness."

We both stood there in our own thoughts. After a moment, he reached over and squeezed my shoulder. I smiled at him, then he headed back to work.

As I went back to my office, I caught movement outside the window. The dark car was back across the street. I looked in vain to see if I could find Hank's guy anywhere, but I knew that was futile. They were good at their jobs.

I picked up my phone, thinking I should call the cops, but remembering that Hank's guy was out there, I set it back down. When my next appointment showed up, I noticed the car was gone, and the patrol car was passing by. Good. I could breathe a little easier for a moment.

Chapter Twenty-Seven

~Clint~

We didn't find a match with the fingerprints from Joanna's house. There were so many people who came and went from her place, it was difficult to pin down who was supposed to be there and who was not.

"Hey, Hartley."

"Hey, Walden."

"I just heard, no leads on those prints."

"Yeah, frustrating."

"I think we might have been too quick to rule out Hank. His guys are professionals. This was definitely a professional job," Terry commented.

"The inside of that house didn't look like a professional job to me. Hank's guys are smooth. They don't trash stuff for no reason. They have a mission, they find it, they get out. Only the lack of prints makes it seem professional."

We were both silent for a moment, caught up in our own thoughts. Terry was the first to speak.

"So, you don't think maybe Laney...?"

I had to think about that. Laney had a motive for killing Jeremy. She had also buddied up to Joanna pretty quickly. However, if they were close, Jo might tell her anything she wanted to know. I just had a gut feeling it wasn't her.

"I don't think she did it. They're friends. You've seen that for yourself."

Terry nodded his acknowledgment. Again, we got lost in our thoughts. I had no new ideas. I wish I could come up with something, anything. A knock on my door made us both look up.

"Walden, Hartley... Need you over on Collins. Drug bust in progress, and they need backup," Lieutenant Brant said.

We were instantly up and headed to our car. At least this was something to distract from Joanna's break-in. I could focus on something else and maybe clear my head.

Later that evening, I met up with Kelly. I hadn't seen her much, and we had talked even less. I had a feeling that this was going to be the night we broke up. I was dreading it and also ready to have it behind me.

I pulled up at her house and took a deep breath before I headed to her front door. I knocked and waited.

"Hi, Clint." She was wearing a fitted sundress that hugged her in all the right places. One thing I could say about her is that she was gorgeous.

"Hey, ready to go?"

"Actually, can we talk?"

Ah, so she was going to end things.

"Sure."

She stepped back so I could enter her house. I followed her to the living room. She offered me a drink, but I turned it down.

"So, I wanted to talk to you." She paused, looked down nervously, and then back up. "I think you and I both know this thing between us... isn't working, right?"

"Yes." I wanted to say more, but there wasn't much else to say.

"So, we are done?"

"Yeah." I felt my body instantly relax.

"Well, then this is easy for both of us." She exhaled with a smile. "I'm sorry to drag it out. I should have told you sooner, so you didn't waste your time coming over."

"Oh, that's... it's okay. I understand. It was a conversation best had in person, anyway."

"Thank you. I guess our mothers won't be happy." She laughed awkwardly.

"No, they probably won't. I better go then." I stood and then turned to her. "Take care."

Once outside, I felt the relief rush through my body. Free at last.

Back in my truck, I didn't know what to do with myself. As I was trying to decide, a car pulled into Kelly's driveway, and a man stepped out. He looked in my direction as he walked to her door. When he knocked, she greeted him affectionately. Then she noticed me, causing her to jump slightly. She gave me an embarrassed smile.

She hadn't wasted time getting into a new relationship. I gave a two-finger wave before putting the truck in gear and driving away. She could explain to him who I was.

I decided to go out for a drink and dinner by myself, turning the truck toward Quench Bar. It was a favorite of mine.

Chapter Twenty-Eight

~Joanna~

Despite Jeremy wanting to give up on this thing, I wasn't. I wanted to do a little more digging. I asked around and found that Butch was known to hang out at Quench Bar. It had started out as a bar but morphed into more of a restaurant as the area's demographics changed.

I asked Micah and Josh to go with me. I knew Josh would love getting out for some investigative fun.

I had never been here before and didn't realize it was going to be so busy. The bar area wasn't full, but the restaurant side was packed, and of course, we had planned to eat dinner, so we had to wait for a table to open.

While we waited, I walked through the bar, looking around. I wasn't sure who I was looking for. I hoped he had a sign that said, "Hi. My name is Butch," though I knew that wasn't realistic. Failing that, I'd have to ask around.

Before I could approach the bar to ask, our name was called, so I headed back to join the guys. It wasn't the best table, but at least we were in, and I could see most of the bar area from my seat.

The waiter took our drink order, quickly ran through their specials for the night, and then headed off to get our drinks. We scanned the menu, quickly deciding on some shared appetizers. Chris, our waiter, brought our drinks and took our order, then retreated.

"So, any ideas who we're looking for, Boss?"

"No idea. I tried to look him up online but kept hitting roadblocks. I'm assuming Butch is a nickname, and he doesn't use it on social media."

Micah nodded. We looked around and casually made small talk while we all scanned. While I was looking around, I noticed a familiar face: Detective Clint Hartley.

"Oh, dang! Don't look, but Detective Hartley is here." The guys, of course, turned to look. "I hope he doesn't notice us."

About the time I said that, the detective's head turned, and he looked right at me. A bright smile spread across his face, and he headed over.

"Well, well, well, who do we have here? Nancy Drew and the Hardy Boys?"

"Har-de-har-har. Very funny, Detective."

"I'm just teasing. I haven't seen you all here before. Curious to know what's going on. This doesn't have anything to do with Jeremy, does it?"

"Just friends hanging out," I said.

"Yep, heard good things about this place." Micah chimed in.

"I thought we were going to find that Butch guy?" Josh said, blowing our cover story.

"Babe!" Micah scolded him.

"Knew it." Clint had that arrogant smirk on his face. That annoyingly sexy smirk.

"Fine. Yes, Jeremy business, but also here to enjoy the food."

Chris came over. "Hey Clint, will you be joining them?"

"Um, yes, yes, I will." Clint slid into the booth next to me. "Thanks, Chris. Can I get an iced tea, please? And... what did you guys order?"

"Appetizers to share."

"Oh, awesome. Bring... something different from what they ordered. Whatever you recommend."

"You got it. I'll bring your drink right out."

"So, you come here often?" I asked.

"Yes, ma'am. Great food, great staff." Clint replied. "So, Butch, huh?"

"Yeah. Do you know him?" I shifted sideways to see him better.

"Yep. Why are you looking for him?" He narrowed his eyes.

I brushed off his suspicious look. "I was given his name. He used to be in the gambling thing with Jeremy. I heard they didn't exactly get along, and it was suggested that he could be a suspect."

"Not giving up the murder thing, huh?"

"Nope. Not until I know different."

He shook his head. Further conversation was stopped when Chris showed up with our food. I didn't realize until that moment how hungry I was. We all dug into the wings, potato skins, and quesadillas. We also had Clint's nachos still to come.

Between bites, the guys talked about sports and music. I listened and ate myself stupid. I was definitely going to come back here again. I was fighting the urge to lick the crumbs from the plate.

"Ms. Joanna, want to know where your guy is?" Clint whispered close to my ear.

I looked over at Micah and Josh. They were murmuring to each other.

"Yes, is he here?" I whispered back and looked over at the bar area.

"Yep, just arrived."

He pointed to a tall, burly guy. He had the look of a lumberjack. I shuddered at the sight of him. The thought of going to talk to him was suddenly terrifying, and I couldn't identify the reason why.

"Oh... Um, yeah, he looks like a 'Butch.' It fits."

"You ready to meet him?"

"I guess..." No, not really.

"If you're nervous, I will be right there with you." His soft tone sent shivers down my spine, and goosebumps formed on my arms.

"Okay." I stammered out.

We slid out of the booth and wove our way through the restaurant to the bar. Butch was standing with a few others, laughing and enjoying a game of darts. I looked back toward Micah and Josh. They were staring wide-eyed after us.

"Hey, Butch," Clint said.

"Well, hey there, Detective. What can I do you for?" He eyed me up and down and slowly licked his lips. A chill ran through me.

"Ms. Joanna and I are looking into some leads on Jeremy Landon's murder." I tried to hide my shock at Clint's statement. Was he finally starting to believe me or was this just a show for Butch? "We were hoping you could help us with any information you might have on him. I know you used to gamble with him at Hank's."

Butch excused himself from his friends and gestured for us to step away from them. His expression was stoic.

"I thought his death was an accident," Butch said when we were out of earshot of his friends.

"Some information has recently been brought forward that has reopened the case."

"If you're hinting that I know anything about it, I don't. I didn't like the guy, sure, but I didn't kill him." He shifted his weight from left to right.

"Any idea on who might? He wasn't exactly a liked guy." Clint remained cool and calm.

"I honestly have no idea. It could be anyone. He cheated. No way he was that good at poker."

"So, no names at all? I thought we had a long-standing relationship, Butch. Need I remind you?" Clint's tone was sharp but calm.

"No, no, I would give you information if I had any. I always have, Clint. You know me, right?" He pleaded, wringing his hands nervously. Was Butch afraid of Clint?

"Alright, well, I appreciate your time. If you get wind of anything, you know how to find me."

They shook hands, and we headed back to our table. I looked back once at Butch, and he was giving me a death stare. Yikes! I moved closer to Clint and was thankful I hadn't had to talk to him.

Back at the table, Micah and Josh remained quiet.

"That went well. Don't you think?" Clint asked.

"No, I don't. He didn't give us anything. It was pointless. The only thing I learned is that he was a waste of time."

"Just wait."

He took a long sip from his glass, then snagged one of the last nachos.

Moments later, Butch appeared at our table. "Detective?"

"Oh, hey, Butch. Did you remember something?" Clint asked.

"Yeah, but..." He looked at Micah and Josh.

"They're safe to talk in front of. They're part of Joanna's team."

He looked at Micah and Josh again, then at me, and squared his shoulders.

"Look, I didn't do it, but as you said, he wasn't liked... have y'all looked at Greg more closely? He was always popping off about what a dick his brother was. Still does, actually."

"You think he's serious enough that he would do something like that?" Clint asked.

"Uh, yeah, maybe. He has a bad temper. I've seen him go off on guys for slacking. He can be scary, even to someone my size."

"Thanks for the information. We'll look at him."

"You won't tell him I said anything, will you? I mean, he's my boss, and I really need that job. I have a baby coming soon, and I can't get fired."

"No problem. I don't give my sources." Clint looked at each of us around the table for confirmation, and we all nodded our agreement. He then looked back at Butch, "how is Nina doing?"

"She's good, and the baby is growing. I can't wait to meet him."

"Good, man. That's good. Well, thanks again."

Butch nodded, then shuffled back to the bar. I don't know why I had been nervous about meeting Butch. He seemed like a big teddy bear, at least toward Clint. I wonder what their relationship was. Had Clint busted him for something? Did he owe Clint for saving him? I would probably never know, but clearly, there was some fear and respect between them.

With that bit of business completed, we wrapped up our dinner. Clint ended up paying for all of us. We stressed he didn't have to, but he insisted as he handed his card to Chris with a wink.

"Thank you, Clint. It wasn't necessary, but very nice of you." I said.

"Anything for our local celebrity."

I blushed. I hated being called a celebrity, even in jest. We all walked out. Micah and Josh got in the car while I turned to speak to Clint.

"I really appreciate your help today. I'm not sure I would have gotten anything out of him without you."

"Yeah, no problem. He and I go back a few years."

"And thanks again for dinner."

"Yeah, my pleasure." He stepped a little closer with a soft expression, and the gleam in his eyes made me too aware of my lips. "Any time," he whispered softly.

With that, he tipped his head and walked to his truck, leaving me standing there, confused with my mouth open.

I climbed into the car.

"What was that about, Boss?"

"I have no idea."

Chapter Twenty-Nine

It had been a few days since the Quench Bar. I had thought about what Butch said about Greg. If a guy like Butch was afraid of him, maybe this was our killer. He could be the one following me and trying to scare me.

Greg was the first person I had talked to about Jeremy, apart from running into Laney that one day at the grocery store. He had a lot of reasons to want his brother dead, right down to Jeremy being the favorite son.

I can only imagine what it must have been like for Greg growing up in Jeremy's shadow. Then to have the family forgive his brother so quickly for nearly killing their grandmother.

I was working in my office, preparing for an appointment. As I typed an email, I heard a knock at my door. I checked the time. It was too early for the Carters. Micah and Tessa would normally just let themselves in on workdays, so it couldn't be them.

I tiptoed to the window to peek out and was relieved to see it was just Laney. But that was strange. She hadn't called or messaged that she would stop by. Something must have been wrong.

I quickly walked to the door. "Hey, Laney. Is everything okay?"

"Hm, no. No, not really. Can I come in?" She looked back over her shoulder.

Little alarm bells sounded in my head, but I tried to remain calm.

"Sure, come in." I stepped to the side. "Can I get you a drink?"

"No, thanks. This won't take long. I just wanted to ask you something."

"Oh, sure. We can sit in my office if you would like."

Once we were seated, she looked around, conflict flashing on her face. Something big was on her mind. She remained quiet, only looking at me for a moment as she fidgeted with the hem of her shirt. I was about to ask her what was bothering her when she broke the silence.

"This isn't easy for me. But I was talking with Greg, and he said you were investigating Jeremy's death as a murder."

Uh-oh. I had thought this might come up at some point and had been dreading it. There was no avoiding it now.

"Yes. I was."

"He also said you were looking at him, Aaron, and Hank as suspects," she said through tight lips as she crossed her arms over her chest.

"Yes. That's sort of true. They all had motives, but after talking to them, I decided that they weren't likely to have done it."

"And that's why you were asking about his parents? And the gambling club information was about this, too?"

"Yes. I'm sorry. I should have told you."

I felt some relief that the secret was out but guilty that I had upset Laney. She had enough in her life to deal with, which is why I hadn't burdened her with it in the first place.

She nodded and started fidgeting with the hem of her shirt again. It was almost like she had more to say but was having a hard time getting it out. Finally, she looked up at me. Her eyes blazed with anger, which sent dread down my spine.

"And you thought I was a suspect too?"

There it was.

"I never thought of you as a suspect. Not at all."

"Don't lie to me. I have enough fake friends." She had tears in her eyes. Automatically I offered her the box of tissues. She took one. "I really thought... I thought we were friends, but you were just interested in my motives and backstory."

"Laney, we are. I never suspected you. Jeremy never did, either. That was the first thing he said to me. He thought it might have been the others, but not you. I swear."

She looked at me. A tear fell, and she wiped it away with the tissue. "Really?"

"Yes, I promise. We never even considered you."

I told her how Jeremy found me, asked me to investigate what he thought was his murder, and the leads we had dug up that led to nothing. I could see her processing this.

"And I agreed to do it... Oh, gosh, I'm sorry." Now I had tears in my eyes. "I never told you, but I was married... Your story and mine are so very similar."

Tears formed in my eyes. I tried to fight them back, but a few stubborn ones slid down my cheek. Now it was Laney grabbing the box of tissues and offering one to me.

"Oh, my! What... what happened?" she asked.

"I was young. It was my final year in college when I met Ted. He was a bit older than me. We had a whirlwind relationship. We were married days after I graduated college, and he took a job here in Creekview since I had a job lined up here myself." I wiped my eyes. I hadn't cried over Ted in a few years. It was due, I supposed. "He traveled a lot for work, or so I thought. Turns out he was cheating on me the entire time. Several different women."

"A cheater like Jeremy. Jo, I'm so sorry."

"Yeah, it's been hard hanging out with Jeremy, trying to help him with all this... but there's more to Ted's story." I sighed. "Like Jeremy, he died."

She gasped and took my hand.

"He and one of his girlfriends were out of town. They had been out drinking at a club, and then on the way back to the hotel, got into a car accident. It killed them both."

"Oh, Joanna. That's awful."

I nodded and wiped away a few tears. I hadn't told anyone this story in years. It wasn't something I shared often.

"After they died, her family sued me. I guess they wanted someone to pay for their loss. I had to spend a small fortune in lawyer and court fees fighting it. I won, thank goodness, but with that added expense and all the debt Ted racked up on his cheating trips, I was in over my head. I'm in a much better place now."

"I'm so glad you told me. I know exactly how you feel, and you know exactly how I feel. I mean, different story, but with so many similarities."

"Yes. So many." I paused, thinking about what to say next. "I started doing the medium thing to help get myself out of debt. It was a power I had but hadn't really used in years. It just seemed like something I could do to help myself at first as a side gig, for extra cash, but then later, obviously, full-time. I had also hoped I could find Ted. I had so many unanswered questions. When Jeremy found me and told me his story, I thought of you immediately. How you would have a lot of the same feelings and questions. I knew I had to help."

"I'm so sorry for marching in here all dramatic like this. You know what I've been through almost more than any other person." She smiled at me. "I just got to listening to Greg and shouldn't have. He's losing his mind. I think his debts and work are really weighing on him. I told you before how much of a mess he's been, not eating, not sleeping. He's paranoid and quick to anger. Frankly, he scares me." Her voice came out shaky and breathless.

"That's crazy. I'm sorry." I didn't mention that someone like Butch was also afraid of him. It would only make her more anxious.

We sat in silence for a moment. I was relieved she felt better about our friendship again.

"So, do you still think Jeremy was murdered?" Laney asked.

"Um, no. He gave up on the idea and accepted it was an accident."

"That's so sad. But do you think he was murdered?"

"I honestly don't know. It really looks like an accident, but I just have this nagging feeling."

"Did he tell you about the previous accident at the lab?"

I gasped and sat forward. "No. Do you think it could be related?"

"Maybe. It was a year ago. One of our lab assistants died the same way. A mix of drugs, seizures, cardiac arrest. It was horrible. Renee had been at the lab for several months and was experienced. I don't see how she could have had an accident like that. Then when the same thing happened to Jeremy, it was suspicious. I was too heartbroken at the time to think about it. But I have thought about it a few times since."

"I know nothing about these types of accidents. What type of investigation was done? Wouldn't this be something that might shut you down?"

"After Renee, not much was done. The usual police investigation. Then the FDA came in and went through our safety procedures and interviewed all the employees. It was determined to be a tragic accident. They came back after Jeremy and gave us a warning. We are basically on probation. One more accidental death and we are shut down."

"Wow. Do you think they were accidents?"

"Given our safety procedures, I would like to say no, but with two deaths... it's hard to say."

"And if not an accident, any ideas on who would have done it?"

"None, and no proof it was done intentionally."

"Is there anything you can tell me about Renee?"

"Not much. She was just an employee. I didn't know her well. I don't work in that part of the lab. She was a tech in the area where Cate works, so she might be able to help you. They were good friends."

"Okay, I might reach out to her."

"Well, I had better get going. I have a doctor's appointment to check on this little one." She held her stomach as she stood. "I'm so sorry again for storming in here all emotional and pointing fingers. I'm so very glad we are friends."

"Me too."

We hugged, and she left.

I had to do some research on that case and see what happened. It had to have been in the news, but I couldn't recall hearing about it.

I had to wait until after I'd seen the Carters to start Googling, but once the appointment was over, my research began. I wasn't a medical expert but could see the two deaths were alike. As Laney had said, both deaths featured a mix of drugs, creating a gas and then death. I didn't have time to do research on Renee right away.

It was sad. She was young. Her pictures showed a beautiful woman with a sweet smile.

I wished I knew how to get in touch with Jeremy to ask him about this development. It wasn't like I could call or text him, and I had no idea where he went when he wasn't with me. For all I know, he was hanging out in a cave or something.

I was shutting off my computer and cleaning up my desk when I heard a car pull up outside. I wasn't expecting anyone. I stood to go peek out, but before I could reach the window, there was an urgent knock on the door.

For a split second, I froze, then continued toward the window. I did it oh so carefully, not wanting whoever it was to see me.

It was an angry-looking Greg, and parked in my driveway was a car that looked identical to the one that had been parked across the street.

His banging grew louder. I had a sick feeling and didn't want to answer the door. I quietly snuck back to my bedroom to text Micah, Tessa, or Audrey. Anyone I could think of who lived close enough to get here. My brain didn't go to the logical choice of the cops.

He knocked again with growing impatience. A few of the dead people in the house agreed that I shouldn't open the door. It was weird to be in a room full of people that couldn't help me. He knocked harder. I felt a mild panic starting to bubble up in my chest.

"Joanna, I know you're home." From my bedroom, his voice was muffled, but I heard that part clearly.

Damn. I still didn't want to answer the door. I needed some kind of backup in case this went badly. I needed to call the one person who I knew could help.

Chapter Thirty

I was sitting at my desk, going over the reports I had written on the Landon case. I had already reviewed the video footage but didn't know what I had hoped to see differently. Joanna believed this somewhat blindly, claiming a spirit was directing her. True or not, someone did slash Laney's tires and break into Joanna's house, so I had a duty to look at this closer.

Butch hadn't been a lot of help, but his suggesting Greg Landon made sense. I had double-checked Greg's alibi for the day of Jeremy's death. If we worked on the assumption that the chemicals had been set up, the alibi at the time of death didn't matter as much as the time leading up to it. We didn't have that information.

"Damn." I slammed my fist down. At the same moment, my cell phone rang. It was Joanna. My heartbeat quickened. "Jo?"

"I need your help, please," she whispered.

"Are you okay?"

"Greg Landon is banging on my door and threatening me. Please, I need you to come over."

"Why didn't you call 9-1-1?" I grabbed my keys and waved at Terry, who was standing across the room from me. "Hold tight. We're on our way."

I stayed on the phone with her as we got into the car, trying to keep her calm and, truth be told, myself. If I could hear her voice, she was okay. I could hear Greg in the background, yelling and banging on the door. What was he so angry about?

Terry called dispatch to get a patrol officer over there ASAP. I just hoped there was a car closer than we were. I tried to be calm and keep her talking while we waited. Finally, dispatch confirmed that there was a car just a few blocks away, and they were heading Joanna's way. I felt better and let her know help was coming.

We continued talking while Terry drove until she confirmed the uniformed officer had arrived. I was finally able to breathe.

"We're just a few blocks away. Let the officer know that we'll be there shortly." We disconnected.

"So, what do you think Greg wants with her?" Terry asked when I was off the phone.

"No idea, but I could hear him in the background." My mind was telling me all kinds of stories, but they were just that: stories. The main one being he was unstable and could be his brother's murderer. Could he have been the one to break in the other night?

We finally pulled up at her house. One officer had him cuffed and leaning against the patrol car, questioning him. Joanna was standing on the sidewalk near her front door, speaking with the other. I could see the relief flood her body as her face relaxed and her shoulders lowered.

"Clint, thank you." She came to me and wrapped herself in my arms. Second hug this week, but this time I didn't want to let her go. However, she ended it. "I'm sorry to keep doing that. I just really appreciate you sending help. I didn't know what else to do. He scared the crap out of me, and you told me to call you if something else happened."

"True." I wanted to hold her again, but I kept my arms at my side. Terry went to speak with Greg and Sergeant Jones. To Sergeant Nunez, I asked, "Did he say anything about why he was here?"

"Jones has been speaking with him. I came to get a statement from Ms. Webber."

"Okay, let me figure out what is going on." I looked at Joanna. "Why don't you go sit inside? I'll come in after."

She nodded, gave Greg one final look, and went into the house.

Sergeant Nunez and I joined Terry and Sergeant Jones by the car. They were talking with Greg. He was insisting he hadn't done anything wrong.

"I just wanted to talk to her. Is that against the law?"

"No, that's not, but making death threats is. I could hear you through the phone."

He looked at me, appearing to puff up his chest. I matched his stare. He was a man that tried to intimidate people. I wasn't one to be intimidated easily.

"She wouldn't open the door."

"And that means you can call her a bitch and threaten her life?"

Our staring contest continued. He wasn't going to win.

"My girlfriend was here earlier. They've been spending a lot of time together. Plus, this one says she has been speaking with my dead brother. Do you believe this shit? I'm losing my mind here."

"That still doesn't give you the right to terrorize her and say you are going to kill her." Terry snapped.

He also shouldn't be telling the cops he was losing his mind, especially if he ended up snapping. We would have his motive.

"Someone broke into her house a few nights ago. You wouldn't know anything about that, would you?" I said, then waited to see his reaction; however, he seemed unfazed.

"I don't. And I have an alibi with witnesses if you need it."

"I'll let you know."

Since Joanna had told the officers she wouldn't press charges as long as he would just leave, we couldn't hold him. I wanted to at least take him in for questioning, but if Joanna didn't want to push the issue, I couldn't make her.

The officers gave him a warning to leave her alone. He agreed but cursed as he climbed into his car and drove away. The patrol officers left right behind him, leaving just Terry and me.

We went into the house to check on Joanna. I knocked and then opened the door.

"Jo?" I called out.

"Yes, I'm here." She emerged from her office. "Is he gone?"

"Yes. We issued him a warning."

"Thank you. I don't want to cause drama."

I tried not to laugh; I got the impression she liked drama considering what she did for a living. I kept my opinion to myself, though. It was no laughing matter. This was dangerous and real.

I explained to her Greg's reason for being here.

"I disagree with you on not pursuing a harassment charge, so I could question him, especially on the break-in."

"You think he could have done it? I got the impression he would just barge in like he tried to today." She smiled and toyed with a piece of her hair.

"Well, you've got a good point there. I still think it would have been worth talking with him."

"Do you want us to stay a little longer?" Terry asked. "I doubt he'll come back, but do you have a friend that can stay with you or somewhere you can stay?" Terry sounded as concerned as I felt.

"I'll be fine. I'm supposed to be going out with friends this evening." Joanna paused. "But now I might just go to my sister's."

I nodded and told her not to hesitate to call us. We said our goodbyes. I paused at the car, not wanting to leave her.

"We need to look closer at Greg's involvement in Jeremy's case." Terry's head snapped to stare at me.

"Are you serious? You really are starting to believe this murder theory of hers."

"Yep. I am even more so after this. I mean, think about it. The car following her is the same make, model, and color as Greg's. Then the break-in may or may not have been him, and then this crazy outburst. What do you think?"

As we drove away, my phone rang. Unknown number. "Hartley," I said, answering it.

"Detective, Hank here. I wanted to check on Ms. Joanna."

"She's fine. A little dust-up with Greg Landon, but overall, fine."

"I have Travis down there right now. He said Greg was banging on the door and screaming at her."

"So, why didn't he come to her aid?" I ran my hand across my face.

"He's my least experienced man, a complete newbie. I gave him instructions to stay out of it. Just observe."

"And what would have happened if Landon had gotten in? You would let her get killed?" My blood was boiling.

"No, I had others on the way. But then Travis said the police arrived, so I called them back. When he let me know you were leaving, I called you to check on her. So, there you go."

In my head, I counted to ten. This guy always pushed my buttons. We had a long history, with him barely toeing the line of legal activity.

"Hank, could you promise me, if you have men in the area, that you will help us protect her, please?"

"That's why I have men there."

I thanked him, and we said goodbye.

Terry and I headed back to the station. I had to do some more digging into Greg Landon.

Chapter Thirty-One

~Joanna~

As soon as Terry and Clint left, I messaged Laney to let her know what had happened. She replied instantly, saying that Greg had already called her, yelling and threatening her. She wasn't going home and was staying at her mom's; that way, she wasn't alone, at least until Greg calmed down. She didn't need the extra stress of him stopping by her house angry.

I told her I was going to Audrey's. We agreed to check in with each other later.

Next, I called Audrey. She didn't hesitate to invite me to stay. She was ready to come get me to ensure I made it safe and sound.

"I'll be fine," I promised.

"Okay, just please be careful."

I packed a bag and grabbed my laptop. I looked around at my house. What if someone broke in again? I hadn't yet replaced my television, computer monitor, or any of the smashed artwork. I would, but I was heartsick over it all and still felt vulnerable. It had once been a symbol of my freedom and new life apart from Ted, but the house didn't feel like my safe place anymore.

I drove over to Audrey's, lost in my thoughts, not watching for cars. Since it appeared that Greg had been the one following me, I hoped the police warning would stop him from continuing. I thought about the things he yelled at me, threatening to kill me. I shuddered thinking about it. His tone was so full of rage and anger, and I believed at that moment, he was fully capable of carrying out his threats.

If he was this angry with me for asking a few questions, I could definitely see him killing his brother over experimenting on and nearly killing their grandmother. It made sense.

I arrived at Audrey's, and she rushed out, throwing her arms around me.

"I'm so glad you're here. I was so scared for you. Break-ins, a stalker, Greg Landon... and he threatened you?" She grabbed my bag out of my hand, leaving me holding the one with my laptop. "Come in. The boys are so excited to have Auntie Jo-Jo here tonight. They haven't stopped talking since I mentioned it."

I nodded and followed her. A wave of exhaustion washed over me. Was this my life now?

"I have dinner almost ready. Spaghetti. I know it's your favorite. I already had it planned. Must be fate." She winked over her shoulder at me.

I flashed her a weak smile.

"Um, you didn't say anything to Mom, did you?" I asked.

"Of course not. This isn't my first rodeo, Jo."

"Auntie Jo! Auntie Jo!"

I was swarmed by little boys as soon as we stepped into the house.

"Hey, boys."

As fast as they were there, they were gone. Running, laughing, and squealing. I could feel my body relax. The innocent sounds of children had a calming effect and grounded me in the moment. I was safe with people that loved me. I had a lot to be thankful for.

Audrey walked me to their guest room, setting my bag down.

"You know where everything is, but if you can't find something, let me know."

"I really appreciate you letting me stay. Things have been crazy."

"I wish you had told me about this stuff sooner."

"I know. I should've. I just didn't realize how serious this was, not until the break-in and then this Greg thing today."

"All very scary. Being followed, watched. Jo, that's scary. Hopefully, now that Greg has been confronted, it will stop."

"I hope so."

She left me to settle in, which took all of two minutes. I didn't plan to get too comfortable. I really wanted to go home. I stepped over to the window. Nothing to see but the perfectly manicured lawns of Audrey's neighborhood. Much different from where I lived. This was all new. Young trees and freshly planted landscaping that hadn't quite grown in yet. All the houses, more or less, looked the same.

I took another minute to breathe, count to ten, and refocus my brain. Maybe I should listen to my mother and look for a nice safe accounting job. My current work seemed to be getting me into a lot of trouble that I wasn't mentally prepared for. Now out of debt, I didn't need to do this any longer, at least not for the money.

I went downstairs to join the family for dinner. It was fun, and the food was delish. My sister was an excellent cook. Stan told "dad jokes" through the whole dinner, making the boys giggle.

"By the way, Jo, I'll get that security system installed for you tomorrow. The same one we have. Then I'll show you how to use it."

"Thanks, Stan. I really appreciate it."

I really had the best brother-in-law. I wished I could find one just like him for myself.

After dinner, I played with blocks and cars with the kids, then helped bathe and put the boys to bed. My heart swelled with love for my two nephews as I tucked them in for the night.

"Makes you want to have little ones of your own, huh?" Stan had snuck up on me as I watched them.

"Ha, I wish. I've gotta meet someone first."

"Not necessarily." He walked away, humming.

Why was everyone pushing me to have a child without a partner? It wasn't that I couldn't do it; I just wasn't sure I was ready for the responsibility. With or without a partner, kids were a big decision. Looking at how messed up my life was at the moment, a kid would not fit well. How scary would it be to be going through this and trying to protect a small human?

I joined Audrey downstairs. She was half-watching TV and half-reading.

"Did they go down okay for you?" She looked up from her eBook.

"Yep, no trouble at all."

"They are good boys." She glowed with love when she spoke about her kids.

I pulled out my Kindle, and together we read in peaceful companionship. My phone chimed. It was Clint.

Just checking on you

I blushed as I read it, and a slow smile spread on my face.

All good here

At your sister's?

Yep

Good. Call if you need anything

"What are you over there grinning about?" Audrey asked, "who is that?"

Uh-oh. Busted.

"Nothing. No one."

"It doesn't look like nothing and no one to me."

I shrugged and went back to my book. I felt Audrey stare at me. Then she sighed heavily before going back to her book. I could feel her eyes peering at me from time to time, but I continued to ignore her, at least for a few suspense-filled moments.

"Okay! It was the Detective... Clint. He was just checking on me."

"I knew it was a guy. He's super cute." She squealed.

"I'm not interested, and besides, he has a girlfriend." I wasn't actually sure if he had a girlfriend, but I had seen him with that one woman before. It was clearly a date, and they seemed familiar, so I just assumed.

"Well, you should tell that to your face because it's saying you're interested."

"It lies," I said flatly and tried to refocus on my book.

"Maybe you are just lying to yourself," she teased me. "I'm heading to bed. Good night, sis."

"Good night, sis."

I decided to follow suit and go to bed. Once in my room, I pulled out my computer, wanting to do more research on Renee. I hadn't really had a chance to research Renee much before Greg started banging on my door. Maybe there was some connection between the two of them.

But after various searches, I couldn't find anything new and no obvious connection to Greg.

Switching over from murder, I looked at a job site, just to peek. I found several listings that sounded interesting, but I hadn't done accounting in years, and they all wanted recent experience. Tessa did the bookkeeping for the business, and I just reviewed her work as a double-check, so I knew what was going on. Would that count?

I shut down the computer and got ready for bed. Despite all the stress and worries about who was stalking me, I managed to fall asleep and slept my first solid night in a week.

When I woke, I felt more focused and ready to get back in the game. Overnight, I had come up with a plan to investigate Renee's death.

The boys' voices could be heard from downstairs. They were asking for me, so I pushed myself out of bed and got myself ready. I packed up my bag, planning to go home tonight. Hopefully, I'd be safe.

Once I was ready, I headed downstairs to find coffee and see my nephews.

"Auntie Jo-Jo!" Dylan ran to me, throwing his arms up. Sweetness. I picked him up, and he hugged me, then grabbed the sides of my face with his sweet toddler hands. "Hi, Auntie Jo-Jo."

"Hi, Dylan. How are you today?"

"I eat pancakes."

"Yummy." I carried him into the kitchen, where Harris was still eating.

He smiled around a half-eaten pancake. I set Dylan down, and he went to play with his race cars.

"Mornin', sis. Coffee?" Audrey was already grabbing me a mug.

"Yes, thank you."

"Did you sleep well?"

"Like a baby." I sipped the coffee. This was not the cheap stuff. This was the grind-your-own gourmet stuff. "Mmm. This is good."

"It's from The Jumping Bean."

I nodded and watched Dylan playing on the floor. Audrey was making pancakes and chatting with Harris about a cartoon. I wasn't familiar with it.

"Hello, family." Stan came into the room. The boys lit up once again.

"Daddy!" Dylan was on his feet and launching at his dad.

I watched them share a moment. Audrey handed Stan a cup of coffee and was rewarded with a kiss. He joined Harris at the table.

A pang of jealousy pinched my heart. This was what I had hoped to have once upon a time. A simple moment with a man I loved and children to share it with. I had been stupid to trust in that dream, but obviously, it was attainable for some. Maybe even for me someday.

I was starting to feel like a third wheel. This was their family time, and I was intruding on it. I tried to drink my coffee faster so I could get a move on with my day. However, this wasn't the kind of coffee you gulp down. With each sip, I found myself wanting to savor it more. I might have to splurge on some expensive coffee myself.

While I enjoyed the coffee, I grabbed my phone and sent a text to Laney. It was close to 8:00 a.m., and she should be at work. I needed to go to the lab and look around since I wasn't familiar enough with the layout and wanted to see what it looked like. Perhaps if I saw where the different drugs were kept, where they were mixed, and finally where both Jeremy and Renee died, I could put some ideas together.

Laney replied that she would be happy to give me a tour. We planned to meet at 10:00 a.m. at Landon Medical Research and Laboratory. Good, I would have more time for this yummy coffee.

At exactly 10:00 a.m., I pulled into a spot labeled "visitor." At her request, I messaged her that I was here. She replied that she would meet me at the security desk.

In contrast to Novak Labs, this building was not as modern and didn't scream money. This was what I pictured when I thought about medical research facilities: all industrial, plain, and beige.

"Hi, welcome to Landon Medical Research. Can I help you?" the security guard at the reception desk asked.

"I'm meeting Laney Landon."

The guard looked at her computer screen and back at me. "Ah, okay. Joanna, right?"

"Yes, that's right."

"Let me get you checked in and then let her know you are here." She reached for the phone.

"I'm here, Sandra. Hi, Jo." Laney said, stepping into the lobby.

"Hi, Laney." I smiled at my friend.

"I'll just need your id, Joanna." Sandra, the guard, smiled.

I handed it to her, and she ran it through a scanner that then printed a visitor badge.

"Here you go." She passed it across the reception desk to me.

"Thanks so much." I pulled the backing off and stuck the sticky badge to my shirt.

She buzzed me through the security barrier.

"Let's start with the offices," Laney suggested.

I followed Laney as she showed me through the hallway to the offices.

"This was Jeremy's office. We haven't used it since... I actually haven't even been in here in a few weeks or more."

She pushed the door open. The smell of it was stale and unused. Like the rest of the facility, it was plain, but there were a few personal items on his desk. A picture of him and Laney. An ultrasound picture in a frame. There were still some documents on the desk as if waiting for him to come back. On the walls were framed copies of his degrees and a couple of framed motivational posters.

"Oh, I should have taken this plant out." She walked toward the window where there was a dried-up old carcass of a plant. "Do you see anything that could be a clue in here?"

I didn't, but I really didn't know what I was looking for, having never done this before. Plus, I'm sure the police had already taken any evidence.

"Would Jeremy have kept any records or files about Renee's accident?"

"He might have. We can look, but more than likely, HR would have all that stuff. We can ask after."

We started looking through his files. Nothing too interesting. Copies of expense reports, budget planning, copies of FDA applications for various products, among other things.

"Doesn't look like anything here." My shoulder slumped a bit. Not that I thought it would be easy to find clues.

"HR then," Laney said.

I followed her through the hallways. Laney said hi to various employees walking past us on the way to the HR office. As we turned a corner, a familiar face came into view.

"Joanna. Laney. Hello."

"Hi, Cate," Laney said.

"What are you doing here, Joanna? This isn't the most interesting place," she said sweetly with a light laugh.

"I was showing Jo around. She was curious about how things worked here." Laney answered for me.

Apparently, Laney didn't trust Cate, and I wasn't going to correct her. Honestly, I didn't know who to trust, so the fewer people that knew about this, the better. And to be fair, it wasn't a complete lie, it just wasn't the whole truth either.

"Oh, I didn't know you had an interest in pharmaceutical products. It's kinda boring. I only do it because it pays the bills."

"I guess Laney makes it sound interesting." I quipped.

"Ah well, she did train me here; I know she can make it sound better than it is." Was that a dig or a compliment? I couldn't tell, but Laney smiled at her.

"You were a good student."

"Thank you. Well, I gotta get going. Need to check on a shipment. Toodles."

We continued on our way. Laney waited until we were out of earshot.

"Sorry to lie, well, sort of," she whispered, "but I don't trust her."

"I figured."

She opened the door to an office labeled "HR." We stepped into what appeared to be a small lobby or waiting room with two additional doors, one open and the other closed. A head popped out of the open one.

"Hey, Laney. What can I do for you today?"

"Hi, Diane. I was hoping I could look in the files. I just had a question about Renee's accident."

"Renee? Really?"

"Yeah, I know it's been a while, but there was just something about it that has me thinking about Jeremy's accident."

I guess Laney trusted Diane, at least enough to tell her exactly what we were looking for.

"Hmm, now that you mention it. Wow... You know where everything is but let me know if you need help."

"Thanks, Diane."

I followed Laney through the closed door. It led to a large windowless room with wall-to-wall metal filing cabinets with a counter area in the middle. She headed straight to a specific drawer. She pulled out a folder and then a second. I saw the names on them: one was Jeremy's and the other Renee's.

"I didn't know that one day I would be running all this," Laney said as she stepped over to the tall counter, setting them down, and started flipping through Jeremy's until she got to what I can only assume was the company's accident report. She did the same with Renee's.

"Okay, yes, here we go. Same exactly. Mixing the same chemicals, same reaction, same death. I can't believe I didn't think to look at this more closely sooner. I guess grief had me in its grip."

I nodded. "I assume this isn't a common type of accident, right?"

"These are the only two like this that we have ever had. We lost one other employee in a freak forklift accident several years ago, but otherwise, we have a high safety record. We have been in business for nearly ten years. Not to say that there haven't been some near misses, but we have always been able to render aid in time. You know, things like a spill or a cut. Nothing serious."

I thought about this for a moment. It really did seem suspicious.

"What's your staff turnover like?"

"I would have to ask Diane for sure, but we have mostly added staff. Not too many leave. A few, but not on bad terms."

There was a connection between the two, but on the surface, nothing seemed obvious. Should I mention this to Clint? Why hadn't they connected the two together already? My only thought was that nobody else found it suspicious.

Laney put the files back, and we exited the room. She stepped into the office to speak to Diane. Laney explained that we would like to keep our visit confidential. Nobody can know why we were here.

"Of course, Laney. You're the boss, and my job is to keep these types of conversations confidential."

"Thanks, Diane. You're the best."

We walked out of HR and almost right into Cate. Was she following us?

"Oh, hey, y'all. What're you doing in HR?"

"Just talking to Diane. I had a question about maternity leave. It's coming up for both of us."

"Yep, that's why I'm here." She smiled and started to pass us. "Maybe I'll run into you both again before you leave, Joanna."

"Maybe," I said with a half-laugh that I hoped came across as casual.

My heart was beating so fast. Something about running into her again felt odd.

We walked off in the direction of the labs without another word. We both kept looking at each other nervously and looking back.

"Maybe I should go," I said.

"No, let's not let her ruin things. That was probably just a coincidence."

Probably, but it had the hairs on the back of my neck standing up.

We walked to an area where Laney gave me a white coverall with a hood to cover my hair, gloves, and covers for my shoes. We then went through a sealed door and into a "clean room." Laney explained it had special filtration to keep airborne particles from just freely flowing into or out of the mixing area. The first door shut before the next one would open. It felt super-secret and sterile.

I could see why Jeremy didn't think Butch could have gotten into this part of the lab without assistance or being seen. He would have had a lot of steps, and unless he had the special badge that Laney had as not only a chemist herself but the CEO of the company. Butch would definitely not have that level of access.

As we walked around the lab, Laney then showed me the various stations and work areas. Various chemicals were kept in one spot and mixed in another. Everything was clearly labeled. Even my untrained eye could see what was stored in which container.

I met several of the chemists and was able to ask questions about the process. They were happy to answer them, at least at a high level. Marcus was the most helpful. He walked me around to each station, showing me the various tools and processes.

"This is very interesting. Thank you for sharing."

"No problem. I'm happy to teach others about it." He smiled widely.

"Can you tell me about some of the safety practices that are in place?"

"You mean if we have an incident, like an exposure?"

"Yes, I suppose. Or, like what happened with Jeremy, what would have happened had someone found him sooner?"

The color drained from his face, and the smile fell. I made a mental note of his reaction. I'd have to ask Laney or Jeremy more about him.

"Had someone found Jeremy, we'd have switched on the ventilator to air out the space of the gas. Then we'd determine which drugs he was working with and find the correct MSDS. Oh, that's the material safety data sheet. It lists all the safety information about the chemicals and the right procedure for dealing with an exposure. Some require a full shower, some will react to water, and so on. We would also have called 9-1-1." He paused and looked at me. The color was returning to his face. "I still have some guilt that Jeremy died while he was only trying to help me out. We were behind on an order, and he was trying to help us get caught up."

That explained why he went ashen when I mentioned Jeremy's name. I had been hoping for a lead in this case.

"That's understandable. I'm sorry." I said. "I really appreciate your time in answering my questions."

"You're very welcome."

After the tour and speaking with the employees, I felt like I had a much clearer picture of how things worked. This had either been an unusually sloppy day for the lab or murder. How could someone come in and think anything else? Looking at the health and safety record, with the practices that were in place and then how everything was set up, this "accident" couldn't have happened twice.

Even if it was an accident for Renee, perhaps someone set up the same conditions to make it look like Jeremy did the same thing. Two accidents just didn't seem right, at least one was intentional.

Laney walked me out, ensuring that I got signed out with security.

Thankfully, we didn't see Cate again, but I couldn't shake the feeling she was watching us. Why did she suddenly give me the creeps? Was it her silky-smooth manner? Her fake smile? Or was this whole murder business making me paranoid?

As I stepped out into the parking lot, another familiar face came into view: Nina.

"Hey, you're that medium that was asking about Jeremy."

"Hm, yeah, hi."

"What are you doing here? More investigations?" she asked sharply.

"No, no, just meeting with Laney Landon."

"Really? That's odd."

"We're friends. I'm interested in her work." I tried to sound casual and like this was an everyday thing. "So, what're you doing here?"

"Bringing my boyfriend his lunch." She held up a fast-food bag. "Is that okay with you?"

"Of course. Sorry."

"He said you and that detective were asking him a bunch of questions. You need to butt out of things, or you'll get yourself into some serious trouble. Causin' problems for innocent people. Who do you think you are?" She snarled and stepped close to me.

"Oh, I'm nobody. I'm sorry."

She was a good five inches shorter than me, but at this moment, she seemed larger and had me backing up a few steps as she got angrier.

"I have a good thing going, and I can't lose this man because you think that snake was killed. Butch didn't do it, and that's all you need to know."

I tried to back up further.

"I understand."

I tried walking away, but she blocked me, giving me a final stare-down before she stepped to the side and then made her way into the building. I quickly walked the remaining few feet to my car.

That was intense. I wanted to shake it off.

Instead, I focused on what I had learned on my tour today and digest this new information. My gut feeling was that Jeremy was murdered. Still, I had nothing concrete, and I wasn't trained in this type of thing. Without something concrete, it was all speculation.

I had a few errands to run, including picking up my new televisions. I wanted my house back to some kind of routine, even if it was a new normal.

Chapter Thirty-Two

~Killer~

She was getting too close. I was going to have to keep an even closer eye on her. Why was she nosing around everywhere?

I paced around my apartment. This was not how things were supposed to happen. I had gotten away with Renee's murder. Jeremy's had been an accident though. It wasn't supposed to be him. I was going to fix that soon, but I had to bide my time now that she was so close.

There was a knock at the door. I opened it.

"Hey, come in."

"Hi," he said, slipping his arms around my waist. "Mmm, you look so good."

"Thanks, so do you." We shared a long, slow kiss. "I missed you."

"I missed you too." A few more kisses. "Dinner smells good."

We sat to eat our food. I had ordered in, not being much of a cook. In fact, I hated cooking. Such a domestic activity.

"Is this from Anthony's?"

"Yep. So good, right? They have the best chicken parm."

We ate, making small talk about this or that. Nothing special. We had been together for a while now, and honestly, we both had only one thing on our minds.

"So crazy how that medium was nosing around today." I said.

"Yeah, she was very interested in how the lab works."

"So, what do you think?"

"About?" he said around a bite of food. Internally, I cringed but smiled sweetly at him.

"About her asking all these questions? Like, why?"

"I just figured Laney was having a tough time accepting Jeremy's death. I mean, she has a baby on the way. That can't be easy, losing the dad so suddenly. Maybe Joanna is helping her come to terms with things."

"Maybe." I chewed slowly as I thought about what he said. "She's got the detective involved too. As you know," I added as an afterthought.

He didn't know I had the same issue as Laney and the other one. The girlfriend Jeremy didn't think I knew about, but I did. And this guy here thinks this was his baby, and I wasn't telling him any different. Jeremy was gone and couldn't help.

He didn't know about Jeremy and me, and I certainly would never tell him. I didn't allow him at my doctor's appointments, even though he had asked. I'd lied and said because we weren't married, it wasn't allowed. The idiot bought it.

We finished our meal without much more conversation. I could see in his eyes what he wanted. Honestly, I had lost my appetite for both my meal and him.

"Are you finished?" he asked.

"Oh, yeah, I'm sorry. I'm starting to get tired." I pushed the food around on my plate.

"Aw, well, you are growing our baby." He reached over, cradling my stomach. "Let me clean up. You go watch TV and put your feet up." He took our plates and headed to the kitchen.

I plopped myself on the couch and clicked on the television to my favorite celebrity reality show. Mindlessly, I watched while surfing through my various social media accounts on my phone. I flipped through one of my friend's recent selfies. She was such an attention whore.

"Ugly... duck lips? What are you, twelve?" I mocked as I continued scrolling through her pictures. "Ugh, look at this one. That pose is so last year."

"All cleaned up in there." He snuggled up next to me, but I moved away.

"Sorry, I'm not comfortable tonight. The baby has been moving a lot." I flashed him my sweetest smile.

"That's okay. I'll give you a foot rub." He moved down to massage my feet.

After he was done, I begged him to go get me some ice cream, which he did. He would do anything I asked. While he was gone, I could finally relax and think.

I didn't trust Laney and Joanna. They were up to something, but I couldn't put my finger on what. Maybe I should kill them, too. I could do Laney easily at the lab, but Joanna would be trickier.

He returned with my ice cream. A pint of banana chocolate. He brought me a spoon and a napkin.

"Thanks, babe. This is my favorite." I opened the ice cream and began eating my treat. "Mmm... this is so good."

I mostly ignored him while I ate and watched my show. He played on his phone and waited. I knew what he was waiting for, but I was no longer in the mood, wanting instead to be alone. I had every intention of sending him packing when I was done using him.

Once I finished my ice cream, I started making some fake yawns and stretching, hoping he would get the hint. I might not want him there, but I didn't want to be mean.

"I guess you want me to go, huh?"

"What? Oh, I'm sorry. I'm just so tired today." I rubbed my stomach gently to visually remind him that I was growing a baby.

"Does that mean you want me to go?"

"Aw, baby, I don't want you to leave. You know I love having you here." I gave him my best pouty face.

"I'm not playin' with you. Either you want me to sleep over or not."

Did he just raise his voice at me? My bitch switch flipped. "Fine. I want you to get out! I don't want you here. Raising your voice at me. That's uncalled for. I'm pregnant."

I pushed up from the couch, not as dramatically as I would have liked, given the nearly full-term baby in my stomach, and stomped to the front door, swinging it wide. I gestured for him to leave.

He stared at me with rage. "Gawd, you are such a bitch sometimes. I'll be glad when you have that kid, and you get back to normal."

He stormed past me without a kiss goodbye. I slammed the door behind him to show my disappointment and hurt.

Tears started to form in my eyes. I hated crying. I was not that girl. This baby wreaked havoc on my hormones.

The baby kicked me. I took it as a little hello and an "I love you."

"Aw, sweet baby, I love you, too. I'm so ready to meet you." I caressed my stomach lightly. Another hello kick.

I thought about him again. He frustrated me to the point of rage, but it wasn't going to matter soon. I didn't plan to stay with him much longer. This baby didn't need a daddy so badly that I would stay with this loser.

Chapter Thirty-Three

~Clint~

I was out on another first date. Why did I bother? But this was just another attempt by my mom at setting me up. When would she run out of friends with single daughters?

We were at Spades. I didn't understand the appeal of this place, but Amber seemed to like it as much as Kelly had.

"So, tell me about yourself, Clint," she asked as she pushed a stray hair behind her ear.

"What's to tell? I work, and I go home." I shrugged.

"No hobbies?"

"I like football. I play with some of the guys in the department sometimes, but mostly just watch. What about you? Tell me more about you."

She went on and on about this and that. I only half listened to her. She seemed comfortable talking about herself. I asked questions here and there to give the impression that I was listening. It was my superpower.

"Oh, darn, I finished my drink. Would you mind getting me another?" She shook the empty glass.

I nodded and headed to the bar to order.

"Hey, Detective." Greg Landon appeared to my left and walked with me the last few steps to the bar.

"Hey."

"Girlfriend again?"

"Sort of. First date. You?"

"Business." He gestured to his table. "I wanted to apologize for my behavior the other day. I didn't mean to scare Joanna. I just wanted to talk, swear. I should have controlled my temper better."

"Yeah, well, you didn't need to stalk her for the last few weeks either. She has been scared out of her mind. And do you know anything about the break-in?" Since I didn't get a chance to question him as I wanted, I figured I'd take this opportunity.

"What? I only went there that day to talk to her. I haven't been following her, and I certainly never broke in. If I have something to say, I say it right to someone's face."

"She identified your car as the one that has been following her for the last several weeks."

"It's a common model. A lot of people in this town have dark blue
BMWs. It could be almost anyone. Heck, my 80-year-old neighbor has
one. My doctor has one. My mother has one, but a different color. It
wasn't me. That was the first time I had been to her house."

I stared at him. Having been trained to read body language, I
could usually tell if people were lying. He was not lying, or he really
believed his story. I studied him for a moment longer.

"Shit." That meant she was likely still in danger.

I thanked Greg, grabbed Amber's drink, and delivered it to her.
Then I texted Jo to see where she was. When she didn't answer, I
messaged Terry.

"Are you okay, Clint? You seem distracted."

"I'm sorry. I just got some news about a case. I was messaging my
partner to let him know so he could handle it, and then I'm all yours
again." It was a lie. If Jo said she needed me, I was out of here.

"Oh, no problem," she said, then went back to telling me about
her job.

I kept peeking at my phone, looking for a reply, but none came.
Where the hell was everyone?

Chapter Thirty-Four

~Joanna~

I was watching a movie on my new television and enjoying the heck out of it. I hadn't realized how outdated mine was. Technology sure has come a long way.

Right at the climax of the movie, there was a knock at my door. I grabbed my phone to check my security camera on the app, so thankful that Stan had gotten this installed. I frowned when I noticed several texts and missed calls from both Clint and Terry. It was on silent, so I could just be alone. Clicking over to the camera app, I saw it was Detective Terry Walden at the door.

"That's strange," I said to the empty room. I paused the movie and walked to the front door.

"Hi, Detective. To what do I owe the pleasure?"

"Hi, Joanna, sorry to bother you. Clint messaged me and wanted me to check on you. May I come in?"

"Sure, come on in. I just noticed all the messages and calls. I had my phone on silent."

"That explains it. He was worried."

"Why? Nothing to worry about. Greg followed me earlier but hasn't tried to talk to me."

"It isn't Greg. He's at the same bar where Clint was. When he asked Greg about following you, he said he hadn't been."

"He's lying... right?" My blood ran cold because I knew what Terry was saying was likely true. "You saw his car. It was the same car."

"It's a common make, model, and color. I checked the registration records for our county. Plus, Greg has plates on his, not the temporary tags like the one following you."

He was right. The car had paper tags while his had vanity plates. They read LANDON1.

"Ugh. I had hoped this was over." I wanted to cry.

He nodded. "We did, too."

"So, you're telling me there's still some random stranger following me, and we don't know who?"

"Unfortunately, yes."

I stared at him, blinking a few times and trying to gather my wits. My brain couldn't process this information.

"What am I going to do? I can't hide in fear forever..."

"We need you to be safe. Are you able to have someone stay with you, or can you stay with someone else?"

"I'm sure I can stay with my sister." I didn't want to, though. Earlier I had felt so empowered and was now crushed.

"I can follow you to your sister's if you'd like."

I thought about it for a moment. I didn't want to live in fear.

"Really, I think I'll be okay here. I have the security system now with cameras, and you have the patrol car going by several times. You don't think that's enough?" I just wanted to be in my own home.

"I mean, it's your call. I can't make you go, but... be safe."

"I'm sure. I'll feel better here, plus I have appointments all day tomorrow. I don't want to rush back."

"I understand. Okay, I'll do a quick security check for you, and then you lock up after I leave."

He walked around the exterior of the house. I watched him on the cameras as he checked the windows and doors. He came back and did the same on the inside, checking that everything was secure. Once he was satisfied, he joined me in the living room again.

"Okay, everything looks good. Make sure your cell phone is on and not on silent, and please don't hesitate to call Clint or me immediately if you get scared. I don't care if it's a raccoon; if you get nervous or scared, you call us."

"Thanks, Terry."

I walked him out, and he made one last plea for me to stay with my sister. I told him I would think about it, but I felt safe enough for tonight, even though deep down, I was nervous. He acknowledged and left.

Nothing seemed out of place or unusual overnight. Thank goodness. I woke at my normal time, got myself ready, then started prepping for my appointments.

About midday, Jeremy showed up. He hadn't been to visit in over a week. I wondered what was going on, but I still had a client. He just hovered around, but I could tell he was anxious to speak to me.

"Stop distracting her. This is my time." My current spirit started arguing with Jeremy.

"This is urgent," Jeremy said.

"I don't care. I have things to say to my family, and to me, that's urgent."

"You don't understand."

"No, Mister, you don't understand!" Mr. Martin was angry. He gestured for Jeremy to leave.

"I... uh... he says." I tried to hear what Mr. Martin was saying. "Sorry, Mrs. Martin, there are a lot of spirits right now. Let me refocus, and I can attend to the others after your time."

Jeremy took the hint and left the office.

Once the appointment was over, Jeremy came storming back in along with Marcus. Wait, what?

"Marcus? But..."

"Yes, this is what I was trying to tell you. Marcus was killed today at the lab, just like I was."

"And Renee?"

"Oh shit! I forgot about her... how could I forget? I was just so caught up in... Never mind. Yes, just like Renee."

Marcus was quiet. He seemed like he was in shock. I'm sure I would be too if I had just died.

"So, any ideas on who killed you?" I asked.

Marcus looked at me and said the one name I wasn't expecting. "Cate."

"The poodle?" I blurted out without thinking.

"Huh?" Marcus looked confused.

Jeremy burst out laughing and gestured to Marcus not to worry about it.

"I don't think it was Cate, but he seems adamant. She just doesn't seem like the type to me."

"What is the type?" I asked.

We all thought. Who really knew? We couldn't come up with any examples.

"I should call Clint." I grabbed for my phone.

"Before you do, there's more. Marcus, go on."

"We were the ones following you, and we broke in. Cate wanted to know if you had files on clients." He looked around, his eyes wide. "I made the guys stop short of completely destroying your house, but they really tore it up. I'm sorry about that. She told me all kinds of lies, and I believed her."

"But the car looked like Greg's. Did you all drive the same car?"

"No, not exactly. A few different ones but all the same make and model. We got them from a chop shop, and she asked that we get ones that looked like Greg's. She doesn't like him and thought it would make it look like he was following you. Which it did."

"I can't believe this. Why would she do that?"

"I have no idea. I realize how little I actually knew about her."

"But why follow me?"

"She told us you were trying to steal her baby. She made me think it was my baby, so I was hell-bent on stopping you."

"That doesn't make sense. Why would I want her baby? I barely know anything about her."

"I honestly don't know. I can only guess that since she killed Jeremy, she didn't want him 'talking,' and since she believes you talk to the dead, I'm guessing she thought you could and would spill the beans." Marcus was starting to relax. His eyes weren't open quite as wide, and he wasn't looking around nervously.

"Wait, I didn't know you were involved with Caitlyn," I said.

"We've been dating for about two years."

"But wasn't she with Jeremy? I'm so confused." I looked from Jeremy to Marcus.

"She made us keep our relationship a secret because we worked together. Now I know the real reason. I didn't even know about him. A lot of things make so much more sense now. She always insisted on using condoms, so when she got pregnant, I was angry at first. We had been so careful, but she insisted it was mine." He looked at Jeremy. "Now, I understand how it happened."

I needed to call Clint. The phone rang a few times before he answered.

"Jo? What's up?"

"Hey, Clint. I have Jeremy and Marcus from Landon Labs here. Marcus is dead. Killed, he says."

"I know. I'm here at Landon's now on the investigation." There was some background noise, and he had a muffled conversation with someone else. "Sorry about that. I can't believe I'm going to ask this, but he's there with you, really? Does he have any ideas?"

"Caitlyn Fitzpatrick."

"The poodle?"

The description was spreading.

"Yes," I said.

"That doesn't make sense."

"He said she had him and a few of his friends following me and that they are the ones who broke in."

"Seriously? Okay, look, I need to wrap up here, but I'll come over there right after."

There was a knock at my door. It was my scheduled lunch break, so I wasn't expecting another client for at least an hour. Micah and Tessa were both coming in after lunch, but they never knocked.

"It's Cate," Jeremy informed me.

"Hey, Clint," I said before the detective could hang up, "Cate is here."

I heard him curse and then call out to Terry.

"Hang tight, Jo. Terry and I will be right there. Don't let her in."

"I'm sure I'll be fine. She's always seemed harmless. Even if she did kill those people, she did it in the lab. I get the impression she doesn't like to get her hands dirty."

"After everything Jeremy and Marcus told you, you still want to chance it?"

"Yes. I gotta go, but please head over." I turned to go answer the door.

Jeremy and Marcus both begged me not to.

"She is a murderer!"

"Don't let her in, you idiot!" Jeremy shouted.

I opened the door anyway. Despite everything, I thought I could keep her distracted until Clint and Terry could get here, and knew Hank had someone watching my house, so I didn't feel alone or unsafe. More than anything, we needed this to end.

"Hi, Cate. Sorry, I was on the phone. I wasn't expecting you." I tried to sound as casual and surprised as possible.

"Hi, Joanna. I'm sorry, I just..." She started crying. "There was another death at work, and I just need to talk to someone not involved. Everyone is so upset, obviously."

"Oh, wow, I'm so sorry. Yes, come in, please." I tried keeping my breathing slow and even. "Do you want some water?"

"That would be lovely. Thank you."

We stepped into the living room, and she took a seat and a tissue from the box I had on a side table. She dabbed at her eyes. I could tell she was fake crying. There was no evidence of real emotion or sadness. I took my time getting her a glass of water.

"Here you go."

"Thank you so much." She sipped it. "Do you still talk to Jeremy? I miss him."

"Um, not really. Not since your appointment." I tried not to look in his direction. He and Marcus were standing to her right.

"Oh, I had hoped." She took another slow sip of water. "How long after someone dies do you see them?"

There it was. She wanted to know if I was talking to Marcus.

"I don't know. It seems to vary depending on the person. A few have been dead for many years before they manifest, and others right away. It depends on their desire to speak to the living."

I tried to say it casually, but I suspected my eyes gave me away, as I couldn't help a quick glance at Marcus. It was just a split second, but enough for her to catch the movement.

"Is he here? Marcus? Is Marcus here?" She looked toward the spot where Marcus was standing.

"Marcus? Um, no. Is he the person that died?" I tried to fake surprise.

She sprang to her feet and was in my face in two seconds. How did she move so quickly, as pregnant as she was?

"Don't lie to me! I know he's here." She was breathing heavily. "What did he tell you?"

"Nothing. He's not here." I lied.

She laughed a wicked, bone-chilling laugh. I realized my instincts on this were way off, and I should have listened to everyone telling me not to open the door for her. She was clearly unstable.

"You're a liar. Just a plain, boring liar!" She started pacing in front of me and mumbling, but I couldn't tell what she was saying.

The couple of times I'd met her, she never acted so crazy. What had changed inside of her?

"Cate, you need to relax, and let's talk about this. There is no reason to get so worked up."

She whirled around, and suddenly she had a gun. Where had that been?

Instinctively, I put my hands up in front of me. "Whoa, Cate... Caitlyn, please. I can help you."

"There is nothing wrong with me. You're the one that needs help." She waved the gun, gesturing for me to stand up. I did. She pulled some handcuffs out of her purse and put them on me. "Now, let's go."

We walked out the front door, and she pushed me into the front passenger seat of her car. She grabbed some rope from the floorboard, then tied me to the car seat before pulling the seat belt around me.

She was surprisingly nimble for nearly nine months pregnant, and she made such quick work of fastening me to the car. Had she done this type of thing before?

I felt a slight panic bubbling up, but if I stayed calm, maybe she would be calm too. My only hope would be that Hank's guy would see us leave, or the detectives would get here before Cate could drive off.

Speaking of Hank, I looked around to see if I could find where his guy was. According to Hank, they had been following me for weeks. He'd said he would protect me, and now would be an excellent time to get involved if they were going to follow through on that.

"Who are you looking for? I know you don't have a boyfriend," she growled at me.

"Just looking." Where was the patrol?

She drove away from my house, taking the back way out of my neighborhood. Clint and Terry would likely be coming from the other direction. She headed away from Creekview toward Buckston. All hope of being rescued faded. It seemed I was going to die today.

Chapter Thirty-Five

~Clint~

Terry and I rushed out of the lab after handing over the investigation to another officer.

We sped toward Jo's. I really hoped she was wrong about Cate. Honestly, I wasn't sure if I believed in mediums or an afterlife or anything like that, but how else could she have known about Marcus Ruiz? We hadn't released any information yet about the death, and the media had only just shown up as we were leaving.

The pieces were clicking into place whether I wanted them to or not. Joanna had known things she shouldn't have been able to know. Details about the case. Information that hadn't been public. And now Marcus's name before anyone outside the lab could have told her.

Either she was somehow involved, which I knew in my gut wasn't true, or she really could talk to the dead.

My chest tightened at the thought of her in danger. I should have made her leave. Should have insisted she go to her sister's. But no, I'd let her stay home alone, and now Cate had her.

My phone rang. I hoped it was Jo, but it wasn't. Unknown caller.

"Hartley," I said.

"Hello, Detective. Hank here."

"Hank, what's going on?"

"That poodle took her. My guy was following but lost them in Buckston."

"Buckston?"

"Yeah. I assume they're going to the chop shop that Cate's friends have ties to. My guy doesn't know where it is, but we're working on it. We'll find her."

"Thanks, Hank." We disconnected with an agreement to stay in touch.

My hands gripped the steering wheel tighter. Buckston. That was at least twenty minutes away, and we were going in the wrong direction.

"So, we're going to Buckston?" Terry asked.

"Yep."

I made a sharp U-turn and hit the gas. Terry grabbed the door handle but didn't complain.

I made some calls to the local PD in Buckston and asked them to start looking and find out what they could tell me about any chop shops in their area. I couldn't have another death on my hands, and especially not our local celebrity.

Our local celebrity. Who was I kidding? She was more than that. Somewhere along the way, between her stubbornness and her determination to help Jeremy, between that smile and the way she called me for help, she'd become important to me. And I'd failed to keep her safe.

The officer I spoke with would get in touch with their lead detective. He would have the detective call me back. In the meantime, they would send out officers to look for Cate's car.

I called our dispatch to let them know where we were going and what was going on. I needed additional backup and resources. Maybe someone in our department had seen them or had leads we could follow into Buckston.

"We'll find her, Clint," Terry said quietly.

I nodded, not trusting my voice. We had to find her. The alternative wasn't something I could think about.

We had a good twenty minutes before we would be in Buckston. This was going to be a torturous ride.

Chapter Thirty-Six

As we drove, I was oddly calm, even knowing Cate was almost certainly taking me somewhere to kill me. She, on the other hand, kept mumbling to herself and fidgeting in the seat.

I remembered what Micah had once said about being able to charm people, so I thought I might try that.

"Tell me about Oakley. Remind me when she's due?"

"Hm? Oh, in just a few weeks. I can't wait to meet her."

"Do you have her nursery set up?"

"Oh yes, it's all pink with gold accents. Perfect for a little girl."

"I bet she'll be beautiful like you."

"I did one of those 3D ultrasounds, and it was amazing. She is perfect." She had this sudden glow about her, and the crazy woman faded. Unfortunately, it didn't last long. The crazy woman came back quickly as she realized what was happening. "Don't try to distract me."

Well, that worked for all of two seconds. I wondered if she would fall for some celeb or tabloid gossip. I didn't get the chance to try, as she pulled into an old industrial business park.

I wasn't familiar with Buckston, so I wasn't entirely sure where we were. She drove through the buildings until she parked in front of a large warehouse. She unbuckled and then untied me.

"Don't do anything crazy. I'm going to come around and help you out." She came to my side of the car and pulled me out. I fell to the ground where she kicked me. "Get up! Don't you run or I'll shoot you."

I struggled to my feet, but with her help, rough as it was, I made it. She immediately pulled the gun out of her bag, pressing it against my side and pushed me forward into the building. If I survived, I was going to be covered in bruises.

Inside, there were luxury cars and trucks in various states of repair. This must be the chop shop that Marcus had mentioned.

Jeremy and Marcus had accompanied us, but I couldn't look at them for validation. I wasn't sure what Caitlyn's reaction would be if she knew. After weeks together, Jeremy knew I couldn't talk to them, but he used the time to explain everything to Marcus.

It didn't look like anyone else was here, and if Marcus's story was to be believed, anyone here wouldn't help me anyway. They were all working with Cate in some form or fashion. I had to hope that Hank still had someone watching me. I just had to stay alive long enough that help could arrive.

"Sit over there." She gestured to a rusty, old chair set against a wall.

As I sat, it looked like my back was to an office. I wanted to get my bearings in case I could escape, but I didn't get a chance to look around more before she tied me to the chair with the same rope from the car. I was no expert on tying someone up, but Cate seemed to know what she was doing. I could barely move a muscle when she was done.

It begged the question, how does one become so skilled in kidnapping? I didn't want to know the answer.

She then began pacing around the shop area, mumbling to herself. What was she thinking?

"Cate, is there some water? You probably need some as much as I do."

She glared at me but then went to a side room, returning with two bottles of water. She went to hand it to me before realizing I couldn't hold it, and so she unscrewed the top and held it for me to drink. Quite a bit dribbled down my face, but I managed to swallow some.

"Thank you. Be sure you drink yours, for Oakley."

She stared at me blankly for a moment before walking to the other side of the room and sitting in a chair against the other wall. I don't know what she wanted with me. She just sat there, not talking, but drank her water as I had suggested.

"Tell me about Renee," I called across to her.

"You know about Renee? Did she talk to you, too?"

"No, I just... heard about her from the news. I thought I remembered hearing that you were friends."

"We were, but she ruined it." Her voice cracked as she spoke. "She deserved what she got."

"I'm sorry. It's tough to be betrayed by someone you care about."

"Bah. She was going to out me to Marcus. He's the only one, or I should say, one of the few that didn't know about Jeremy and me. She was basically blackmailing me all while pretending to be my friend. Everyone pretends. Nobody really cares about me. Only Jeremy cared, and he's gone because of me." A few tears fell quietly from her eyes.

Now I was starting to understand her a little better. She was a woman left behind, scorned, and betrayed. I looked at Jeremy and Marcus. I hadn't interacted with them, not wanting to freak Cate out. In her current state, I had no idea how she might react.

Despite my hands being cuffed and tied, I tried to signal to Jeremy. I had a plan and wanted to get his help.

"You need my help?" he asked.

I nodded slowly so as not to draw Cate's attention.

"Okay, what? Oh, I think I know. You want me to help you talk to Cate?"

I nodded again. Sure, I could make something up to say, but it was better to have Jeremy's experience with Cate here. She would see right through me if I tried faking this.

"Oh, Jeremy... Hi," I said.

"What? Jeremy is here." Her voice cracked. "Jeremy...?"

"I'm here, sweetie." Of course, she couldn't hear his voice; it was my voice. Still, she reacted the way we had hoped.

Marcus wasn't thrilled and walked out. He had loved her, but Jeremy had filled him in on the details of his and Cate's relationship, including the baby's paternity.

"Oh, honey, I miss you. I'm so sorry." Cate said.

"No, I'm sorry. I put you in this position. I wish I wouldn't have left you."

"That was my fault. I tried to... I tried to kill Marcus, but I killed you by mistake. You weren't supposed to be working that day." She was sobbing.

"It's okay, baby. It's okay. I forgive you. It was an accident." I really tried to say it the way Jeremy had.

She looked at me. Her face was red and streaked with tears. "I wish I could hear him. I hate that only you can hear him. I hate it!"

"I wish you could, too. I know it doesn't mean as much hearing me say these words."

"Where is he standing?" I couldn't move much, so I nodded my head to her left side. She reached forward; her hand went through him. "I miss him... you, so very much."

"I miss you, too. But I'm here now."

We sat like this for several minutes. No words, just Cate crying. Then she started to do something I didn't expect. She started labored breathing as if she was...

"Um, are you in labor?"

"No, I can't be. I'm not due for three weeks." She moaned and grabbed the chair. "Okay... maybe. I've been feeling it for a while, but I just thought... oh, gawd."

"Crap. You need to untie me so I can help you. We need to get you to the hospital."

Her crying changed to whimpering like a scared child. She struggled through another contraction before she was able to get up and untie me. Thankfully, I had my phone in my pocket.

I got her to the car and buckled her in. She gave me directions out of this area while breathing through the contractions. Once I got to a more familiar area, I called Clint.

Chapter Thirty-Seven

~Clint~

With Buckston PD's help, we had looked in several areas of Buckston with no luck so far. Hank had a dozen of his guys out here as well. We scoured the industrial parks and warehouses.

"Where are they?" I muttered as Terry drove us through yet another row of warehouses.

"We'll find them."

I doubted Terry was really that confident, but it helped to not be looking alone. Every warehouse looked the same. Every shadow could be hiding something. Every minute that passed felt like an hour.

I kept thinking about the last time I'd seen Jo. Standing in her doorway, that determined look on her face when she'd insisted she'd be fine. I should have dragged her out of there. Should have made her go to her sister's. Now she was somewhere with a woman who'd killed three people, and I had no idea if she was even still alive.

My chest tightened at the thought. I couldn't lose her. Not now. Not when I'd just started to figure out what she meant to me.

We circled back through an area we had already searched when my phone rang. Joanna's name showed on the display.

Relief flooded through me so fast I almost couldn't breathe. "Jo?" I asked as I answered, probably too quickly.

"Yes, it's me. I'm fine. I'm with Cate, and we're heading back to Creekview. She's in labor."

I closed my eyes for a second, letting the words sink in. She was alive. She was okay. "Where are you?"

"I honestly don't know. Somewhere on I-75 between Buckston and Creekview. I am heading to St. John's."

"We'll meet you there. Be safe." I wanted to say more. Wanted to tell her I'd been terrified. Wanted to ask if she was hurt. But she was driving, and she had Cate with her, and there would be time for all of that later.

I turned to Terry and relayed the message for him to drive back to Creekview, straight to the hospital. I then called Hank and then the Buckston PD, slowly spreading the word that Joanna was safe, and Cate was in labor.

The drive back felt longer than the drive out, even though Terry had the lights going. I kept checking my phone, waiting for another call, some sign that Jo was still okay.

We pulled up twenty minutes later at the hospital and rushed straight to the labor and delivery floor. At the desk, we asked about Caitlyn. They said we would have to wait in the family room as she could not have visitors.

"We aren't visitors. We're police officers, and she has committed three murders."

"I don't care who you are. Right now, she's having a baby, so if you could wait to arrest her until after she has given birth." The nurse at the desk snapped.

She placed her balled up hands firmly on her hips, and it was clear she was not going to budge on that. Any other time, I might have respected her dedication to her patient. Right now, I just needed to see Jo. Needed to know with my own eyes that she was really okay.

We trekked to the family waiting room area. The frustration of being so close but unable to see her was almost worse than not knowing where she was. At least when we were searching, I was doing something.

I messaged Jo to let her know we were here. I wanted her to know I wasn't going to leave her. Whatever happened next, I'd be right here waiting.

Chapter Thirty-Eight

"Breathe, breathe. You've got this. You're doing great." I said.

I couldn't believe I was here experiencing this with her. Jeremy was here, too, helping me with what to say. Marcus had decided not to come. I didn't blame him.

"I can't. I can't..." She was holding tight to my hand.

"Cate, she's almost here. Keep pushing for me," the nurse encouraged.

I was coaching her the best I could with breathing and cheering her on, but I've never experienced childbirth myself. I was thankful for Jeremy's presence here with us. He kept me focused while I kept Cate focused. I had never seen anyone in labor before, not even my sister.

"One more push, Cate, and then your daughter will be here." The doctor was in position and ready. Two nurses were waiting: one for Oakley, the other for Cate.

The nurse encouraged me to look as the baby was born.

"Oh wow, Caitlyn, she is... she's here!" I just watched a baby enter the world. Holy moly!

They set the baby on Cate's chest and wiped her down. Cate was crying and laughing as she cooed to her daughter.

"Jo, she's beautiful. Look at her. Oh, Oakley, baby. Hi. I'm your mommy."

"Here, let me get a picture." I took out my phone and noticed that Clint had texted me several times. I smiled before taking a few pictures of the new family, then replied to him.

The nurse took Oakley for measurements and then to the nursery for all the newborn baby things. Jeremy followed the baby to the nursery, letting me know he would be back later. He was a proud daddy.

The doctor finished with Cate. Then the nurse took some vital signs, gave her some pain meds, and then some postpartum care instructions, saying she would check on her again shortly. It was now down to just the two of us.

"Thank you for being here with me. I appreciate it so much." Cate said.

"I'm glad you let me. She is beautiful, and I feel blessed to have witnessed this."

"I'm going to be arrested when I leave... and I was thinking." She started weeping softly. "This is tough, but I don't have family. You know... foster kid, never adopted. Big loser."

"Oh, Cate, no... you're not..."

"No, I know what I am, and oh my god, I killed three people. One by accident, but two on purpose. I'm a monster." She hung her head for a moment as if she had just realized what she had done, and it was truly sinking in. Even with her head down, I could see the tears streaming. "I don't want my daughter to know... and I don't want her to end up in foster care like me. She's only a baby, probably has a good chance to get adopted, but I want to pick her parents. Or at least her mom." She looked up at me then. Her eyes locked with mine.

"Wait. You don't mean me, do you?"

"Yes, if you want to, I'd love for you to take her, raise her, and, depending on the verdict, adopt her. I assume I will get at least life." Cate sounded like she had already resolved herself to that.

I expected that would be the verdict as well.

I didn't know if I even wanted to have kids of my own, let alone to raise someone else's and especially someone who had just kidnapped me with the intention of killing me, or at least I thought she was. Could I do this? Was I crazy to even be considering saying yes?

"Earlier today, you were going to kill me, and now you want me to adopt your daughter?"

She shrugged. "I know. And I know how it sounds, but I have no one else I can ask. I want to at least somewhat know the person I leave her with."

"You don't really know me. We have only met a few times."

"I know you. You're the Medium with a Heart."

I shouldn't be surprised that Cate had latched on to my celebrity status as a reason to connect with me. That was one thing I did know about her: she loved celebrities.

"That's my stage persona, but you don't know me."

She shrugged again.

There was a knock at the door, interrupting our discussion. I needed time to think.

When the door opened, I saw Clint, Terry, and another officer I wasn't familiar with. They were here to start the booking process. They read her rights, explained the process, and how they wouldn't take her into custody until she left the hospital.

Clint pulled me to one side.

"Are you okay?"

"Yes, I'm fine. She didn't hurt me."

"Okay, good. I was worried."

"You were worried about me, Detective? Why is that?" I teased.

He leaned close, so close, I thought he might kiss me, but he just whispered, "I couldn't let our local celebrity die. The old ladies of town would skin me alive."

He winked at me, then walked away.

Well played, Detective, well played. I thought as I watched him rejoin the others.

I stepped back over to Cate's bed. She was crying, so I took her hand. She smiled sadly at me.

"I'll take her." I blurted out before my brain caught up with my mouth.

"You will? Oh, Joanna! That would make me so happy."

The officers all looked at me but didn't say anything. The one I didn't know excused herself and Terry followed.

"Did you just agree to take her baby?" Clint asked.

"Yes, I did. She doesn't have family to adopt her daughter, and so I am." I squeezed Cate's hand that I still held.

"What about the Landons?"

Cate and I looked at each other. I hadn't thought of them.

"I'll work with a lawyer and child services on the legal part, but if it works out, I want her to go with Jo," Cate said.

She looked more at peace and relaxed now that I confirmed my decision.

Clint nodded, but it looked as if he was biting his tongue. He then said he needed to go but would be in touch. He reminded Cate that an officer would be stationed outside of her door.

After he left, I realized I had a ton of things to get ready to bring home a baby.

"Do you want me to stay with you?" I asked.

"No, you have done so much for me today, and after I was so horrible to you. Worse than horrible. I'm so sorry..."

"Don't worry. The most important thing now is Oakley, and for you to rest and take care of yourself." Watching Cate give birth made me more forgiving, I supposed.

"Thanks, and I'll give Oakley extra kisses from you when they bring her back to me," she said. I could only nod a reply as I started thinking of all I had to do. "I know you have a lot to do now to get ready to bring a baby home, but you can have all the things I bought for her. I won't get to see her use them, but knowing she has them is enough for me."

"That's a wonderful idea."

Cate had already given me the keys to her apartment, so I could bring some things that she needed to the hospital. She, obviously, needed her hospital bag. She'd said she had packed it two weeks ago.

"I'll figure out what I need to do to give her to you. I'm sure they will send a social worker at some point, so I'll get things started."

I hugged her before leaving. This day, of all days, had not gone how I thought it would. A workday turned into my kidnapping, and I thought I was going to die.

In the end, I saw a human being born and would be taking that little one home with me. My life was weird.

Chapter Thirty-Nine

Today I was going to pick up Oakley from the hospital. She was four days old and ready to go home. The hospital had kept her a little longer than usual because she was born just shy of full term, but thankfully she was healthy and strong. The paperwork had been started and filed.

I was approved for temporary custody, but the social worker felt confident that I would have no trouble adopting her, especially after she had met with the Landons.

While the family wanted to be part of her life, they all agreed to the adoption. Mrs. Landon was in no condition to take care of a baby, and Greg was the only other fit relative. He had declined, saying I would be a better choice.

Micah, Josh, Clint, and Stan had all helped me get Oakley's things moved from Caitlyn's apartment to my house. We cleared out the bedroom that we used as a storeroom. We would just use the garage for the Joanna the Medium merchandise now.

Cate had been able to stay in the hospital with Oakley but would be moved to the jail today. She fluctuated from calm to depressed to happy at having this behind her. She had some peace at not hiding any longer. I promised to write and send pictures. And, once Oakley was older, I promised to visit with her.

Audrey went with me to the hospital. She was so excited about being an aunt.

"I can't believe you're adopting a baby! I never thought you'd have kids, and now this." She bubbled over with excitement as we drove.

"I know. I'm so nervous but also excited."

I had crammed nine months' worth of prepping for a baby into just days, though it helped that I could use all of Caitlyn's things. I was the queen of research and faking it, so I figured I could do this. It wasn't going to be easy or perfect every day, but Audrey told me all parents think that.

We parked, and I grabbed the car seat, hooking it to the stroller. I had put the going-home outfit that Cate had picked out for her in the diaper bag. We walked toward the hospital's main entrance when I noticed a familiar figure ahead of us.

"Laney?" I called out.

"Oh, Jo, hi." She was waddling and looked pained.

"Are you in labor?"

"Yep. My mom just dropped me off and is parking the car." She took a breath. "Are you here for Oakley?"

"Yes."

She took another pained breath.

"Here, let's walk you up." I looped my arm through Laney's to help steady her. Audrey took over, pushing the stroller.

The girls were going to be just days apart. It was exciting and a little strange. After getting Laney to the nurses and wishing her the best, we headed to Caitlyn's room.

"Knock, knock." I pushed the door open.

"Come in, second mommy." It was the silly nickname we came up with for me, at least until later today.

"Hi, first mommy. And hi, baby girl."

Oakley was dressed in a sweet mint green and pink footed sleeper. Cate handed the baby to me. Oakley stretched and then settled into my arms.

Audrey stood back. She understood this was a tough moment for Caitlyn. She was giving up the baby she had wanted more than anything in the world. The one that would give her a family of her own. My heart hurt for Cate.

I had gotten to know Cate so well over the last few days. We had spent hours talking and getting to know each other. She had truly been a child who had never known love or a family, who had grown into a woman always searching for both.

An officer stepped into the room. He tapped his watch, signaling that we had to wrap things up. Cate grabbed a tissue to wipe her eyes.

"I can never express to you how much this means to me. The last few days have taught me so much. Had I met you sooner, things might have gone very differently for me." She hugged me and then kissed her daughter. "Promise you will send lots of pictures."

"Of course. Please take care of yourself. I will see you soon." I wiped a tear with the back of my hand.

With that, she was gone. We all knew what her future would hold, or at least we had a good guess.

A nurse came into the room, waving Oakley's discharge papers. "Are you ready to take her home?"

"Yes, we're ready, but can you tell me how Laney Landon is? Am I able to see her before we leave?"

"Sure. Do you want me to keep the baby while you do?"

"I'll keep her. I'm the new aunt," Audrey proudly shared.

I nodded my approval. The nurse then pointed me toward Laney's room. This floor was like a maze, so I was glad to have a guide.

I knocked. Laney's mother opened the door. I recognized her from Laney's pictures that I had seen. She smiled and let me in.

"Hi, I just wanted to check on you before I left." I noticed Jeremy standing in the room. I nodded to him.

"Hey. Thank you. How is Oakley?" She seemed comfortable at the moment. Very different from Cate's quick labor.

"She's good. She's with my sister. Cate was just taken into custody."

Jeremy looked down at his feet. I knew that hurt him. He was glad to finally learn how he died, but he was heartbroken to realize it was Cate.

"She must be crushed to be away from her baby."

I nodded.

"Hm, I hate to ask this," she lowered her voice, "but is... Jeremy here."

His head snapped up, and he moved closer to her.

"He is. Right next to you." I gestured.

She looked in that direction and smiled. "I'm so glad you're here. I love you."

"I love you too."

"Thank you for coming to visit me, Jo. I'm not going to make you stay to translate through the whole labor. Just knowing he is here is enough for me. I'll message or call you later, once she is here."

I leaned forward, hugged her, and left her with some words of encouragement. I then headed back to collect my daughter and head home. I stopped in my tracks at the thought. My daughter. It still seemed strange.

A few hours later, we were settled in at home. Then began a parade of visitors, all wanting to meet Oakley.

Once the visitors were gone, I got Oakley settled into bed. I stood looking at her, watching her drift off to sleep. She looked like a little angel, soft and sweet in her pink, fluffy bed.

I went back to the living room to clean up. Once the house was in order, I settled down to read and watch television. I finally felt safe in the house with all the secrets out in the open. Home finally felt like home again and especially with the tiny baby down the hall.

Movement caught my eye, and when I turned my head, I saw the one person I had hoped I'd see again.

"Grams?" Happy tears formed in my eyes.

"Hi, honey."

"Oh, I have missed you. I couldn't figure out how to get you back. I've needed to talk to you."

"I missed you too," she smiled. "I knew it was best to keep my distance. I didn't want to upset your mother. She has always been sensitive to drama."

I nodded. "Where have you been?"

"Around. Close by."

"I have so much to tell you. I just adopted a baby, well, in the process of it."

"I saw. She's beautiful. I'm so happy for you."

"Thanks. She's so amazing."

"Well, I hadn't planned to show myself again, but I've come with a warning. You still aren't safe. There are still people that want to harm you."

My heart dropped. "Crap!"

Before you go: If you loved Premedicated Murder and haven't already received a copy of Unsolved Murder, the prequel to this series check out my website for the offer for your free novella.

www.ejwheltonwrites.com

Note by the Author:

Thank you for reading my stories. This story was so much fun to write and create. It has truly been a joy to bring these characters to life.

This story was a challenge to myself as I wasn't sure I could write a mystery. When one of my aunts asked me if I could and I did.

While I do a lot of research on the details of the book, at times I do take some creative liberties to fit the story. The research is fun, and I enjoy it a lot.

I hope if you have enjoyed this first book in the series, that you will join for the next book, Replicated Murder.

Thank you for your support and happy reading!

9 781956 069020